BEYOND THE LAST ROPE . . .

"Joe's one-handed grip came away and the two slipped. They seemed to hang there for a fraction of a second. Then they were falling. . .

"Gainer did not see them hit the water. One of the men up the derrick ladder shouted that he had seen a head—but nobody ever got a glimpse. It was obviously hopeless. Nobody could survive in such a sea for more than a few minutes!"

Stephen Coulter

OFFSHORE!

AN AVON BOOK

AVON BOOKS
A division of
The Hearst Corporation
959 Eighth Avenue
New York, New York 10019

First Avon Printing, November, 1968

Cover illustration by Roger Kastel

Printed in the U.S.A.

OFFSHORE!

1

THE platform rose from the sea like no monster the sea has ever produced. The sea in its many moods swept against it. It lived with the sea but it was not of the sea and could not lend itself to the restlessness of the sea like a ship.

To the airline pilots who saw it when the sea was running high, it looked like a flying arrowhead, the tip of a great harpoon flying over the waves. Then it was splendid—grandiose—skimming the seamless curves, the veined heaving and pitching swells, driving through the scud and the lashing sprays of the universal, endless movement. The Argonauts were hunting the great whale!

At moments in the northern twilight it was a symbol of other things—conflict and hostility and the feebleness of men; but also the strength of human will. Sometimes, in the squalls, it loomed like the bow of a lost ship beating up to the west. Or in the early morning mists of milky dog-days when the swells rolled long and green, it waveringly floated like a high-plumed and half-imaginary island.

Sounds rose from it, clangs, squeaks and heavy churnings and cadences like choruses of steel flutes. They were damped, absorbed and fogged up, as sounds at sea are.

The platform was a steel triangle, 250 feet long on each side. Forty-two men lived on it night and day, working the heavy oil-drilling gear, tending the machines, eating, watching the sea and sky; and its name, in almost comic antithesis of legend and leviathans and the sea-wrack gods, was painted in white letters twelve feet high on its main deckhouse: Mister Mack.

This morning the sea lay as smooth as marble.

They were driving the long steel stilt-like legs, called spuds, down to the sea bed, implanting them there, then lifting the platform itself on the massive rack and pinion system. The platform vibrated as it rose above the level of the water. A stream of water ballast fell into the sea, hardly fraying in the breeze. Earlier in the morning, Mister Mack had been nosed

500 yards from the last drilling by the bright, busy red and black tug which was now standing off.

The platform had looked like a table turned upside down floating on the water with the three legs in the air. Then they had anchored and started the electric motors and sent the legs down vertically into the sea bed 170 feet below and now the machines were in turn hoisting the platform up the towers of legs still remaining above the water.

At one moment, the gulls overhead soared in fright. Perhaps from above they had seen something invisible to the men? The mishap did not occur for some minutes.

Groups of men stood about on the upper deck, watching until the maneuvering was over. It was the critical period, when the risks were greatest. The shouts of those working mingled with the clank of gear and the grinding of the gearing. The sounds went out over the North Sea and were lost at once.

Gainer, the driller, was posted by the derrick which rose 140 feet above the platform. The derrick had been brought to a position in the center of the platform, blocked and chocked. The massive traveling block and hook which carried the drilling string had been lowered and lashed down inside the derrick structure. Nolan, the tool pusher, was in the raised control room deckhouse watching the inclinometer with Ransome, the chief engineer.

The gearing at the legs was normally operated as a whole, so that the platform remained level and rose on an even keel. But as a result of a faulty connection to the control room which was under repair, they were this morning operating each leg independently.

"All at two hundred twenty-five. Two hundred twenty-five revs," Ransome said into the mike.

The machine rooms were on the deck below. The intercom for the team on the top deck of the platform was turned on full blast, so that Ransome's voice came out in a harsh screech above the general noise.

Two miles to the south the helicopter wheeled in wide circles, waiting to come in and land on the round platform near Spud one. The putt-putt of its engine was inaudible on the platform.

"No three! Sullivan. Hold it, will you? You're supposed to be doing two hundred twenty-five revs."

Nolan, who had been moving behind Ransome, stopped and looked over his shoulder at the dials and inclinometer. He was a smallish lean man with a furrowed brow and a lined face, not bad-looking, an American. He wore dark glass-

8

es, a driller's zip overall smudged with oil, but unlike Ransome had discarded his white plastic hard hat.

"What's he fooling at? Hear this, Sullivan—" he had shouldered Ransome away from the mike. "Did you get two hundred twenty-five or not?"

"Two hundred twenty-five revs. It's what I'm doing."

"It's the gearing again, chief," Ransome said.

"Then cut to two hundred ten. Two hundred ten."

Their eyes watched the inclinometer, the arrangement of three tubes, like arched spirit-levels, in which the bubble must remain centered between marking nodes. "Okay." Nolan stood looking over the other instruments. He fingered his dark glasses, then went to the door.

"Dumb bastard."

"He's all right," Ransome said.

"Dumb bastard."

The top deck of the platform was strewn with heavy gear. The pipe racks, loaded with 30-foot lengths of steel drill pipe, extended in front of the derrick between the port and starboard cranes; and on either side were boxed new drill bits ranged in sizes and patterns, crates of worn-out rusty bits, a battery of fishing tools, reels of cable and hose, heavy-duty joints and spares of all kinds, winches, pumps and the general orderly accumulation of a drilling site.

To the right were the crew's quarters, mess and galley in a long deckhouse and on the opposite side, Nolan's cubicle, cabin and office. Under the helicopter platform were two more small deckhouses, the mud lab and radio room. Hatches and stairways led to the deck below where the mud tanks and pumps, bins, diesel machine rooms and generators were located along with auxiliary power units, stores and so on.

"We're going to forty feet. Right?" Ransome said.

"Right." Nolan turned back to the panel.

Theoretically, the highest waves were between thirty and fifty feet—theoretically.

"Twenty-five feet now, chief."

They were jacking the platform forty feet above the sea where it would be stopped for the drilling.

For a moment, the labouring of the engines continued, then the vibration slowed with heavy shuddering increase. The control room shook. The door sprang off its hook and knocked over a stool. A pot of pencils and a telephone fell with a clatter. Ransome looked startled and was turning to Nolan when both were pitched forward against the control panel.

Outside there was noisy confusion and shouts and the fall of weighty equipment.

"Good Christ!"

Something slashed the control room roof like a whip, bringing down some beaverboard from the ceiling and fragmenting a panel of the security glass. They jumped to the clear window. Outside, the deck ran away in a sharp incline to the far corner. The port crane was swinging violently outboard and some of the piled gear had shifted.

"Spud three! We're on soft bottom!"

The third leg had sunk. It had struck a place where the sea bed was soft—the unpredictable but always present mischance—causing the whole platform to lurch sideways like a tripod table with one suddenly-shortened leg.

"Stop all! Stop all! All spuds stop jacking." Nolan reached to the control panel and threw the red emergency switch marked General Alarm. Bells started ringing all over the platform.

"Cut those goddamned motors! Cut, you dope, Sullivan! Watch out for the pipe!"

There had been a brief alarmed pause after the mishap. Now the crew were recovering from their surprise and racing across the deck, quickly skirting the pipe and climbing over gear that had shifted.

"Keep back! What in hell are you doing? There's enough goddamned weight on the spud! Willis—chase those dopes off. Keep 'em back." Nolan's voice rose.

The seven-ton travelling block and hook were swinging inside the derrick, freed from their lashing by the sudden movement but still held by one wire cable from smashing into the derrick framework. An oil drum, momentarily blocked, broke loose and rolled across the deck, crashing into the crane.

A group was clustered around an injured man. Four lengths of pipe had bounced out of the pipe rack and one had rammed itself into the wall of the mud lab deckhouse like a gigantic dart.

Nolan stood with the intercom mike, staring through the window giving orders. Ransome beside him was on the internal phone to the machine room. The din of the alarm bell was being amplified by the speakers on deck. Nolan swung around and flipped it off.

In the sudden quiet, the sounds came up clearly from the platform. Gainer had left the derrick and was down the nearest hatch to the deck below.

"Get down there and see what's happened," Nolan said to

10

Ransome. He spoke with a slight impediment. Ransome moved fast through the door.

"Where in hell's the damage control party?" Nolan was bellowing over the mike. "Jackson. Where's Jackson? Willis, will you secure that pipe? Hey, Willis—the port stay on the derrick has gone. Jesus!"

It was the wire stay springing free which had slashed the roof of the office. Nolan's face was white. He stopped speaking, turned away from the window. Then he turned back with the mike again. "When somebody's ready, I'd like to know what the hell's going on below. Is it okay if I'm kept informed? I want Jackson on the upper deck. Mr. Jackson report on top deck . . ."

There was a muffled crash from below as some piece of equipment fell.

"What's going on, Gainer? What's happening down there?"

The intercom crackled. "Bloody mess. We're full of mud and oil. Half the mud pond's on the deck . . . and about three diesel drums. Air compressor broke loose—just went over. And it looks as if one of the mud pumps has taken a knock."

"What d'you say?"

"I said the piston's out. Port mud pump. Hey Lofty—"

"Where's Ransome? Gainer—where's Ransome?"

Gainer came back. "Machine room."

"Send Jackson up here, will you?"

"Looks all right, Mr. Nolan," Ransome's voice cut in. "I've got a man hurt."

"Double up the lashing on that travelling block, for Christ's sake," Nolan said. "If we go again it'll be curtains for somebody."

"We going again, chief?"

"Goddamn it, how in hell do I know?"

The gulls overhead wheeled with their mournful two-note cries. Lo—st lo—st. Lost . . . lost . . . lost . . .

2

THE group of men in hard hats, caps and greasy overalls filled Nolan's small office and overflowed at the door. They were angry and impatient and didn't mind showing it. Some of those in front looked from Nolan at the desk to scraps of paper in their hands where they had noted their points of argument. Now and then a man at the back spoke loudly over the shoulders of the ones in front. Gainer was in a corner.

Three hours after the mishap, with the gear secured, they had levelled off the platform, cautiously raised it another ten feet. There had been no further sinking; the spud seemed firmly implanted in the sea bed. In this position, the platform was lower than they had calculated it would be for the new drilling.

Three men had been hurt, one had a crushed foot. He was waiting to be taken ashore by the helicopter which had now landed. The others had gone in by the tug after Nolan had told it that the rig no longer needed its assistance.

There had been a brief interlude after the tug steamed off. Then the crew had blown up.

The accident with the spud had brought the rumbling state of affairs on the platform to a head. The roughnecks, drillers, floormen, electricians—even the geologist—had crowded to Nolan's office with their complaints. The first exchanges had promptly developed into recriminations. Nolan, sitting on the edge of the desk, faced them sourly like the captain of a mutinous crew. He was wearing his dark glasses. It wasn't sunny and they were inside the office. Nolan kept the glasses on. He fingered them occasionally.

"We're supposed to be doing fouteen days, ain't we? Never get relieved on time." This was Wedderburn, one of the electricians. "Always the same old tune."

"You'll be calling over the jet bits in a couple of days and wanting to know where I've lost the bloody stock," the storeman said. "Here's the log-sheet saying we put in for them three weeks ago——"

"How are we expected to work in that space down there with the bloody air conditioner on the blink? The thing's

12

more often broken down than it's working. Lot of foul air——"

"Am I doing the talking or not?" This was Willis, an older man in the front, whom they had appointed spokesman but kept disregarding. Willis had a brown, squarish face with deep lines and a solid manner and he wasn't easily put out.

"You know as well as I do, Mr. Nolan, that we can't carry on in this style. The men have had enough—everybody's had enough." He spoke quietly, wiping his hands on cotton waste. "We're short of any quantity of gear—items we're badly in need of always being left on the dock. We had enough trouble with that last hole to start another now. You can't expect work in these conditions."

"We can drill, can't we?" Nolan said.

"Drill, man——"

"We're entitled to get relieved regular."

"It's always sixteen—seventeen days. Once it was near three bloody weeks."

Willis butted in: "It's quite true. There's been no improvement in changing crews. These man have got families, Mr. Nolan, if you haven't, and you can't ask them to put up with these conditions."

"We'd be a bloody sight better off on the Atlas job over there."

Argo 1, the rival platform of the Atlas Oil Company, was just visible on the horizon.

"And what about the mail?"

"Yeah. I ought to swim out for the stuff," Nolan said. "Or maybe write your long-haired letters myself."

"Mr. Nolan, the Company can't expect the men to carry on without contact ashore. Be reasonable. It's no wonder we can't keep the same men for five minutes. I've had six different men on the rotary in a month—three of them no good."

"Do I have to buy 'em off going to Gulf or somebody else for more dough?" Nolan said.

"And why should we count boat time our time? Fourteen hours to get out here in that boat—in our own time. It's half a day's work. Damn well ought to be paid."

"You knew when you signed on, didn't you?" Nolan said. "Or did they twist your arm?"

"Mr. Nolan, that sort of attitude isn't going to help anybody."

"And then the boat goes into the German side. It happens! What the hell's the good of a German port to us? The captain makes out it's a shorter run."

"You can't have it both ways, can you?" Nolan said.

"What about the lousy grub you was going to improve?"

"The cooks are about ready to quit, ain't they Fred?"

"Where they going?" Nolan said.

"I don't know what you eat, Mr. Nolan, but the food we're getting is something pretty poor and monotonous and the cooks are not going to stand much more bellyaching from the men about it either, I'll tell you that."

"Sure, you gentlemen are entitled to cavier," Nolan snarled. "You're getting the equivalent of first-class shipboard food and you goddamn know it."

"We eat out of bloody cans. Never see a fresh veg."

"Yeah? You think I'm sending in for fresh asparagus maybe every day?"

A face came forward. "You won't keep forty-two men doing this work on deep-freeze, tinned stuff and beans, Mr. Nolan!"

"That's another thing," Willis put in. "We're still shorthanded. We've had this out enough times. Something's got to be done. The full complement of this rig is fifty-two men. It can't be worked properly with less. You know and the Company knows it."

"You getting your bonuses?" Nolan said.

There were loud protests.

"If I got my men out here, they'd tell you to stick your bonuses, Mr. Nolan. I'm working a twelve-hour tour * and by God if there's any more like this morning, there's going to be trouble."

"Sure, I ought to have had second sight and known about the soft bottom."

"The whole damn rig's being run too tight!"

"We're being pushed to hell——"

"No smoking on deck! No smoking down below! It's only just okay if we smoke in the bloody mess!"

"Those crummy old awful old mags," Lockwood, the geologist, said. "And the TV always on the blink."

"No proper washing machines, neither."

As it went on, Gainer watched Nolan's face. Nolan sat listening unsympathetically, conceding nothing. Now and then he passed a hand around the back of his neck and looked up with a furrowed brow. Gainer felt his own exasperation growing. Nolan didn't even raise his voice. He listened to everything they had to say, occasionally putting in acid comment.

At last he said, "Okay. You gentlemen said what you wanted to say. I've heard it. I don't consider it amounts to more than a row of bellyaches. As far as I'm concerned, you get

* Tour—pronounced tower. The shift of a drilling crew.

your orders from me and not from anybody else on this rig. When I think you have legitimate cause for complaint, I'll take action. Now if you don't mind, I've got some work to do and I'd be obliged if you'd clear out and get on with yours."

They paused. They looked at each other. Then they went out with tight lips.

Gainer waited until they had gone. "Well? What are you going to do?"

"What do you think?"

"Radio to the tug to turn round and tow us back."

"Sure," Nolan said. "Oh sure. Like hell."

Gainer gave himself time. He pushed the door shut. It slammed. "You know damn well they're right. There's one reasonable thing to do: pull back to harbour, retool, change the crew."

"Yeah? Then what?"

"Give us all a rest, get some hard and fast arrangement on reliefs and then maybe we can get back to work."

"That sounds like several reasonable things, Mr. Gainer, but I reckon I ain't a reasonable man." Nolan called the senior men he worked with by a formal "Mister," like a sea captain.

"But what do you expect to get? They've got a whole fat list of legitimate grievances, legitimate reasons for howling. I tell you I never saw such an edgy bunch as those drilling crews. The rest of them are sick at not getting ashore—hell, you heard it all."

"This is where we're supposed to drill and where, as far as I'm concerned, we are going right on to drill."

"You make a lot of effort cutting down the time on hole; you'd do better to get the stuff out here on time."

The Company had been complaining about costs going up steeply. But Nolan, an inquisitor over delays, nagged back, constantly attacking the Company's failures to get stores and parts out from shore. Relentlessly he hunted down the reasons for delay, the mistakes on the platform that held up the drilling. Quidd, his clerk, the most hated man on board, spied for him—and of course every shutdown cost Nolan part of his own bonus.

"Is that so?" Nolan said.

"We're in for trouble in a big way unless something's done."

"Thanks for your advice, Mr. Gainer. You can keep the change."

Gainer looked at him. "You can save that stuff for the men, Nolan." He took hold of the door handle, then turned back. "You know damn well this platform is not suitable for this area. It's meant for shallower water altogether, Mexican Gulf stuff—one hundred fifty feet at the maximum and we're in one seventy to one seventy-five. We've got trouble with the gearing on Spud three——"

"We've been through all that."

"——and you won't admit it's because we need a refit. You can't jack her up enough; and we're in flat calm."

Nolan was looking at him obliquely. His forehead furrowed. He adjusted his dark glasses and for a second Gainer thought he looked lonely and scared. But the next minute Nolan said levelly, "I'll be obliged if you stick to your appointed job, Mr. Gainer, and I'll stick to mine, which includes doing any complaining or making any reports about the rig when I think they need making and not before."

"Look, Gene, for God's sake——" With an effort, Gainer relaxed. He spoke in a conciliatory tone. "We're getting nowhere. How about taking it easy? We've got to work together and——"

"You heard what I said, didn't you?"

"I did, but I think you're being unreasonable. I don't think this attitude's going to make it any easier for any of us."

"There's no attitude, Mr. Gainer. Now get out."

"Is that how you want it?"

"You heard me."

Gainer stood there looking at Nolan for a few seconds. "Okay," he said and went out.

The cranes were working and parties of men were moving about shifting equipment. It was mid-afternoon and the October sun was declining in a copper blaze. A steamer trailed dirty smoke across the horizon far to the south. On the circular landing platform above, the Sikorsky helicopter was preparing to leave, the rotor turning. Two men were easing a stretcher with the injured man on it inside while the pilot stood by.

Gainer gave Parrish, the pilot, a sign, walked quickly across the deck to his cabin. He threw off coat and helmet, zipped his overalls, extracted some items from the pockets and pulled off his shirt. He moved with the quick decision of an angry man. In a few moments he was dressed. He took a ready-packed overnight case and was about to go when Peter Guggendorf, the doctor, came in. They shared the cabin. The doctor was new on board.

"You going ashore?" the doctor said.

"Yep. Keep the home fires burning, doc," Gainer said grimly, moving to the door.

"Bring me some tea."

"Okay."

"And some Buck-Master."

"Some what?"

"Buck-Master. Great stuff. Lead in your pencil."

"Okay."

The doctor called after him, "If you can't get Buck-Master, get Tonicate. Terrific."

Gainer went across the desk and up the iron ladder to the helicopter platform. No sign of Nolan.

"You've got another passenger, Ed," he shouted to the pilot, then indicated the sick man. "Who's going in with him?"

"Osborne." Osborne was the temporary sickbay attendant from whom the doctor had taken over. He was now leaving for good. Gainer ducked to enter the machine. The sick man's stretcher was installed with Osborne sitting alongside. Two other men were sitting up front behind the pilot's seat. One was Bradford, the mud engineer.

"Hi." He gave Gainer a hand sign with open palm. Bradford, who was in a dark blue suit, had a narrow black moustache and carefully-combed black hair, gold wrist watch, gold ring and tie chain. The other man was a specialist Gainer didn't know; they were always getting specialists of one sort or another on the rig for a day or so.

"You going in?" Gainer said to Bradford.

"Yep."

Gainer's arm was taken from behind. He turned.

"You got a chit from Mr. Nolan?" Parrish said.

"What for?"

"Everybody who goes ashore's got to have a chit signed by him."

At Gainer's look he shrugged. "You know how he doesn't want any crew flying in."

"I'll sign it. Give me your book."

The pilot hesitated. "You know, Mr. Nolan said—"

"Hell, come on," Gainer said. Parrish handed it over.

As they were taking off, Gainer saw Nolan looking up from the deck. Parrish gunned the motor and the Sikorsky banked steeply, heading west towards the land.

3

THE illuminated glass figures flicked on and off as the lift rose from the steel-and-black-glass entrance hall of the Contram building. At six, Gainer waited while the two girls who had ridden with him got out, then followed. One of them, a long-waisted brunette, gave him a smile of recognition.

"Hello," Gainer said. She wasn't bad.

He turned along the corridor, took a right-angle branch and went up a flight of stairs to the Executive Floor above. This was not served by the lift he had taken and Gainer had not, in any event, wanted to reach the floor by lift since he was heading first for the office of Margie Field, his girl. They had talked in haste on the telephone overnight after Gainer had landed at North Scully, the Company's east coast base. He had been in a hurry to catch the London train.

Gainer was six feet tall and well-built, with light blue eyes and a weathered face. He had short, rough, fair hair. He was thirty-six years old, had been an oilman all his working life and he had the feeling of the man in the field for headquarters. Whenever he came in to the place, it seemed to him to be manned by people remote from the realities which were his daily grind—the dirt, the sweat, the heavy work and the problems which any drilling entailed, a race of desk-sitters, paper-fiddlers, not men who acted. He felt the contempt of the slogging soldier for the Staff, though with Gainer it was qualified since he did not have the simple comforting illusion that the men at the top were all idiots. But they weren't *men*.

The corridor was carpeted in dove grey. Here and there on the wall was a valuable picture. Gainer knocked on a door and opened it on to a big, light-carpeted office with a long window, modern teak furniture and a big pot of flowers.

"Oh, Larry!" Margie was just coming in from an adjoining office. She shut the door behind her, put down the things she was carrying. "Darling." She kissed him quickly on the cheek.

"New smell," Gainer said.

"Like it?" The cool freshness of her teeth and mouth were very attractive. "From Paris."

"Yeah?" He hadn't heard she had been in Paris and sup-

18

posed somebody had brought it over for her. "Are you doing anything tonight?"

"No, but are you sure you're going to be here?" she said.

"I told you."

She looked briefly hesitant, then said, "I had a sort of date but I can put it off."

She was smallish and blonde with depths of burnt ochre showing beneath the lighter ridges of her hair. And even in the setting of the office, she created an effect with the rather hard chic of her dress, her mauve-varnished nails, her wet, slightly derisive mouth. Gainer thought she was looking wonderfully well.

"You still haven't told me what this is in aid of," she said with a little pout.

Gainer lit up a cigarette and exhaled a jet of smoke. The impulse on which he had angrily hastened ashore had weakened. "Sticking my damn neck out. But somebody has to make sense of this drilling."

"What's wrong?"

"What isn't! Nolan's blocking off complaints, we're short of gear, the crew are playing up—and so on. I have to get to somebody who'll take decisions." He looked up hopefully. "Perhaps the old man?"

She shook her head. Margie was the Chairman's personal secretary. "Bad moment."

"Why? What's on?"

The door being flung open cut off her answer and a man in his late fifties with a black check tie and pearl pin surged in from the corridor, leaving the door wide open behind him. "Miss Field, what time is the meeting?"

"Twelve."

"Twelve." His quick flick at Gainer had already passed back to her with inquiry. She said, "This is Mr. Gainer, Mr. Moreno. He's in from Mister Mack." Moreno was on the Contram board, one of the big wheels.

Gainer met the hard grey eyes as Moreno, leaning forward, neck extended, advanced into the room. Moreno had no eyelashes.

"From Mister Mack? Now that's interesting. That's interesting. And are you going to strike oil soon, Mr. Gainer? Are you going to strike oil? H'm?" The professional intimidator, Gainer recognized; the asker of rhetorical questions to intimidate. Moreno had a puffed chest, almost deformed in its massive structure, and no neck.

"I'd like to be able to tell you," he said, grinning and deciding to ham it to elude the pressure.

"So you don't know whether you are going to strike oil?

You're drilling but you don't know whether you're going to strike. H'm? How long have you been drilling, Mr. Gainer? You're drilling but you don't know whether you're going to get any oil? Does anybody know whether you're going to get oil?" A pause—which Gainer didn't attempt to fill. "And how are you finding things with Mister Mack? You can tell me that, Mr. Gainer? What's the situation out there?"

Gainer hedged. He had a strong feeling that Moreno wasn't the man and this not the opportunity. "We've just pulled out to a new site, sir, Block AR 41 on the chart. Put the spuds down yesterday."

Moreno's eyes were closely examining his face. It was an uncomfortable experience and Gainer had the impression that he wasn't going to get away with much.

"Block AR 41. And you're drilling at Block AR 41?"

"We shall be starting tomorrow or the next day. When we've got the BOP packages and so on down there."

"And have you come to report that conditions are favourable or unfavourable?"

Gainer dropped his look to Moreno's black striped waistcoat then looked up again. "Well, sir, we're not giving ourselves the best chance of success out there."

"Ah? Why's that?" Words like bullets. No more rhetorical questions. The pewter eyes were fixed on him and something in Moreno's manner expressed eagerness. Gainer had an idea that for some reason Moreno was anxious to have bad news. Margie had moved around to shut the door to the corridor and was doing something on that side of the room and over Moreno's shoulder, he caught the briefest glance from her which seemed to confirm his thought.

"Well, it's a whole lot of things. we're not getting stores on time. We keep putting in for gear which doesn't arrive, with the result that we're shut down. The relief tour doesn't turn up as regularly as it should and the men don't get ashore to their families."

Moreno didn't appear impressed with these details. Obviously, his look said, there was something more, something beyond this. "But the drilling prospects are favourable or unfavourable?"

"Mr. Moreno, that's a wide question. We haven't got started on this hole yet."

Moreno repeated the words, eyeing him. "Not started yet. You're going to drill at AR 41 but you haven't got started yet. I see." He had obviously gathered his impression; he was not a man you could easily dissimulate from or put something past. He turned away and went out.

Gainer had to wait till Margie had finished on the phone. She hung up, made a note, then turned to him.

"He looks a tough bird," Gainer said.

"I didn't have a chance to tell you. You've arrived in the middle of the civil war. There's a tremendous row going on."

"What about?"

"Mister Mack. Moreno and his group are dead against going on in the North Sea."

"They are, are they?"

She nodded. "Been coming to a head for months and now it's right here."

"What do they want?"

"They want to pull out entirely. They're having a board meeting on it today."

"That's the meeting at twelve."

She nodded.

"Somebody pushing against the Moreno crowd?"

"Of course. The Chairman and Mr. Stoneman—"

A junior executive put his head around the door. She left Gainer's side and hurried out to him. Gainer crossed the office, took an internal phone from the desk and rang a lower floor.

"Perry? Larry Gainer. Hi, you old so and so . . . Sure. Not bad. Yuh, I heard . . . That so? Listen, I wanted to ask you, where's Stevenson? No, the lab man. He's been lab man on Mister Mack but we haven't seen him out there for a week . . . I see . . . Well, if he shows . . . We don't either, and meantime we're operating without a lab man. Okay, thanks boy. See you." They didn't know.

He lit another cigarette. The trouble on the rig and the situation building up here made it imperative for him to see somebody who would take decisions. When Margie came back, he said, "What chance of getting in to see the old man before the meeting?"

"Mmm. Not good. Have you seen Anderson?" Anderson was the company's chief driller through whom Gainer and other men from the field would normally have to pass to reach the executives.

"No. I want to do it without him if I can."

"You're really asking for trouble."

"There's too much stalling already."

Margie looked doubtful. "All right. I'll try. You won't get long." She took him along the corridor, installed him in a waiting room and Gainer sat there, expectantly at first, then, when nothing happened, he got up and stood looking out of the window at the panorama of London below.

A protest march, a small affair of two dozen men and a

few supporters, was heading down Park Lane escorted by a mounted policeman. He could read a banner or two. *Hands off our Five Percent* and *Bendigo Must Go.* Who was Bendigo? In the park beyond, two nurses were talking on a bench while their children chased a dog.

He smoked another cigarette, looked at his watch. Eleven-twenty. It felt like a waste of time. He sat down again, examining the abstract paintings on the walls, a large one in yellows and browns from which a woman's Negroid head seemed to be looking out, the smaller picture a series of identical and geometrically-aligned cubes on a blazing red background, from which he could get neither pleasure nor stimulus.

There was a large turquoise vase of early chrysanthemums with great bronze-looking petals looking extravagantly costly, and on the low, red lacquer Chinese table a pile of the smart continental monthlies like *Domus, Art et Architecture, Du, l'Oeil* and so on among one or two glossy-covered oil journals. The sofa on which he sat was elegant and Scandinavian. And all these arrangements increased his impatience, his sense of the lack of connection between what went on here and their life at the drilling.

Margie had told him, months earlier, about the order of battle lining up inside Contram. But then he had been away on the job and what had happened in the meantime wasn't in the ordinary range of a driller's news. Now it had apparently come to a head-on collision—which was going to make it a damn sight harder to get them to deal with the trouble on Mister Mack.

He reached for the ashtray, stubbed his cigarette and heard Margie at the door.

"Oh, he*llo.* This is a pleasant surprise." It was Diana Corbett, from Marketing. She shut the door and came forward smiling. "Mister Stranger . . ."

Gainer had been running around with her at one time, before Margie. "Hello, Di. You're looking very good."

"Am I? I'm better than you ever found out." She sauntered up, as far as her tight skirt allowed a saunter. "What are you doing here? I thought you were out on the wild, wild waves." She wore her lank, dark brown hair cut around her face with one little point curving on her cheek—a style that suited her perfectly and in some way enhanced the beauty of her mat skin. She had a small mole on her jaw and blue eyes, the whole effect very pretty and ripe with her good poise, but remotely signalling that the playful amusement was misleading. At one time they had spent a couple of nights together which had been very successful but not deeply engaging, and then

22

the thing had broken up for lack of opportunity, since he had been away working; and afterwards he had met Margie. But Di had always been pressing for a resumption.

"I just came in for a conference."

She was wearing a two-shade brown silk dress with rounded neck and short sleeves. She came around the low table, stood close. "You still turning to the right, Gainer?"

He grinned.

"You still building angle, Corbett?"

"Uh-huh." She slid an arm around him, wriggled her hips and pressed herself in. He felt the contour of her still-unsupported and muscular midsection under the silk, and her long thighs. She eased herself away and for an instant he felt her free hand wander—then she stepped back with a little laugh.

"I never see you. Why don't you come around any more?"

"Well, see I only swim in on Thursdays; and then I have to see my trainer. You know how it is."

"You are a bastard. Larry . . ." she purred, moving in again "You're being brutal. You have me all set up for you. Every time I see you I can't get you off my mind for a week. Be nice to me. We made good, didn't we? Wasn't it fun?" She crooked a knee against him, not so close to him that she couldn't start fooling again.

"Sure, but—"

"We didn't give it much chance."

"Di, now come on, baby, this is not the bridal suite."

"Nobody's coming in. I don't see you enough."

"Your boss's going to open the door any minute." She had her tongue provocatively between her teeth, obviously aware of the effect she was producing on him. He took her gently by the waist to push her back but she trod one of her stiletto heels on his foot and said "Let's go out tonight, get a little high and come back and practice the twenty-five positions? Larry, h'm?"

He laughed.

"I have a new flat. You haven't seen it. I'll wait for you. Pick me up at six-thirty."

"Sorry, Di, I can't. I'm tied up. Now look—"

He took her waist and lifted her away and she stood back with her head on one side, looking at him with absolute frankness. "You can't say you didn't like it."

"Boy, you're the devil." Gainer took out a cigarette, lit it and moved across to the window. The door opened. It was one of the junior girl secretaries who worked for Margie, and Gainer gasped mentally. A near miss! The girl looked from one to the other, a bit puzzled; but Gainer thought it was all right.

23

"Miss Field said would you come along at once, Mr. Gainer?"

"Thanks."

Di picked up some files she had put on the table and said over her shoulder, "Ring me before you leave, Gainer, and I'll have that address."

"Sure thing."

She went out. He tossed his cigarette into the ashtray and followed the girl down the corridor, cursing inwardly, then laughing. It wasn't the most composing introduction to the coming interview.

"You have about five minutes," Margie said, leading him across to the Chairman's door. "You'll probably be interrupted at that."

"Anderson in there?"

She shook her head.

Inside, the door was shielded by a high grey screen which they had to negotiate before getting into the office, a long room with an angle at the end, parquet floor, good carpets, shiny panelling and the conventional mahogany furniture. Sir Walter Meldreth, the Chairman of Contram, was sitting back in a high-backed chair at his desk, smoking a cigar and evidently waiting for him.

"Good morning, sir." Gainer stepped briskly forward—hoping Meldreth wasn't going to tell Margie to fetch Anderson, but Margie had tactfully dropped back and disappeared after bringing him in. Meldreth said, "Good morning," beaming and nodding his head in the benevolent and somewhat stupid way Gainer remembered from their single previous meeting. He remained seated and motioned Gainer to a chair.

Meldreth was plump and sixty-fiveish. He had thick white hair, a Groucho Marx moustache in white, and gold-rimmed glasses which didn't look particularly thick but magnified and liquefied his eyes in a curious way so that they swam about behind the glass looking enormous, as if they were in bowls; and though he was impeccably shaved and turned out, there was an effect of bristliness about his chin and jaws and you wouldn't have been entirely surprised to notice a dab of cotton wool on some shaving cut or a blob of egg on the striped waistcoat.

There was something faintly dummy about him, as if he had been a stooge for so many companies that it had somehow ended by expressing itself physically. There was also a patronizing and inadequate element in his manner—in the solidity of his seat in the chair and the peculiar way he shook off the ash of his cigar into the glass ashtray—and Gainer felt that it wasn't going to be easy to convey urgency about Mister Mack.

Yet Sir Walter had the reputation of having been one of the smartest financial operators on the Canadian stock market—a particularly tremendous and never-rivalled placer of debentures in his earlier days. There was obviously more behind the dummy facade. He had a silver-framed portrait of a woman on his desk—an old-fashioned touch—and a galuchat 1925-ish cigarette box, which he did not, however, offer to Gainer.

"Well, now. You've asked to see me about the work?" he said in a plummy voice.

"Yes, sir." (Gainer had decided to plunge straight in.) "We're having serious trouble on the platform and we're going to have worse unless there are quick improvements. I don't know if you know what we're up against?" Gainer paused, hoping they could get to grips at once; but Sir Walter gave him no help and sat puffing his cigar. Gainer could feel no exchange of sympathy.

"We are a dozen men short, sir. You can't work an outfit of that size at three-quarters strength. The result is that the crews won't stay. The crews we started with have broken up, gone elsewhere—everybody's crying out for good floormen or drillers or roustabouts these days—and we keep getting patchy replacements, bad workers, men without the right experience and so on. Even some of these won't stay because the food's bad, mail doesn't arrive, the gear is short——"

"You've had a great deal of shutdown time, Mr. Gainer," Sir Walter interrupted. "we have been losing a lot of time."

"Mostly because we can't get the supplies and services out to us, sir. We've had three different nipple-chasers* and none of them has made any improvement."

"Your maintenance and repair costs are running extremely high. Extremely high. Costing far too much."

It didn't sound as if Meldreth were with him. Not following. Meldreth seemed to be pursuing thoughts of his own.

"For the same reason, sir. We're kept waiting for material which we have asked for six times but which doesn't arrive. Something's got to be done. Half the time when the boat turns up, you find the items you want urgently have been left on the dockside, then when you look for them they're lost. There's a chronic waste of time in getting material out to us. Ten days ago, we asked for extra pump liners and rod packing for the circulating pumps and we haven't got them yet."

---

* Nipple-chaser—not necessarily a sex fiend but a man whose job is to procure and deliver tools and gear to the rig.

"Isn't any investigation made when this happens?"

"*We* investigate, sir. We've been doing practically nothing else lately, chasing repair parts, finding out why they haven't arrived, why this or that failed. Nolan has a clerk—Nolan's the tool pusher—who needles everybody whenever there's a failure and gets the men on the raw. Somebody's going to kill him one day."

"That's Mr. Nolan's responsibility, isn't it?"

"Yes, sir, it is. All I'm saying is that if somebody here doesn't do something, the downtime's going to get worse, the costs are going up further, we're going to have much more trouble with the men——"

A panelled door behind Sir Walter's desk had opened swiftly and a desiccated man in black came in. He emanated a chill. He stopped, drilled Gainer with a look, then bent in a self-possessed way at Sir Walter's ear and said something of which Gainer caught only the sibilants. When Sir Walter replied, the man looked up again at Gainer.

"This is Mr. Stoneman, our managing director," Sir Walter said.

Gainer, who had never seen Stoneman before, got to his feet. Stoneman reputedly was head man. Gainer half expected some exchange of greetings. Stoneman simply gave a nod and Gainer sat down again. A cool bird. Stoneman had a leathery face composed in ridges which folded, as soon as he opened his mouth, like the folds of a hard, dried, petrified concertina. Gainer had the impression that there were cracks and fissures in the folds, but he couldn't be sure. Stoneman had small brown eyes and thin, faintly purple lips. He was fiftyish, obviously controlled Meldreth completely and he had, by merely entering the room, brought the interview into a different mood.

"I've been telling the Chairman, Mr. Stoneman,——"

"You come from Mr. Nolan?"

"No, that is, I——"

"Then why are you here? Why are you away from your job? Aren't you the driller? You have left in fact without authority."

Gainer guessed that Nolan had radioed some message about his arrival. "Mr. Stoneman, I have a responsibility, as you're implying, and I'm fulfilling it here for the moment more effectively than I can on the platform by telling you that conditions on Mister Mack are about as bad as they can be."

Meldreth was going to speak but Stoneman stopped him with a gesture. "Go on." His lips were like a crack in a board.

Gainer went through the facts again—the constant breakdowns in the shore-to-platform supply line, the reduced and piecemeal crews they were working with, the storage space piled up one week, empty the next through bad organization, the frequent lack of tools, the poor food, the discontent, Nolan's pressure for faster work and so on. He warmed up as he spoke and was getting a good deal of thrust into the recital when Stoneman interrupted him.

"Nolan doesn't give anything like so black a picture."

"I beg your pardon?"

"I said Nolan doesn't think it's so bad."

"I can't account for what Nolan says."

"But he is the Tool Pusher. He's in charge, isn't he? You do what you're told." It was offensively said.

Gainer shifted in the chair. He wasn't going to be trodden on.

"So I repeat—why are you here?" Stoneman said.

"Mr. Stoneman, the men are being driven, they are everlastingly being harassed and told to cut time. How do you expect three men to do the work of four and keep it up for twelve hours at a run—we've had men running on that damned platform—then listen to a bellyful of sour abuse and criticism which ought not rightly to fall on them because they're short of equipment and things are damn badly organized? It's unreasonable. It won't work, Mr. Stoneman. Every time they get ashore there are half a dozen who pick up their pay and don't come back and on the next tour we get weevils * for floormen!"

Stoneman was leaning on the desk. He was a man who had learned long since to control his anger. It left his face a shade greyer. "Are you complaining of speedy work?"

"Speedy work! Good God——"

"You are now costing ten times more than a shore rig, Mr. Gainer, and costs are still rising astronomically. Your downtime has doubled in the past month——"

"On account of——"

"——and whether you personally like it or not (Stoneman had loudly raised his voice) in those circumstances you are bloody well expected to move fast! Mr. Nolan is investigating failures in supply and he reports that drilling can and will continue. And that is fully what we intend. Is that understood, Gainer? Fully what we intend!"

The leathery creases multiplied. The eyes hardened. He looked the hatchet man, all right, Gainer thought. He wished he had Stoneman out on the rig for a week. Meldreth was

* Weevil—inexperienced rig worker.

simply a figurehead. And he saw, of course—in the light of what Margie had said about the struggle going on inside Contram over the drilling—why Stoneman should be set against giving any ground to his complaints, even though the thing was illogical. He could hardly say this. But he thought he could try to get a rise out of Stoneman on it.

"If Nolan's investigating, why are there so many breakdowns in supplies?"

"Mr. Gainer, I don't appreciate your tone."

Gainer looked straight at him. He reached deliberately into his pocket for a cigarette and took one out. Stoneman watched him in silence, then, as Gainer produced a lighter, said, "When you are in this room, you do not smoke unless you are invited to."

Gainer flushed, put the cigarette back. Stoneman went on. "This office has approved every item that Nolan has asked for."

"We had a further mishap yesterday——"

"We know it."

"—which has increased the difficulties."

"All the more reason why you should be on board."

Gainer gave himself time. Slowly Stoneman said, "This is a very competitive business, Gainer, and we are not in it for our health. Or for yours."

Gainer said, "I'd be doing less than my duty, Mr. Stoneman, if I didn't tell you that it is a serious mistake to use that platform for drilling in the condition it is in and at that depth. It has never been entirely suitable and we are now going into the winter."

With a small gesture of impatience, Stoneman turned away, then swung back. His hand gripped the desk edge hard. "The drilling is going on and there is going to be no bloody nonsense and no further waste of time! Get that into your head!"

It was not pleasant. Gainer controlled himself. He said quietly, "I'm giving you my opinion, Mr. Stoneman, that unless we can get a better platform or do an extensive overhaul of Mister Mack, we'd better pack up."

"Pack up!" Stoneman's mouth was a blue crack. "When we want your advice on conducting this company, Mr. Gainer, we'll invite you to sit on the board. Until then you have a contract to drill and drill you bloody well will or we'll know the answer. So now I advise you to get back to your platform, Mister Driller, or there will be plenty of trouble and it will be very unpleasant. Good day."

Gainer stood up. He was on the point of saying, "There's

28

certainly going to *be* trouble, and I hope you get it." But Stoneman was offensively waving him off.

Gainer felt maddeningly frustrated and baffled at how the thing had gone so wrong—as if he were contending with the Company instead of serving its interests. Standing in front of the desk, he flicked his lighter, slowly lit his cigarette, turned and walked the length of the office, hearing Stoneman's low rasp talking to the Chairman. He shut the door deliberately —holding off the infuriated desire to go back and redeem Stoneman's dismissal—and saw Margie looking up from her desk.

"How did it go?"

"I've just been thrown out. I hope it won't be long before I punch Mr. Stoneman on the nose."

"What happened?"

The Chairman's buzzer went. "Tell me later." She collected a sheaf of papers from the desk and moved towards the door.

"See you tonight." He went out.

For safety's sake, Bradford had decided not to telephone from his overnight hotel. He turned off the Euston Road towards Russell Square. The London morning sky was pale blue. He had got in on the last overnight train at three a.m. and had been fighting down a desire to phone Judy ever since. Better later. Get the business end settled first or he'd never manage it.

He walked down to Russell Square Underground Station and went in. The phone boxes were occupied. He waited till one was free then went in. The phone was sticky, the glass blurred. He left the door open while he dialled. Then when the Atlas operator answered, he put sixpence in, quickly pulled the door to and said, "Mr. Raymond please."

"Mister?" the girl said.

"Raymond."

Pause. "One mo—ment please."

There was a longish wait and clicks. "Are yew holdin'?" said a voice.

"I'm waiting for Mr. Raymond."

"One mo-ment."

The first girl came back. "You're waiting for Mr. Raymond? Who wants him?"

Bradford said, "It's personal."

Another wait. The girl came back. "Mr. Raymond's in a meeting. Can I leave him a message?"

Bradford thought: meeting at ten to ten in the morning? Unlikely. "Tell him Brad called. I'll ring again."

Quickly she said, "If you'll wait a minute, I might be able to pass that in to him."

Bradford held on. It was a cover-up. He got another sixpence ready. But the girl came back almost at once. "Mr. Raymond says he's very sorry he's tied up but would you have lunch with him?"

"All right. Where?"

"He said the same place as last time. Half-past twelve. Is that all right?"

Bradford thought fast. What was it called?

"The Hansom," the girl said, as though she'd been primed.

"That's it. Yes, all right. Half-past twelve." He rang off.

He was a bit nervous. Did the girl know the place? Maybe it was Raymond's regular lunch hang-out? Couldn't be, for a thing like this. He wanted to phone Judy like hell but it was no good. It would have to wait until afterwards.

4

THE board room was in a blue haze. The long table had been in order when the meeting had begun but now the ashtrays were overflowing, the blotters were scarred with doodles, screwed-up paper was lying about and the water carafes were empty.

Similarly, the attitudes of the fourteen members of the board who sat around the table had passed from cool expectation, in which they had arrived, to tension.

At the head, Walter Meldreth was rolling his cigar in his mouth and flicking vaguely at the ash in the ridges of his waistcoat. Stoneman, on his right, was leaning forward, keyed up, cupping an ear to the man opposite.

The discussion had clearly marked out the two opposing groups. On one side were Stoneman, Meldreth and two supporters. The other side was led by J.B. Moreno, the most powerful individual member of the consortium which had launched Contram into the great competition for North Sea oil. Around him were four other directors, the chief of whom was A. Douglas Veitch, a small-boned man with slicked-down black hair who sat on Moreno's right.

At this strength, therefore, Moreno's side outnumbered Stoneman's five to four.

The five other members of the board had not yet finally declared themselves and by the natural coagulation of the other two groups, were seated together in the middle of the table. These undeclared men included Warren Neal, the only American on the board, and Henry Bream. Bream was the most important of the neutrals because of his certain influence over one, if not more, of the others.

Twice since the meeting had begun, Moreno had almost succeeded in bringing the issue to a vote. Stoneman had managed to defer this; but the Moreno group obviously felt they could carry the day and were increasing the pressure.

At the moment the room was filled with a general hum of voices as the men talked to their neighbours or across the table. The discussion had been interrupted by Moreno's assistant bringing in some documents which Moreno had wanted to examine on the spot. When the door shut again, the general buzz continued for a moment longer, then faded as the men's attention came back to the business in hand.

Bream adjusted his glasses and looked down towards Moreno.

"I'd like to be clear, J.B., about what's entailed in your proposal. Are you suggesting that we should——"

"Not suggesting. We don't suggest anything. We've got to the point now where we insist. This North Sea venture must be closed down, here and now. The thing is running away with itself. It's absurd—look at it! You have the figures in front of you. Whatever Stoneman may say, we have spent far, far too much on operations and neither I nor any of my associates had any intention of getting in this deep for what we've got—and so far we've got absolutely damn all out of it."

"The end of Contram operations, you mean?"

"I do!"

"You're complaining of costs, J.B.," Stoneman said from the other end of the table. "But whose idea was it to buy up Trevis and Baker—and Hartford Cement?"

"Or sign those contracts with Hydrotex?"

These were references to the board's early and enthusiastic attempts to keep off rivals by tying up supplies, auxiliary equipment and means of study—hiring out cementing companies, surveying specialists, logging firms with a limited amount of specialized gear and so on, to prevent competitors using them. It was a classic method—and under the skillful guidance of Veitch and Moreno, Contram had hired these specialists, covering the operations with a multiplicity of subcontracts which had successfully masked the real purpose from their competitors. And since there had been very little of the specialized gear needed for offshore drilling on the European market when the rush for North Sea oil had begun—and American equipment was all employed—they had believed they had leapt ahead and gained important advantage. But they had failed.

"The contracts with Borg-Harris and Nunroe have cost us £2 million—of which we're not likely to get back more than £300,000."

There were general shuffles and murmurs.

"But good God, Cardinal Oil were pushing all they were worth for the equipment," Veitch said. "We had no option. Either we kept them out or stayed out ourselves."

"In the meantime, it's cost us £2 million and the fact is we didn't block Cardinal for more than three months."

"I hadn't realized this." Bream looked shocked.

32

"It's going to cost us more like £2½ million before we've finished with the subsidiary deal with Lavaca Tools.

"Calculated risk," Moreno said rapidly. "Everybody agreed. Well worth taking. Quite a different thing from this other. It's an open end."

"Yes, but you can't set the £2 million against Mister Mack's operations," Stoneman said; and it was clear from the looks of the neutrals that he had scored a point.

"Nobody knows where we're going," Moreno said.

"And where d'you think you're going unless you drill?" Stoneman shot back.

Veitch was tapping a pencil. "Have my colleagues had the document I asked to be circulated?" He meant the neutrals.

Bream shuffled the papers in front of him. "Far as I can see, we've drilled three holes, all dry."

"At a cost of £1 million a hole," Moreno said.

"Three million pounds worth of hole in the sea bed. And we're expected to go on?" said Veitch.

Meldreth coughed. "These are the costs we have to expect."

"Walter's right," one of the others said. "We obviously had to expect this sort of outlay."

"I contest that," Veitch said. "We were after a British concession and you know it. The basis we were operating on and the justification for the very heavy initial investment was a worthwhile British concession, which, I remind you we were pretty well guaranteed. Our influential chairman and managing director were supposed to have it in the bag. We took up this German area, or Dutch area—whenever they decide whose it is—as a very secondary interest, very secondary, not as the main investment, and directly against the advice of some of us. We have not got a worthwhile British concession. We were offered a block of no use to anybody; and the proof is that nobody else has even considered taking it up. We are not going to get a concession—at least, not one that's any good. In my view, it is therefore rash, disproportionate and entirely unjustified to make the sort of investment we are now making in this area, and we should cut our losses forthwith and pull out."

"Hear, hear," from one of the Moreno supporters.

"Absolutely. Fully support that," from another opposite. Stoneman noted that Bream, the all-important neutral, was looking at Veitch and nodding apparent agreement.

There was the sort of brief, ominous silence that could lead so quickly to capitulation by the weaker members.

"That sounds like a late backdown, Mr. Veitch," Meldreth

said. "What would you say if we were to strike oil next week?"

There was irritated shuffling of papers at the other end. Veitch ignored him, smashing a quarter-smoked cigarette into the ashtray. Abruptly he flared up, "We're running at operating costs of £6,000 a day. There is nothing hypothetical in that."

"Mr. Veitch expects one hundred percent built-in certainty." The edge on Stoneman's voice had teeth. "The only man in the oil business who never operates on less."

Veitch looked mutely savage, but a couple of the neutrals smiled.

Meldreth said, "I called in one of the drillers and questioned him today. He reports extremely favourable conditions on the new site. Extremely."

Three of the undecideds looked up brightly at him.

"I'm having a report put in," Meldreth added.

"Yes, but it's one hundred twenty miles out and unless we got a big strike it would simply not be worthwhile at all, that distance from the shore. Too costly to exploit." This was one of the Moreno supporters.

"Even a moderate strike wouldn't pay," Moreno said.

"And has anyone," Veitch said bitingly, "has anyone yet worked out what to do about the very high workover costs on offshore wells—the service and repair once they are completed and operating? Holes plug up, equipment breaks down and so forth and I'm told the problems of getting back on line could be immense."

"I find our legal people have serious doubts about our German position," Bream said. Bream was a sad, beaverish-looking person—a large expanse of oval face, receding chin and downfalling fair moustache.

Stoneman was controlling his impatience. "We have secured ourselves through our influential friends in the local German Laend government."

"I don't think 'secured's' the word, is it?" Veitch said. "We've got a concession to drill in a disputed area—an area which the Dutch and Germans are both claiming and where the Dutch contend we have no rights. Not much security—and we've spent £7 million."

"The Dutch are going to involve us in a heavy lawsuit as soon as they get the chance." Moreno drew on his cigar. "This accommodation with our local German friends, as you call them, is going to be worthless once the Dutch put the pressure on."

Stoneman's eyes were going from one face to the other. The offensive was being pressed all along the line.

"And have members of the board studied the report we took earlier on the last two holes drilled?"

Bream said, "They seem to have had a difficult time drilling them."

"Difficult? There's been a loss of material at which the board may rightly be appalled. The report, by the way, is an expert piece of camouflage, but if you sift the figures carefully you see we have lost material worth something like £375,000. In two holes— £375,000!"

"It's sometimes inevitable in these conditions," Neal put in. "To a large extent, the North Sea is pioneering."

"We can't go on at this rate for a secondary interest," Veitch said. "£375,000 on top of £3 million operating costs —another £3 million-odd for contracts and agreements, £2 million more for the platform—*and no oil!*"

There was a murmur of assent at that end of the table. Moreno said in a loud voice, "We've chewed the cud long enough. I want a decision. Operations have to be wound up. We have to liquidate for the best we can get, forthwith—and we'll take a show of hands on that now."

Raising his hand, Moreno looked around his supporters.

"Order!" Meldreth called out. "This is the chair."

"Point of order!" There was a chorus of protest from the other end.

But Veitch, Moreno and three others had their hands up. Two of the neutrals followed suit.

"Seven for," Moreno said. "How many are there? You two gentlemen there—Mr. Bream? Can we have your vote?" Eight would be the majority.

"Order. Come to order!" Meldreth was hammering the table. Stoneman was on his feet.

"The Chair!" But Moreno went on counting. Bream and his companion were noncommittal.

"Mr. Neal?"

Neal said, "This is out of order, isn't it?"

Moreno's face darkened. For a moment he looked as if he were going to get up. But he stayed where he was. He didn't count the remaining four. Seven to four and three waverers. Moreno gave Stoneman and Meldreth an ironical bow.

"Your point of order."

For some minutes after this, ordered discussion broke down and there was a general buzz, with members of the board talking right and left and across the table. Finally Neal made himself heard.

"I'm told Atlas are pressing their drilling very close to our area."

"They're alongside, in the Dutch sector. They've got a full Dutch government permit."

"Yes. They believe it's a very promising zone—overlapping into our area. Topaco are beginning to drill south of us, too—on the Dutch side again."

"The drillers all agree it's very promising," Meldreth said. "Very promising."

"Very promising! Is that what you heard from the driller this morning, Walter? Let me tell you I saw that driller, too, and he was full of trouble." Moreno was leaning forward. "Why not tell the board? They think nothing of the chances out there with that platform. I want an account of what he said. Let the board hear."

Stoneman and Meldreth exchanged a glance. What did Moreno know? Was this a preliminary to an attack on the platform?

Stoneman said, "You know as well as we all do, J.B., why that platform was bought. It was our chance to get ahead in this very highly competitive enterprise in the North Sea. And you, among others, advised us urgently to grab Mister Mack —yes, yes to *grab* it—when it came on to the American market. We were in. We were ready to go. Everybody knew that there were no other platforms available in Europe or the States which could drill at this depth. There was a world shortage of material. We had every reason at that time to think the British concession was coming off—and in any event, we had this excellent German area. We were damn lucky to get Mister Mack and you know it. The platform is operating well and it will go on operating."

"Yes, yes but—" Bream looked down the table towards Veitch. "This Dutch lawsuit is very disquieting. What are they saying?"

"This is a bloody race, Mr. Bream!" Stoneman banged the table before Veitch could answer. "A race! Don't you understand that? It's the biggest race you've ever been in———"

Murmurs. "There's no call to———"

"But that's just the fallacy," Bream said. "There's no premium on North Sea oil. Nobody's going to get a better price for the first pristine barrels."

For a moment, Stoneman looked as if he was going to choke. He was unable to speak. Then he had himself in hand. "Whoever strikes first in this area, is in, Mr. Bream—*in*, and it means the big prize! This is one of the greatest commercial prizes of our time, good God! Contram will be in *possession*. They won't be able to touch us. Legal tittle-tattle? Rubbish! We'll be sitting on the property which we have discovered and developed. They'll never get us out. No court will give them a finding. The first company to strike oil gets it. The first company to strike gas gets the big pickings, the first and finest contracts, the top of the market! We know it. Atlas knows it. And so do Texite—which is why speed is vital—vital!—and why they are using every weapon to force us out!"

Veitch's voice cut through the others. "We agreed to an investment of £7 million. We've exceeded that and our agreement has therefore lapsed."

"I move the Chair put a formal vote," Moreno said. "There's been enough of this."

Stoneman caught Meldreth's eye.

"I think we should break," Meldreth said quickly. "Meeting adjourned for twenty minutes." He pushed his chair back and rose and before Moreno could react the others were on their feet with him. Stoneman was moving towards the neutrals.

The board dining room was next door and led out to a reception room where the Company's guests were usually entertained. The members of the board dispersed into these two rooms. Stoneman and his group marched straight through to the reception room, leaving the dining room to Moreno and his supporters. The air crackled with hostility. A small lobby cloakroom between the two could serve as channel of communication—if there was to be any communication.

The board room waiters, at any rate, passed from one room to the other with drinks. Meldreth told them to take orders for sandwiches and ordered one foie gras with bacon on rye, one smoked salmon on toasted wholemeal and an underdone beef with asparagus tips and paté on wholemeal for himself. Twenty minutes was going to last as long as necessary.

Stoneman had cornered two of the waverers whom he had hustled through with him. They all had drinks in their hands and Stoneman had the two seated on one of the modernistic sofas, facing them in a chair. Meldreth moved away; the operation was on and he did not want to get hurt in it. Stoneman was going to pull him in soon enough in any event.

He contemplated a chair but decided against sitting. He thought the shape of the chairs was ridiculous—shallow cones into which you stuck your backside and sank back. But the designers had assured him they were "swish"—the vogue word of the moment—and he had let himself be guided. Brenda, the little girl whom Meldreth was keeping in some style in a room in Charles Street, told him he was "swish" too. It made Meldreth feel younger and buckish.

Standing apart, sipping his martini, he watched Stoneman.

Stoneman was leaning forward, speaking rapidly, now and then making a gesture. In moments of animation his face looked like a badly cracked oriental mask. Meldreth thought he was a very dangerous man. At one period he had been mortally frightened of Stoneman but he had since "accommodated himself," as he put it. Now he simply wanted to keep away from Stoneman in his worst moments, do as he was told and hope for no trouble. The week before, he had signed three blank debenture certificates Stoneman had put in front of him. Stoneman had made it clear that he wanted no questions. Meldreth had asked none. At these bad moments, he reminded himself of Stoneman's periodic generosity, of his lack of pettiness and his courage. Stoneman had adopted a blind child and was, Meldreth had heard, subsidizing a settlement for Indian immigrants.

On the other side of the room, Neal the American was standing with one of the others. Meldreth felt that Neal, who was doing the talking, was essentially won over. That made seven to five, with Bream and another waverer the deciders. Bream was the key neutral. One or two of the other waverers would follow his vote, it was plain.

Meldreth discarded his cigar and steered across the room for another martini. He looked forward to the sandwiches. He took a close personal interest in the board's catering department and saw that they obtained the very choicest things.

When the sandwiches came, he had his carried to a side table and stood, with his customary Pimms, munching. The foie gras was from the little French shop he had discovered in Cunliffe Street. The girl with the big bosom had served him on the last two occasions now. She was French. He had playfully said a few words about *très enchanté* and *très charmante*, at which she'd given him a big smile. He thought she'd noticed his interest; the way she looked at him as he went in now. Her bosom was glorious. It made him weak at the knees to contemplate it. He had trouble keeping his eyes on the lovely galantines and things. He was sure she deliberately wore no brassiere to give it the wobble.

Meldreth felt himself blanch a little at the thought. She must be about eighteen, possibly seventeen—or younger—they matured early. He would go in again tomorrow for some small thing, say how good the foie gras had been, slip her his number discreetly, and ask her to ring him up one evening or come out.

Stoneman and the rest were still cornered, talking intently, and had been joined by Bream, for whom Stoneman had evidently been biding his time. Neal had disappeared.

Meldreth eyed the silver tray on which one more sandwich,

delicately decorated with cress, remained. The chef had got into the agreeable habit of sending him little surprises. Now and then when the lunches were not too formal, or when he lunched alone, these little things would appear. He had to watch his weight. He wondered if the French girl thought him too fat. Perhaps it was the reaction from business cares but he couldn't get her off his mind. He swore she'd sharpened that carving knife the other day just to joggle them in front of him.

He looked down at the dish again. He felt he could eat an entire plateful of these delicious trifles. The Pimms glowed inside him. The voices of the argument were distracting. He leaned forward and took the sandwich. H'mmmm. Duck liver, sliced grapes and crumbled egg on soft toast. Delicious! "Aggh", he crummily murmured as the waiter exchanged his empty Pimms pewter mug for a chilled full one. He could hear the argument still going on, Bream's voice naggingly doubtful. They were evidently having trouble convincing him.

Meldreth looked at his watch. They'd been out twenty-five minutes. He could give it another fifteen. He put the last morsel of sandwich into his mouth (he really must tell the chef to repeat that), and turned towards the group.

Stoneman was speaking about costs. "The economic operating cost we are now running at."

Somebody at Meldreth's ear said, "Could I have a word, Walter?" It was Neal. Meldreth looked at Neal's brownish, pleasant face. "And Stoneman?" Neal said quietly: "Urgent."

Meldreth nodded—moved in. Stoneman disengaged himself, handing over the argument to one of the others.

One minute later, they were alone by the window, listening to Neal. Their heads were down. Neal spoke in a whisper. He had been out of the building and used the telephone.

"I've just had a tip-off that Moreno and Co. are in indirect contact with Atlas. I've heard it before but I just got the confirmation. They are working through Heldig in Amsterdam. Atlas has pledged them control of a big area if the Contram drilling fails and we pull out."

Stoneman was immobile. His eyes were fixed on Neal's. "What's the reliability?"

"It's true all right. I had it from someone I trust absolutely."

"They want to sell us out to the Dutch?"

"That's correct."

"Then Atlas moves into our area and helps the Dutch press their claim?"

"Right." There was a pause. Neal drew on his cigarette. "If it's any comfort to you, my information is that they didn't begin with this idea. It's only since the British concession fell down that they've let themselves be got at by the Dutch."

"Can I use this when we resume?"

"No. I had to swear it wouldn't get back to my tip-off, and it would if you spilled it now."

Stoneman was silent. Meldreth could see the faint whitening round his mouth which signalled the inner fury. "Selling us out to the Dutch, the bastards. . . . When you heard this——" He stopped abruptly. Richards, the company secretary, had approached and was hovering a few feet away.

"What is it?"

"Mr. Moreno sends his compliments and says he would like to resume immediately."

"Tell him we'll be in."

They let Richards move off.

"If he gets a vote now, we're beaten," Meldreth said. "Salaman looks as if he'll vote with us but you can't be sure. That'll be six—with you, Mr. Neal. (Neal nodded). They seem to have seven. Bream has just gone in to join them, what's more."

Stoneman looked around.

"Just gone in," Meldreth said.

Stoneman suddenly gripped their elbows, making Meldreth wince. It was a gesture he hated. "Go over there and join them. Keep 'em busy. Don't let them go in."

"What are you going to do?"

"We have to stall for another full twenty minutes. Do anything, but don't let them go in."

They moved towards the others. Meldreth glanced over his shoulder as they reached the group in the middle of the floor and saw the outer door swinging after Stoneman.

Meldreth racked his brains for something outrageous to say, another attack that would hold them—keep them arguing here. The discussion was dwindling away. The group was beginning to erode and members drift towards the communicating door. Unless something happened soon they would be beyond control. Twelve minutes had passed since Stoneman had gone.

Meldreth began to feel the small uneasy constriction in his chest. He wondered what Stoneman was doing. He believed it was something entirely unscrupulous, which would involve him. He could do nothing about it; life would be misery in the cold without the concealed fees, the company-paid apartment, the massive expenses, the travel, the Rolls and the delicious young playthings these attracted. He thought with an inner twinge of the girl in the Cunliffe Street shop. Even if

40

none of these existed, he wouldn't be able to do anything. Stoneman was not a man to be trifled with.

Out of the corner of his eye he saw Richards, the secretary, approaching.

"Mr. Moreno says he wants to begin, sir," Richards said.

Meldreth nodded, said nothing and turned back as if he were absorbed in the exchange among the three neutrals which had suddenly livened.

A minute or two more went by. Then Stoneman strolled in, perfectly casual, as if he had just been to the lavatory. Meldreth tried vainly to get some sign from his face. Stoneman unhurriedly joined the group. He lit a cigarette. The next moment he had slightly detached Neal from the rest and under cover of Meldreth's bulk was speaking to him in a rapid whisper.

"Go in. Talk to Veitch. You want to know more about the lawsuit. You're dead worried. Let them think you can't get assurances from me and you're shifting to them. Say there are two more doubtfuls here trying to make sense out of us but can't."

"Right."

"Wait! As soon as you see Bream move—but *not* before— tell them he is for *us*. For *us*. Understand?"

"Okay."

They moved apart. Stoneman interrupted the discussion, taking the group's attention. When Meldreth looked around, Neal had gone in to the other room.

Meldreth wanted another drink but checked himself. The Moreno group already numbered seven, and if Neal persuaded them that he was won over, they would reckon that they had a majority.

In a moment Richards came out of the enemy room conducting Bream. Bream had a worried look. They went towards the outer door. Meldreth pretended not to notice. Stoneman's back was turned but he immediately interrupted the discussion and leaned forward, gripping Meldreth's coat lapel in witness.

"We have had two approaches from the Americans for an interest. We can bring it off if we're not damn fools enough to pull out." It rivetted their attention.

"What? Who from?"

"Then why not tell———?"

"For God's sake," Stoneman's whisper was hoarse. "I wouldn't tell my wife. One thing I do know; they have independent seismic charts showing our area as the richest of the whole eastern side of the continental shelf. This is in the utmost confidence among ourselves here and I ask you not to pass it on."

It was a lie, Meldreth knew—a complete fabrication.

Stoneman swung around. "We can't wait for them any longer. They'd better be ready. Let's go in."

Meldreth saw that Bream had followed Richards out.

They marched through to the board room where the others were waiting. There was a general murmuring shuffle and shifting of chairs.

"About time too," Moreno said.

"I want to protest, Mr. Chairman, at the unnecessarily prolonged adjournment," Veitch chipped in. "It's now ten past—"

"All right, all right," Stoneman said testily. "Last time you called an adjournment, everybody fell in with it."

Neal, who had been leaning over the table speaking earnestly to Veitch before this, resumed his seat. He kept his head turned towards Moreno's end of the table. Moreno was looking around the faces. Richards came in and bent to Meldreth's ear.

"Mr. Bream has been called away, sir. An urgent message. Private, I believe. He didn't leave any message."

"I see," Meldreth said blinking benevolently. "Could I have order, gentlemen, please? Thank you. I have just been told that Mr. Bream has been called away on an urgent private matter. He left no message about coming back. I don't propose to wait. I don't think the sense of our meeting—"

"Haven't we had enough of this shilly-shallying?" Veitch said. "The proposal we've been discussing—J.B.'s proposal that Contram should close down North Sea operations has got to be put to the vote *now!*"

"Very well," Meldreth said. "Very well. First I have Mr. Stoneman's proposal which was tabled before yours, J.B.— namely, that Contram carry on——"

"What do you mean, before ours?"

"There's no other motion before the meeting."

"Yes there is."

"Well, I'm damned!"

Loud protests from Moreno's group. Firmly, Meldreth's voice made itself heard. "Members may not have been paying sufficient attention, but Mr. Stoneman's motion that Contram continue operations was read out at the start of the meeting and I now put it to the vote."

Moreno, with open palm, was quieting his supporters, saying it made no odds.

"All those in favour?"

Their eyes took in the raised hands. There were five. One

more—Salaman—hesitated momentarily, his face flushed, then raised his too. That made six.

"Against?"

They raised their hands—six.

"With my casting vote, motion carried seven to six," Meldreth said rapidly. "Other business?"

"But—" the members at the far end of the table were expostulating.

"Move to adjourn," Stoneman snapped.

"Seconded."

"Meeting adjourned."

They got to their feet. Moreno sat stock still for a moment, then got up too. He was full of anger. He walked around the table and paused, looking at Stoneman. Meldreth thought there was going to be an outburst. Then Moreno stalked out. His friends trooped after him.

Stoneman was standing by the window of his office. He had his back to the light and Meldreth was glad he couldn't see his face clearly. The outline and the voice were enough.

The other members of the Board had dispersed and Stoneman had started a long discussion about the platform and supplies to it. Meldreth had listened uneasily. The lie about the American approach entailed risks. It was bound to get back.

But he was worried more about what Stoneman had done to eliminate Bream from the meeting. He did not often have these anxieties; but this time he couldn't dispel the feeling that Stoneman had been more than usually underhanded.

Stoneman knew something about Bream and had used it at that moment. That was obvious. He remembered Bream's look of pain as he had gone through—to some phone call, some summons from outside? Meldreth believed it had been some piece of blackmail.

Cautiously, he had tried to probe. Stoneman had said, "I don't think you're being very clever, Walter. If I were you, I'd keep my nose out."

"It's simply that——"

"You were told Bream had private business to settle, weren't you? That's good enough for you." He paused with his eyes on Meldreth. "Isn't it?"

"Uh—of course."

Now, from the window—their discussion having turned to the platform—Stoneman was saying, "And you will tell those bloody drillers that there had better not be any more hold-ups. Send Nolan a message to speed up. I want an investigation of every delay, every lost item, every slip-up, every shut-down. I want the reports sent here to me at top speed."

"Moreno's at the back of those stores hold-ups."

"I know it," Stoneman snapped.

"I believe he's also been tipping Atlas to buy off the men when they come ashore."

"We'll look after Moreno." Stoneman lit a cigarette, took two paces, turned around. "We are not by God going to be squeezed out. We're in too deep now to give up. The data say the oil's there and those drillers are going to strike it if they have to dig it up with their bloody hands."

Bradford, the mud engineer, sat on the bar stool sipping his drink. He was trying to look at ease. Like an habitué of the place. It was a private lunch-and-dinner club, The Hansom, but it was early yet and only two or three people had arrived.

The girl sitting round the bend of the bar looked like a regular member. She twitched her skirt down towards her knees again. It was a very tight skirt, it wasn't near her knees and she didn't try very hard to get it down. When she had tried it wasn't nearer.

Bradford lit a cigarette, glancing at the new customer—a bit like Gainer—who had just come in. It would be too damn bad if Gainer turned up here. There was hardly a chance of it, though. He hadn't expected Gainer to come ashore in the helicopter. Bradford had handed him a line about coming in for some surfactant—a special mud ingredient they would be needing. Gainer hadn't seemed suspicious. Why should he be? He couldn't know anything.

Two more men came in from the street, letting in the bright daylight and the midday traffic noise from Oxford Street round the corner. Bradford remembered that on his previous lunch-time visit the place had been full. It was decorated in the style of 1900—dark green tasselled drapes, dark wallpaper, gas jet globes, old-fashioned mirrors, plush banquettes and brass fittings and there was a big brass 1900-ish nude as a lamp on the bar.

Bradford thought it was very high-class. It was a symbol of his moving up in life. He examined his bitten nails. He was wearing his big bold signet ring on his third finger (gold wristwatch, of course) and he had had the works at the barber's while he had been waiting, so he smelt all right too.

"The other half, sir?" The barman gave him a smile.

"Thanks." Quickly, Bradford reached for his glass with the dregs of vodka and lemon. The barman was reaching for it too. Bradford snatched his hand back. The barman withdrew his. Bradford stood looking at the glass, then took it, drained the dregs and pushed it across with a grin. He coughed. Okay okay. After all, they had expected him. He had arrived early but the barman had greeted him genially and said that Mr. Raymond had left orders for him to be looked after until he got there.

It was now twelve-fifty. Bradford hoped it wouldn't be much longer. Raymond wouldn't have suggested their meeting here unless the place were safe. Still, if one oilman used it —if you could call Raymond a genuine oilman—others might. And you never knew who was working under cover. Come to that, "Mr. Raymond" might be a surname or Christian name. Everybody called him Raymond.

"And there we are, sir," the barman served the fresh drink. "Olives? Chips? A few smoked salmon or caviar canapes while you're waiting?"

"No thanks." Awkward to eat; but he felt richer.

Three more men had come in. The girl opposite was still alone. Bradford thought she was classy. Was she making an offer? He could probably have her. They had private rooms here. Raymond had joked about it, offering him a girl, when they had met here last time and Raymond had put the general proposition about Atlas. Bradford had been tempted by both—Atlas and the girl. The lunch had been extravagant, the drinks marvelous; he felt good. What had he got to lose?

In the end, he had not committed himself about Atlas. Raymond had said frankly that he was connected with Atlas and that Bradford could help them in any number of ways. Atlas were powerful. They would make it very worth his while. Bradford hadn't accepted, had left it at that, and Raymond had laughed and said okay, Bradford might as well have fun with the girl all the same. He was ashore. Relax.

This had been one of the club girls they had talked to before their lunch, a slim, racy blonde with a purse mouth. They said that meant the goods. She had joined them at coffee and offered it openly while Raymond was talking to somebody at the next table.

"How about you and me going to bed, handsome? I've got all afternoon and they'll let us have a room here. H'm?" Then, when Raymond had signed the bill and they were moving away from the table, she had said, "Come on, we can make afternoon-music."

He had damn nearly gone with her.

Bradford drew on his cigarette. Maybe she'd be in today. He looked around. Couldn't see her yet. All the men looked well-heeled and the girls were obviously expensive. It was a place for people in the money. He eyed the girl's legs opposite. The drink was good.

The anticipation of meeting Raymond and the easy luxury of the surroundings had pushed his immediate problems to the back of his mind—the chronic debts, the boredom and irritation of his wife, the extreme pressure Judy was now putting on him to throw over everything and take her away.

Judy was a chick. He was crazy about her. He knew he was crazy about her. She was terrific. When he was with her, he knew he'd do anything for her. She said they had to get away, the two of them. He hadn't said anything to her about the Atlas approach, only that they might have a chance to go away together soon. She hadn't let him alone since then; and now he had decided that the sooner he did break the better.

Atlas would do him extremely well—a big sum in cash, according to Raymond, and a job in some pleasant part of the world, away from these old scenes. Mexico maybe. He reckoned he could be top man of an area with plenty of leave, a house and so on. He'd given Judy a glimpse of it. She'd been terrific.

Bradford alternately watched the girl opposite and the door. The place was filling rapidly now. The girl was searching in her handbag for a match for her cigarette. Bradford was about to move around with his lighter. Then he saw Raymond in the entrance.

Raymond got rid of his coat and came up. He stood very close to Bradford, shaking his hand and showing his gold teeth and saying in a sort of confidential croak, "Well, well, hello. I hope you haven't been waiting too long? Did Angelo look after you?" He made it sound like a State secret. He sounded as if he had chronic laryngitis.

"Sure. Sure."

Raymond was heavy, dark and broad faced and had an odd peppery smell along with the smell of alcohol. Bradford thought he had had a quick one on the way here, probably a quick two. Rubbing his hands together, Raymond ordered a double Vat 69 and the same again for Bradford.

"I've already had two," Bradford said.

"Then this'll be three. You can take it." Raymond laughed and slapped him on the back. His mouth opened wide, like a frog's. It was a big mouth. He caught Bradford's glance at the girl, leaned in close and grated, "Did I interrupt something?" He laughed wheezily again. "You're a great boy, Brad."

"Good morning Mr. Raymond. Everything all right?" The club manager had danced up.

"Thank you, Cecil."

46

"Whenever you're ready, Mr. Raymond. No hurry."

When he had gone, Raymond said, "I've ordered a private room. More comfortable. And you never know, Brad, you might want it afterwards, eh?" Another laugh.

The lunch bar was already full and noisy with customers, new arrivals, waiters. As they finished the drinks, two thickset men pushed through and joined them. Raymond introduced them. They were obviously from Atlas, though of course Raymond didn't say so. In the bustle Bradford didn't get their last names. One was called Harry, at all events, and the other Ambrose. They didn't want to drink and Raymond immediately signaled to the manager who led them all through the curtained archway to the private room.

It was thickly carpeted and done in the same mock 1900 style with two ample padded settees, a chaise longue, potted palms and suggestive pictures. The table was laid for lunch. Before they sat down Raymond led Bradford to the far end and showed him the bidet and washbasin behind the screen. More laughs.

At lunch they drank Brut Heidseck Monopole '55 from magnums. The food was excellent. Harry and Ambrose were pleasant in a heavyish way but Raymond kept up a line of entertaining and wheezy stories. None of them said anything about Atlas or Contram. When they reached cigars and liqueurs, Bradford was wondering what the idea was.

He felt physically heavy and in need of fresh air. He was sober but he felt he had smoked too much and the closeness of the room and the unaccustomed richness of the meal had him muzzy.

Then Raymond said, "Well, now Brad, you're coming over to Atlas. This is what we're here for. Atlas can do with men like you. We'd like to see you with the real opportunities in front of you. We're big and we're developing and we're the sort of outfit that naturally ought to attract young men with talent and foresight and ambition, the men who want to break out of the old rut and get into the top money class. Eh, Harry?"

"That's right," Harry said.

The top money class. Yep. Bradford drew on his cigar. The top money class was right. They'd said it.

"Brad knows we want him to help us get that Contram rig out of the way." Raymond was speaking across to Ambrose, as if he were explaining the situation for the first time. This way it sounded a bit bogus. "He's said he's ready to, haven't you, Brad?"

Bradford hadn't said so. But he supposed this was Raymond's way of smoothing the path, eliminating the awkwardness of a direct "Will you or won't you?" It was really being done for his benefit. And anyway, he *was* going to.

He said, "Yes."

"You are?" Harry said.

"Yes."

"Fine."

Harry and Ambrose nodded. Harry was gently swirling his brandy in a big snifter held in his palm.

"It'll have to be worthwhile," Bradford said. He gnawed at a nail, checked himself.

"I dare say we could make it that." It was spoken in a slow, condescending way and raised a few basso chuckles. Bradford couldn't help feeling a bit small.

He reached out, tapped the ash off his cigar. He caught a critical flicker in Ambrose's eyes watching the gesture. They weren't rushing it.

Ambrose said, "What do you think of as worthwhile?"

"I was thinking of Mexico," Bradford said.

Silence.

"Say Superintendent. To start with," Bradford said.

They watched him, expressionless. Ambrose said, "You may not know it, Mr. Bradford, but there's a lawsuit being filed over your drilling."

"Oh."

"Contram doesn't stand much chance of winning."

Bradford nodded, feeling unable to reply. The thing made him seem at a disadvantage.

"Atlas would find it convenient, shall we say, to have your operations delayed until we were ready to come into court."

"I see."

"Or we may need to get rid of Mister Mack altogether."

"Altogether?"

Raymond put in, "Ambrose simply means, Brad, that as chief mud man, you're in a better position then anybody else to knock out Mister Mack."

Bradford took a sip of brandy. He tried to make his movements look easy and relaxed. As he tipped up the big snifter to drink he could see them all watching him.

He wanted to say something tough like, I'm greedy or I need big money, but he didn't have the nerve. "What's it worth?"

"A substantial sum. In cash."

"For instance?"

Ambrose said, "Ten thousand pounds."

Bradford swallowed. He tried to keep his expression deadpan, looking at the screen across the room. With £10,000

48

and Judy he'd be going places But places! He hoped he wasn't showing any eagerness. He said "You know what the drilling costs a day?"

"We know."

Harry said, "We'd make it ten with the possibility of another two thousand five bonus."

"I even think we could guarantee the bonus if it came to a final job."

"Final?"

They nodded.

"Final would mean what?"

"No more Mister Mack."

"Yes." Another silence. "I'd need a down payment."

"We can discuss that."

"What about Mexico?" Bradford said.

Ambrose said, "We'd send you to Mexico, Mr. Bradford. You'd have a very good job there. We couldn't place you with Atlas, of course; it would be too obvious. But you'd be very adequately situated."

"What position?"

"It would be very adequate, taking into account the cash settlement."

There was a pause. "Suppose there's a blow-out?" Bradford said.

Ambrose said, "We've considered the possibility." Raymond smiled sarcastically. "Mister Mack would have to get off the hole pretty quick, wouldn't it?"

Bradford said, "I mean, could be a blow-out with gas. Then maybe they'd be blown off by the explosion."

"Accidents happen."

"Or fried, if there was fire," Harry said.

Bradford looked at him. "Yup," he said.

"You'd need have no fear for your safety," Ambrose said.

Bradford looked at his nails. His hands were shaking. "How do I know that?"

"It would be in our interest to look after you, Mr. Bradford, wouldn't it?"

Yes. It was what Bradford had thought of too. It could mean a big income for life. If they didn't want to pay up, he could squeeze them. They'd be dead scared he'd spill the beans. He and Judy would be sitting pretty for life. He stared down at his narrow strips of nails, longing for a bite.

"Okay," he said.

Harry said, "I think it's important now to get a solid agreement between us. We can discuss method and times in a moment. Let's get it clear. We're agreed, aren't we, Mr. Bradford, that you will undertake to stop Contram drilling from

49

Mister Mack and if necessary knock out the platform for a consideration of £10,000 and a £2,500 bonus in the second contingency."

"Cash. And a senior job in Mexico within two months."

"Agreed."

Ambrose and Harry hitched their chairs round on either side of him. "It will be a precision job, Mr. Bradford."

They were all looking at him closely.

Margie had two rooms at the top of a block of service flats, a narrow and not particularly well-kept-up building which, for some reason, she had a great affection for. Gainer went through the bare, rather gritty hall and climbed to her floor, high up at the top. When he rang, she called out, "Darling, is that you? I'm not ready, wait a minute"—unlocking the door—"My hair's a fright." He heard her retreat to the far room.

"All right, trumpeter. Sound the charge."

He went in.

"Get yourself a drink," she called out. "There's some soda in the kitchen cupboard if there's none there. What news?"

"Oh, nothing. I've been chasing supplies all afternoon. Oh, we've got a new doc."

"M'mm." She had a pin in her mouth.

He looked around. There were the usual small areas of disorder which Margie left behind her—magazines sprawled on the deep green silk sofa, a half-empty box of chocolates with the brown crinkly papers strewn, a pile of gramophone records slithered out of their covers, some clothes, in purple wool, that looked expensive and chic, left thrown over a chair—all of this expressing her and her peculiar mingling of frailty and poetry and moments of ingénue innocence with her smartness and sophistication.

"Make me one too—a little martini," she called out.

He went over to the drinks trolley, stacked with half empty bottles and bottles with a mere drain in. "Where are we going? Do you want to do a show?"

"Can we just go somewhere and dine—maybe dance? I'm not energetic enough for much."

"There's that new place, the Ecluse."

He went through the corridor to the kitchen for ice—the kitchen also in mild disorder, a pile of her silk underwear and stockings spilled like some costly liquid on top of the washing machine and lipsticked cigarette ends stubbed out in the juice of meals on one of the plates.

She had a vagueness about things like this which he found touching. It wasn't as simple as neglect or idleness but part of an essential innocence in her; and yet, of course, she lived alone like this, was professional in her job and obviously had to deal with the practical and even dismal side of life.

She had been married for a couple of years to an American who wrote for the big magazines and who was always making rows with her about her untidiness. They had divorced and she joked about it—apparently she hadn't been much in love with him—but to Gainer it had in a curious way increased her attractiveness perhaps by suggesting hard luck and the stupidity of her husband, the obtuseness of the world in not seeing her delicacy and her fine spirit, some element of female defenselessness.

Gainer had been seeing her steadily now for eight months. As far as he knew she lived on a fairly usual pattern. He had had hints of other men in the background and she was too attractive not to be pursued. Yet she seemed to take Gainer —as perhaps she took others?—with amused playfulness, a non-involvement that baffled him, though she had moments of deep seriousness—unexpected moments of moving poetry! —when she listened to him, her beauty heightened by the fragility and the cute courage she conveyed. And of course they made love. All the same, there was something which escaped him.

When he got back to the living room with the ice, he heard the shower going from the bathroom. He mixed the drinks and sat with his, leafing through the magazines—the pictures of girls in their smart new clothes, a London interior in neo-1925, with friezes and low beds and low round tables and the general effect of living close to the floor.

Where he sat, the light was a standard stalk with a purple silk shade bending over the back of the sofa. He leant forward to the ashtray and caught the deep blue darkness tinged with red beyond the window where the lights from other interiors and cars would be shining and lighted shopwindows offering the rich excitements of winter, the doorways of clubs and bars with their inviting glow, the great varnished mercantile paintings glimpsed in first-floor rooms from the pavement, the hint of fogginess. The flat felt snug; the martini, for which he had used one of her deep claret goblets, was having its effect and Gainer felt good.

The hiss of the shower stopped and a few moments later he heard her in the bedroom.

"Do you want that drink?" he called out.

"Oh, I forgot. Pass it in, guardsman."

He poured it—a small one—dropped the twist of lemon rind in and took it over. "Here." Her naked arm, looking round and fragile, came round the door and took the glass.

"Yum." She left the door ajar.

He wondered if it weren't the moment to go in and make love to her—hadn't the shower perhaps been a little invitation?—but the telephone rang and she took it, saying in an urgent little voice, "Hello? Who is it?"

Gainer turned away and put a record on. It was some jazz medley and the first tune was an old Armstrong number, *When Your Lover Has Gone,* which he hummed with smiling pleasure. *What lonely hours, The evening shadows bring*—the bass clarinets in the middle eight bars!—pouring himself the rest of the drink from the crystal mixer. There was a little tinkle as Margie rang off and the tune changed to Mel Tormé singing *Moonlight in Vermont.*

"You haven't told me about the meeting today," she called out.

"Oh my God; it wasn't so good."

"When are you going back?"

"Tomorrow—when I've chased a few more things." He was half expecting a little exclamation of disappointment but she said nothing—and he felt a momentary sag. He carried his glass over, gently pushed the bedroom door and went in. She had brushed her hair and was standing in her pants, sipping her drink.

"Oh—Larry!" She laughed, turning towards him, crooking her free arm across her bosom. She was smiling. He thought she looked adorable—frail and amused and pretty; and when he put his glass down and took her bare shoulders, she didn't resist much.

"Darling—what are you doing? Now go and fix another drink and—Larry—darling—no . . ." responding to his kiss, resisting again and tangling his hair as he bent and kissed her breasts.

There was a ring at the outer door. She made to disengage herself and he said, "Don't answer."

"It's no good, it's Mike. He knows I'm in."

"The hell with Mike, whoever he is."

"Larry, now come on." She laughed, reached up and smoothed his hair into place. "I'll send him away in fifteen minutes but now go and let him in while I dress."

"To hell with him. Let him break the door down."

"We have the whole evening. I'll send him away in fifteen minutes." She freed herself and pushed him to the door. "Tell him you're waiting for me and we're going out. Please Larry."

"Fifteen minutes and he goes out on his ear." She shut the door behind him.

He lit a cigarette, turned up the pick-up volume and began to mix another drink; but Mike rang again.

"Okay. Okay!" Gainer called out. He threw open the door.

"What's goin' on? Somebody got a pardy? Hya, Mac. Dint you hear me? Where's Marge?" He came in. He was about thirty, crewcut, American, good looking and well built.

"Margie's dressing. I'm taking her out."

"Oh. Well, sure. My name's Mike Welsh. Hi."

"Mine's Larry Gainer" They shook hands with terrific masculinity.

"Have a drink?" Gainer said.

"Thanks," Welsh said with a grin. "I know the way." He crossed to the bedroom door and called out, "Hi, Marge. How'sa bewdaful? C'n I gedda bewdaful fingertip 'n say hello?"

She opened the door a crack and put her face to it. "Hi, Mike. Get yourself a drink. I won't be a minute."

"You're looking bewdaful, Marge, you honey bee there."

She shut the door. Gainer slammed the volume up to a blare and sat down with his cigarette and drink. He was exasperatedly jealous. He hadn't heard of Welsh before and wondered sickeningly if he was the explanation of the scent from Paris she had been wearing. Had she been to Paris for a weekend with this lout?

Welsh was obviously familiar with the flat (he was pouring himself a stiff whiskey) and didn't mind showing it. He was well dressed in a button-down shirt and grey flannel suit and looked like money. And above all he was on the spot while Gainer was away on the bloody platform.

Glass in hand, Welsh walked out to the kitchen for ice. He came back frowning at the record player. "My Gud, how do you like that junk? Somebody must've given it to her."

"High-class, isn't it?" Gainer shouted.

"Uh? Does it have to be so loud?"

"Great, eh?"

"I said does it have to be so loud?"

"Get that trumpet?"

"*I said—*"

"Margie wants to annoy the neighbours."

Welsh looked as if he wanted to turn it down but didn't quite have the nerve. "What do you do for a living?" he shouted.

"Painter. Nudes. What do you?"

"Business machines."

"Oh bewd—beautiful."

In a minute, Margie came out looking fresh and clean in a

little black dress with two bows and a long turqouise necklace and a bracelet.

"Goodness." She put her hands to her ears at the noise and Gainer went over and flicked the control.

"That ought to settle 'em. I know Mr. Welsh will excuse us but we ought to be going, Margie."

"Hya, Marge, bewdaful." Welsh was bending over her, keeping her hand in his and Gainer thought she looked up at him with evident pleasure. They were obviously on a firm footing.

"I just looked in," Welsh said. "How'd that evening go, the other night? I heard it was noi—sy." He pronounced the word in two emphatically distinct equal syllables noi—zee.

"Oh it was getting like that. We left, though." She turned to Gainer. "This was a party Mike was coming to the other night but he couldn't. I went with some of our friends."

"Hey was Hank there?" Mike said eagerly.

"Oh yes!"

" 'n Loo?"

"Uh-huh."

"Gee. Musta been some pardy."

The glimpse of her evenings with men while he was absent was galling. She seemed to like the way Welsh kept pawing her arm.

They sat down and Welsh kept up his idiotic patter, dragging in other people Gainer had never heard of and going into their mysterious doings in immense detail. Margie had another martini, a bigger one. After a while, she switched the conversation by asking about a film which had just opened but this immediately sent Welsh off into another long flight of enthusiasm (it appeared he had once worked in films).

At last Gainer persuaded her that they wouldn't get a table unless they went. Welsh, a little tipsy, took a prolonged and maddeningly affectionate farewell of her, snuzzling her neck and then insisted on waiting and accompanying them downstairs. He had a long midnight blue Buick with cream upholstery at the door and offered them a lift but Gainer said thanks, they'd get a cab.

Gainer was morose as they rode to the restaurant. Margie kept laughing and saying, "But Larry darling, he's harmless. He's nice and harmless. You looked so jealous!"

"You seemed to find him pretty interesting."

"But I told you. I sort of had a date with him anyway. I thought he was pretty sporting. Heaven knows what you'd have been like in his place."

Oh hell, were they going to quarrel? The evening was off on the wrong foot after such promise. But when they reached the Ecluse and were installed—the place was smallish, they had a good table and there was a smart crowd—the edge had gone. She looked extremely glamourous and he said she was more adorable than any model he'd ever seen, at which she laughed.

Sometimes her mouth reminded him of the girl's in the Vent Vert ads, with her great curving sweep of green hair and her pouting moist-mauve lips. Gorgeous! But the roundness of her eyes, which was really what helped her look of innocence—perhaps abused innocence—wouldn't have done for that sort of sophistication at all.

"Well, anyway, you always make me feel terrific," she said.

They ordered dinner carefully, then she asked him about the interview with Meldreth. He told her and went on to recount briefly how Stoneman had appeared and the result.

But now all this had receded, since for Gainer, the interlude of Mike had thrown up too sharply his own situation with Margie. Were they or not going to get married? There was something unresolved in their relationship. She seemed not to mind keeping things as they were; and perhaps if it came to a decision, they would break up, which would make him miserable. Yet he had been jealous and furious and thought she was more desirable than ever tonight.

There was a flourish from the band and the compere appeared announcing the first half of the floor show. This turned out to have a comic who did sensational tricks with a trio of talking myna birds and then went on with a long and dazzling Perelmanesque monologue which had the audience weak with joy. After this the band changed to a Negro quintet.

They got up and danced. He said, "Who do you play that old Armstrong tune for?"

"Oh, *What lonely hours, The evenin' shadows bring?*"

He grinned.

"Well, who's the lover who keeps on going?"

"Kick me, my gal. You're wonderful." But was it him, after all?

Later—it was half-past one and there was still a full crowd—they began to talk about when he could come in again and this led on to what was happening on the platform and so on. What had been the outcome of the board meeting? She said she hadn't heard of any change. She asked about Nolan. Gainer explained that he had known Nolan for years and worked with him, like many oilmen had with each other in different parts of the world.

"Why?" Gainer said, faintly curious at her interest.

"I don't know. He seems a tough egg. You know, that look."

Gainer laughed. "Yes, I see what you mean. He's all right. When did you meet him?"

"He came into the office one day. Seeing Mr. Stoneman."

"Well, I tell you. He's a marvellous driller. One of the very best there is, or ever has been. I was working with him down in Guatamala about two and a half years ago; then he dropped out of circulation. Boy, was I surprised when I heard he was Pusher on this job."

"You were?"

"Well, you know. He's all right now; but he used to be a complete nut. He did pretty hair-raising things. When you have a drilling camp and the crew have maybe brought the well in after a lot of slogging and then they move into the nearest town to celebrate—things are wild. But Nolan used to frighten the hell out of the lot. He was a terrific gambler. He had these obsessive fits and when he was in a card game or drinking he couldn't let go till he'd cleared himself out, signed up IOUs till they wouldn't take any more or knocked himself cold.

"We were drilling up at Puerto Ignacio for Zentaco and the Company kept needling us about getting results and you know, Nolan drilled to twenty-one thousand feet. Twenty-one thousand! Wouldn't stop. And we knew it was dry. Crazy! He used to have a sort of compulsive-obsessive thing which he was liable to attach to anything if he was in the mood. There were other things too—totally illegible handwriting for instance. And he always seemed to be on the edge of some terrific outburst. But it never happened. And he's a great oilman."

"We bought him over the heads of half a dozen other companies you know—all the majors."

"Sure." Gainer nodded. "Any of them would want him. He's the top. He's great. Did he tell Stoneman what he'd been doing for the last couple of years?"

"Not that I heard. Working for somebody else, I suppose, if he's so good."

"Nope. He wasn't pushing or drilling. He's too well-known. I'd have heard. Perhaps all he needed was a lay-off. You know what this game is. Perhaps all I need is a lay-off to hang around with you a bit, sweetheart."

"You don't have to ask me."

She kicked off her shoes ."Maybe you ought to go, Larry." They were sitting on the sofa over last drinks. He pulled her over to him and kissed her. Her lipstick had already gone in their kissing and she was a little untidy.

"This is where I put you to bed, my gal and then get right in with you."

"Oh dear, well if it has to be, Samson, let's get there. I'm dead." This was purely defensive coquetry. She led the way in. He picked up his half-empty glass, turned the living room light out and followed her. She was already peeling off her dress.

Gainer arrived at North Scully by train next morning from London and took a taxi out to the Contram wharf. North Scully was the east coast base from which Contram operated supplies to Mister Mack; the other base was on the German coast.

Gainer was feeling buoyant though the prospects ahead on the platform looked grim. Stoneman's reception promised nothing good and Gainer had not been able to discover anything definite about the missing lab man. His inquest on supplies had led to the usual complex buck passing but he had succeeded in having one of the Mister Mack supply boats sent at once with some of the urgently needed items.

At the wharf he was glad to find that the boat had in fact left overnight, taking the men of the relief tour. Action at last! It almost looked as if Stoneman had intervened. His cheerful feelings were justified. His visit apparently hadn't been in vain.

Margie! He kept thinking of her. He sniffed his coat cuff where some of her powder had fallen . . . faintly Margie.

He spent a short time in the Pay Office, then had a message phoned to the helicopter pilot confirming that he would need to be flown out later in the morning. Then he settled down with Voyss, the Number Two at the base, to try to sort out some of the supply difficulties. This took a couple of hours. They had a beer together in the wharfside canteen, then Gainer took his grip and got a lift on a truck to the helicopter landing ground near by. The Sikorsky was there and the maintenance man but no pilot. The maintenance man didn't know anything.

Gainer walked over to the second shed. Parrish, the pilot, had left a message with a storeman that he would be back in fifteen minutes.

Gainer made sure the cases of items he had ordered had been loaded into the aircraft, then strolled out, lit a cigarette and waited.

The rain had stopped. It was the usual wharfside scene of trucks, cranes, railway containers, fork-lifts, tarpaulin-covered stores, stacked crates, drill pipe, oil drums, brightly painted storage tanks, mud, sludge and oil puddles.

He liked the hard industrial pragmatism of all this, the outdoor roughness, the smells and grease and heavy work, the effort, the absence of comfort and the machines and equipment which he found symbols of the "real" world. He had hated the periods he had sometimes had to spend in oil firms' offices and been restless to escape to a drilling.

But now Margie had him hooked! He could marry her and still be a driller; but he knew it wouldn't work. He couldn't see her in one of the company prefabs out in some bush zone with the other oilmens' wives for company. She belonged to a bright metropolitan world of smart magazines, London shops and parties and maybe dopes like Mike. Yet he was seriously in love with her. He wasn't simply going to be able to eliminate her from his mind and had to resolve it somehow.

He dropped his half-smoked cigarette into the mud and trod on it. He tried to turn his thoughts away from her. He strolled back to the shed.

A grey Ford Taunus was coming along the road on the other side of the Company's wire fence. Gainer waited, thinking it was the pilot but the car didn't stop. As it passed, he recognized Sam Bruce, one of the Atlas drillers, at the wheel. He yelled but Bruce didn't hear.

He had heard that Bruce had recently joined Argo 1, the Atlas rig drilling near Mister Mack. He watched the car. The Ford covered the two hundred yards to the open wharf alongside the North Scully inlet and pulled up. Gainer was puzzled. The Atlas shore base was eight miles north along the coast at Aldwick, on the other side of the North Scully inlet.

There was still no sign of the Sikorsky pilot. Gainer walked out through the gate towards the wharf. Bruce got out of the car and after looking around for somebody stood leaning against the front wing evidently waiting. Presently he saw Gainer approaching and lifted a hand in salute.

Gainer came up and they shook hands. "Well, how's the boy?" Bruce was a thick-chested, blue-eyed Canadian of thirty-five with whom Gainer had worked many times. Gainer liked him.

"I heard you're on that Atlas rig, what's it called, Argo 1?"

"Yeah," Bruce said. "Just joined. Ten days ago."

"What you doing here?" Gainer said.

"Yeah." Bruce chuckled, nodding. "Damn nearly enemy territory, eh? Don't tell anybody but we've rented a new supply boat service which happens to have lost the Atlas wharf on its second trip and Sinclair's been over to give 'em hell.

Just waiting for him now." He looked out across the inlet. "I guess this is where he meant."

"Sinclair's pushing with you?"

Bruce nodded. "Well, well. How's the boyo? Still turning to the right?" He was punching Gainer's arm.

"Oh, can't grumble, as they say. I heard you were going over to Gulf after that nice Bengolo job. Somebody said you were all streamed up about it."

"Who was that?" Bruce was grinning.

"Cameron, I think."

"Sure I was. But then I had two months in Bahia." He grinned again. "Oh boy. Terrific. Just terrific . . ." They laughed. "Yeah. She had a title and a Victoria, you know one of those old horse buggies with springs. Jeeze, those springs . . ."

They stood talking. Presently Bruce snapped his fingers as if he'd just remembered something. "*Say*—I hear you got Mr. Nolan pushing with you out there? That right?"

"Yes."

"Is *that* who started this shooting? I heard about that."

This was a reference to an incident some months before between Mister Mack and Argo 1. Sinclair, on Argo 1, had been in a drilling emergency and sent his helicopter over to Mister Mack for a loan of a circulating-pump relief valve. In spite of the two firms' rivalry, the request between drilling men was within accepted practice and established custom. But when the Argo helicopter had approached Mister Mack, Nolan had warned it off on the loud-hailer. The helicopter pilot had continued to circle overhead, relaying his request by loud-hailer too, whereupon Nolan had run into his cabin, reappeared with a pistol and fired off several shots, shouting abuse to the pilot about coming over "spying."

"Well, whadyaknow. How is that little jerk?"

"He's all right," Gainer said. "No, honest, I mean it. He's all right."

"Doesn't sound like it."

"That helicopter thing was exceptional. He's back to the old steady. Off the booze, never touches it. Won't let anybody else have a snifter either."

"He still calling everybody Mister?"

"Oh sure. Wears dark glasses all the time now, too."

"Yeah? You remember that time in Lobitos with the municipal fire engine?"

"None of that now. Hell, he hasn't had a chance—I may say he hasn't been ashore more than four or five times. I mean, that shooting was a bit of clowning. He couldn't have

59

hit the thing. He's getting all hell from the Company. Looks as if the real wild stuff's a thing of the past." Gainer didn't know why he was being more affirmative than he felt; it just happened sometimes that you were.

"Yeah? Well that'd be something. Nolan the nut wises up. What's he been doing?"

"I don't know," Gainer said.

"But that's it, boy. Nobody heard of him for a long time —and now here he is again. Must be a coupla years he's been out of circulation."

"I thought he was dead too," Gainer said.

"Yeah. Where's he been?"

"He said something to Jackson, that's our Number three —you remember Jackson, there's a wild little bastard if ever you saw one—he said something to Jackson about being down with some sister of his in Kentucky."

"My God, a female Nolan! Can you imagine that? Do you reckon it's true?"

"How can you tell?"

"Or was it some girl?"

Gainer shrugged. Bruce said, "Well, if it was she must've had the equipment. Last time I saw him he was bent for hell. And I mean by the main gate."

"Well, he's okay now. Say, Sam, whatever happened with Harry Callum after that blow-out? I heard they pulled him in."

"Yeah, yeah. Poor guy. It was terrible bad luck."

Gainer caught Bruce's look past him and turned. Sinclair, the Atlas Tool Pusher, was coming up, a few paces away.

"Hello, Ted." Gainer gave him a grin.

Sinclair's face froze. He was an older man, in his fifties, with craggy eyebrows and a square face. He wore a trilby and raincoat.

"We can do without your company, Mr. Gainer." His look was hostile. Gainer, momentarily taken aback, glanced at Bruce. Bruce blinked, looked at the ground.

"What's the matter? If it's—"

"I said we'd feel healthier if you'd bugger off."

"This is a public wharf," Gainer said. "I can contaminate the air just as well as you, Sinclair. What do you think we were doing? Exchanging dope?"

"Nolan would like some of ours, wouldn't he?"

"Look, Ted—"

"Clear off, or I'll kick you in the drink."

Gainer, furious, was up to him in a step, catching at his coat collar but Bruce's shoulder intervened. There was a brief shoving scuffle and curses. Sinclair slipped and went down on one knee. Then they were standing, a foot apart, glaring at each other. Bruce looked very embarrassed.

Sinclair shook Bruce off and drew back. "I hope to God you have trouble, Gainer—and plenty," he said. "Send your helicopter over to us and see what we give him." He savagely wrenched open the car door. Silently Bruce got in on the other side. As Bruce engaged the gear, Sinclair wound down the window. "And I hope Mr. Nolan takes you all where he's going."

Gainer stuck two fingers up as the car splashed away.

5

THE green and white Sikorsky dropped and bounced in the air, flying a bumpy passage back towards Mister Mack.

Looking out of the bubble beside the pilot, Gainer could see the great steel triangle of the rig in the distance—the symbol of so much that he was bound to, that he loved and hated and admired and that made up his life.

It was an industrial unit, a work site, a sort of factory on stilts stocked with unlovely pipes, cement mixers, mud pumps and so on—yet for Gainer it embodied a mystique, a spirit which meant an entire approach to life and, though he would never have admitted it, romance.

Men worked on the rig like wrestlers. They hauled at the heavy drilling equipment for twelve hours on end with a precision that could be counted in seconds.

Gainer had once seen a visitor flick his wrist and time the driller, the three floormen and the derrickman breaking out a string of pipe. They were pulling each ninety-foot stand of steel pipe, weighing half a ton, unscrewing it and lifting it and standing it back in the derrick in fifty-five seconds. The visitor went around the rig site and came back three hours later, stood timing the men again. Fifty-five seconds. He went away and came back four hours later, timed them once more. Fifty-five seconds. They were the same men. They had five more unbroken hours of it to do the same pace.

The drilling teams—the driller controlling the hoist drum of the draw works, the three other floormen and the derrickman high up in the derrick—knew each other like boxers. Each of them knew how much to an ounce his companion pulled, the strength of his legs, the weight of his shoulders, how quick he was on his feet, how sure his eye.

Each knew when one of the others slackened off with his weight, when he was not shouldering hard enough on the backup tongs, when he was not bending fast enough to take his share of the heavy slip. They lived with each other and by each other—as a team; and when there wasn't a team, when one man gave something short of all his strength, they all

62

knew it. Then they were just four men. They were not a drilling team.

The team made judgments in inches. The driller let the travelling block drop full speed to within inches of the floormens' heads below. The rotary table whipped around the triple steel handles of the slip six inches from the men's feet moving on the oil-slippery floor alongside. The men did not actually *run* at the work but it was very close to running.

The crew was divided into three tours—two working on board, one off duty ashore. The two tours on board worked alternately twelve hours on and had twelve hours off, did this for two weeks, then had a week off ashore. (This was the principle, though Mister Mack had been having difficulty in getting reliefs to and fro on time.)

The five cooks, kitchen staff and stewards served meals every six hours around the clock, at noon, 6 p.m., midnight, 6 a.m., mostly standard meals of steak and chips except for breakfast. The moment a man stepped off the rig into the boat to take him ashore he was in his own time.

The platform had two working decks and a third deck composed of ballast, fuel and water tanks. Steel ladders down open hatches connected the two upper decks.

The top deck was mainly given over to storage of steel drillpipe—30,000 feet of it laid in thirty-foot lengths in two racks—heavy steel drill collar*, a few lengths of casing, used when the sides of the well hole had to be cemented, rows of bits—hard rock bits, soft formation bits, cone head bits, reamers—in brightly painted boxes arranged by size and type, fishing tools** and smaller gear. There were fixed, electrically powered cranes on two sides and the deckhouses containing the dormitories of the men, offices, control room, mud laboratory (where the rock cuttings were analyzed for traces of oil or the promise of it) and radio room.

The derrick rose at the base of the platform's triangle, 140 feet high. The floor was twenty-five feet above the main deck with a wooden ramp sloping down from it to the main deck for pulling the lengths of pipe and casing up and down.

The derrick floor was the centre of all the activity of the platform. Here the rotary table, lying like a wheel, flush with the floor and spun by a chain drive from the main draw works compound, turned the string of drill pipe with the bit at the bottom which drilled the well hole. At one side of the floor, the driller stood at the draw works controlling the rotary table and the drum hoist from which were suspended

---

* Heavyweight pipe used just above the bit.

* * Fishing is retrieving broken pipe or other items from the hole. A "fish" is any object accidentally lost in the hole.

the travelling block and hook and all the drill pipe in the hole.

Below this top deck was the mud and machine deck divided by steel bulkheads into seven compartments. The men who worked in the confined spaces here among the machines had no daylight, since there were no portholes. They were supplied with air through the air conditioning system. The deckhead in most spaces was 7 feet 4 inches high. All seven compartments of this deck were encumbered with machinery —six DC and six AC generators, three twenty-foot electric switchboards, two big circular tanks for cement and four for chemicals, two Halliburton cement-mixing machines, water distilling plant, air tanks for the air compressors, washing machines and stores.

One big compartment contained the main mud tank with the two powerful mud pumps attached and the two smaller mud mixing tanks with four small pumps, another a working area for the mud engineer and, next door, the engine room. Heavy girders ran from deckhead to deck. The machines and bulkheads made it impossible to see for more than a few feet from one spot.

Besides the crew, there were usually two or three specialists from technical firms on board for a night or two while they did a specific job; six spare bunks were kept for them.

The platform normally carried supplies for two to three months, but this had broken down because of the internal conflict in the company.

The Sikorsky banked over the platform, hovered vertically above it for a moment, then slowly descended.

Gainer craned around now with the binoculars focussed on the Argo 1 rig in the distance. He could see the crew moving about the faint wisps from the diesels, the ballast falling into the sea. He thought he spotted a length of drill pipe flung down the ramp from the derrick floor; it looked as if they were pulling pipe. They had a white crew motor boat coming in and their helicopter was about two miles off, heading for land. He made out what looked like a supply boat alongside the legs on the far side. Busy, thought Gainer.

The Sikorsky touched down and the pilot cut the rotor. The clanking subsided. Gainer stuffed the binoculars into the pocket, took the bag of mail he had brought in, unlatched the door and got out.

He stood there, struck by some aspect of things he didn't immediately grasp, then saw that it was the lowness of Spud three. Normally the helicopter landing platform would be somewhat below the tops of the spuds. Now the spuds were down so far that the platform was practically level with them. They were in deep water for this platform all right.

Gainer looked at Number three spud. It was distinctly farther down than the other two and had much less spare leg protruding above the top deck. A supply boat was along side, a long low black motor vessel with clear after deck and forward super-structure. The port crane of the platform was unloading from it. The platform diesels were not going and there was none of the squeaking and screeching of the brake on the main cable drum, the everlasting and inescapable metallic music with which the driller lives. They were not yet drilling.

. Gainer glanced at the derrick. It had been moved on the skid rails to the drilling position at the end of the platform. Inside the framework, the great block and hook were hanging free with multiple wire lines running down beneath. It looked as if Nolan hadn't finished installing the G and A, the complex guideline and alignment structure and the blow-out preventer * stack on the sea bed. There was probably also the television hook-up to complete. They couldn't start the new drilling until all this was in place. The starboard crane was working deck stores.

He called out to the pilot that he would send a man up to unload the plane, and climbed down the ladder to the main deck. The crew were moving about at work. He looked into the messroom. Four men were reading magazines.

"Mail!" Gainer called out and threw them the bag he had brought. There was a yell.

Outside, he walked aft and looked down at the men working on the scaffolding below the derrick. They were fitting the fourteen-foot high casing of the BOP package and he saw the guidelines of the G and A running into the sea. This meant that they had already sunk a short length of thirty-inch conductor pipe to the mud line of the sea bed, drilled out under it for about 300 feet—the entrance to the drilling hole—and lowered and latched the G and A framework on to it. They still had to make the various joint connections and lock them in place and then fit the BOP. It was a lot of work to have got through already.

Somebody down there was bellyaching over the job. Gainer recognized it was Briggs, the foreman. Briggs had evidently come aboard with the relief tour. Gainer cursed inwardly. Briggs was a troublemaker. Gainer had been hoping he wouldn't reappear. They kept the throw-outs that other rigs wouldn't have. You bet.

_____
* Blow-out preventer (BOP). A device to shut off a violent escape of gas, oil and sometimes water under pressure.

He crossed towards his cabin between items of gear.

"How goes, Joe?" he sang out to Joe Havenga, the negro cathead man. "Oh Frank," he beckoned to Frank Curtis, the man with him, one of the roustabouts. "Mind going up and unloading the Sik? And get my bag, will you? Mail in the mess."

"Okay."

Nolan came up the small booby hatch. He was in overalls, his greasy peaked cap, the peak pushed up, and his dark glasses. He stopped, looking Gainer up and down. He stood gripping the handrail. His brow furrowed. He was slowly chewing gum.

"Glad to have you back Mr. Gainer. I trust this isn't just a courtesy call we're being favoured with?"

"Look, Gene, it was a misunderstanding. I think—"

"No misunderstanding. There's one Tool Pusher on this rig and that leaves no room for subordinates to take charge."

"It seems to have produced results, at any rate."

"Meaning Mr. Gainer can get results when the Pusher can't?"

"For God's sake—"

"Above all," Nolan raised his voice. "It doesn't leave any room for goddamn stool pigeons."

"What? What do you mean?"

"You hear. Stool pigeons."

Gainer was stung in spite of himself. "Who is?"

"Shooting your mouth off to the Company about the trouble we're in—Spud three going down, men hurt, more downtime* and the lousy platform we got."

"You know that's a damned cheap bit of distortion!"

"I know you went shooting your big mouth off with no authority."

"You can stick it." Furious, Gainer went to push past. But Nolan caught his arm.

"I don't take that talk from you or anybody, Mr. Gainer."

"What do you reckon to do about it?"

Nolan fingered his dark glasses. He said quietly, "I can shop you. I've got the law with me here. You know? I can run you off this rig. I can run you out of the Company and I can see that the Company gets you warned off every offshore rig that's working for dangerous conduct."

"Well, for Christ's sake! What's got into you? Who do you think you are?"

"You want to find out?"

---

* Driller's abbreviation for shut-down time, i.e. time when no work is being done.

66

Two roustabouts, carrying a chain and pipe slips were wanting to get by. There was hardly room. Gainer said "Go to hell, Nolan," turned and walked away.

He crossed the deck to his cabin. He could feel Nolan's glare after him. He was so angry he could hardly think. He slammed the door. He itched to light a cigarette but Nolan only allowed smoking in the mess. What was Nolan thinking of? Did he really believe he had some sort of legal power on the rig as Pusher—like a ship's captain? It was ludicrous. Delusions of grandeur! Nolan certainly had Stoneman and company behind him—Gainer imagined their exchange of radio messages—and they could sack him. But this talk of the law was idiotic.

He broke open a packet of Chiclets and fumblingly stuffed some into his mouth, dropped some, furiously kicked them aside, pacing the three short steps to the door and back. The whole thing was ridiculous—comic. He wasn't positively sure what the situation was—somebody on the rig, he supposed, had the power. Could it be Nolan? But for God's sake, to play it up like that! Nolan knew damn well that no oilmen worked remotely in that style. You couldn't run a rig like a bloody warship. On the other hand, after seeing Stoneman, the hatchet man, Gainer didn't need convincing that they would be ruthless if he broke his contract. They would smear him and make it hard to get another job quickly. Was it best to clear out now and go back on the supply boat? Maybe he could have gone to Atlas—but not after this afternoon.

Somebody knocked on the door. It was Frank Curtis with his grip. "Oh thanks, Frank," Gainer said.

"Mr. Nolan's compliments and where's the lab man?" Frank said.

Mr. Nolan's compliments, for Christ's sake. At that, it was better than having Quidd, Nolan's clerk, coming creeping around. "My compliments to Mr. Nolan (Frank grinned) and his guess is as good as mine. I couldn't find out."

"Oke."

"You'd better start saying 'Aye, aye, sir.'"

Frank threw him a chuckle and went. Gainer shut the door and began to change. He chewed. He tried to expel the episode from his mind and switched on his little Jap transistor, thumbed the wheel, twiddled and caught a good jazz group. *I Should Care.* It summoned up a girl and a club in Singapore. He sat on the bunk, whistling, stripping his trousers. It had been a good time. It helped to chase Nolan from his mind.

Besides the two-tiered bunk, the cabin had one tubular steel chair, two narrow steel lockers, glass, tip-up wash basin unit and wall flap. It was painted a hygienic sick-green and there was a tiny dog-eared rug with a permanent crease across it. When the diesels were working at full power on a round trip—hoisting the full length of drill pipe and returning it to the bottom of the well bore—the walls vibrated. Gainer was usually too slogged-out to notice.

Standing in his pants and socks, Gainer washed at the metal wash basin and took a set of clean blue overalls out of his locker. He was shelving a decision and he knew it. Hell, he was the driller. He had a responsibility towards some of the good fellows on the rig—Joe Havenga, Frank, Chalky White and the others.

The door opened as he finished dressing. It was Guggendorf, the doctor. "Hello, you're back." He came in. "How was the trip?"

"Oh—bad to excellent. All shades."

"Have you seen Mr. Nolan?" Guggendorf said. "He seemed pretty worked up about your going."

"We exchanged a few civil words."

Guggendorf gave him a quizzical look and grinned. He had a big head, a moon face and gold-rimmed glasses. He was thirty-one years old, plump, genial and intelligent, a Swiss from the Grisons, with a gift for English. He had joined the rig four days before Gainer's departure ashore—completely green as he cheerfully admitted. He had never worked on a drilling rig before. He was picking up the jargon and the attitudes.

Gainer had been astonished to find a Swiss in the job. "What the devil's a Switzer lad doing this far out? No hotels, no sairvice?"

Guggendorf laughed. "That's just it. They're what I'm escaping. You've never experienced the horrors of cantonal life, I can see. I hope you never have to."

They had several long conversations on this theme. Guggendorf was voluble, cheerful and expressive. He was a man of wide outlook and lively mind and he found life in his own country uncongenial.

"The apple-pie order, the neatness, the efficiency—it's so fine on the surface. You can't grasp the oppressiveness if you only pass through or visit the place. But try living there. You get claustrophobia—at least, I did. There's a mental climate which is absolutely stifling—the closeness, the bourgeois respectability—I'm a Protestant but I've lived mostly away from home among the Catholics so I suppose I'm a bit more sensitive. But you have no idea of the intensity that commercialism and self-satisfaction can attain. The interlocking of interests, of families and the results they give rise to are monstrous. What can you do when you want to make a career? You immediately run into the vested interests, the corporations and what-all and you must intrigue to get inside, to become one of the accepted—it's worse than England. Worse than the English class system."

"Well, that's a national neurosis now," Gainer said.

"Well, I tell you, I have a horror of my fellow countrymen, which is why I can't live there." Guggendorf laughed.

He had an unquenchable curiosity about drilling and kept questioning Gainer. "What's a grief-stem?"

"The kelly. That's the heavy square pipe you see being drilled down above the pipe."

"What's a squeeze job?"

"Hell, are you planning to run a drilling under Mont Blanc?"

Gainer liked him. They got on very well together.

Guggendorf threw some letters and a rolled magazine on the flap. "Mail, would you believe it?"

"Yep. I brought it off. Anyway you've only been here a dog watch. Wait and see how long it takes sometimes."

"Did you bring my tea?"

Gainer slapped his forehead. "Oh hell, I forgot, Doc, I'm sorry. Clean out of my head."

"Doesn't matter. I'm down to my last. I shall soon be facing those canteen bags on string. No Buck Master either?"

Gainer looked guilty.

"Never mind," the doctor said.

"How have things been?"

"Oh, well I couldn't tell you much. I believe they've been doing something with the BOP and that. We seemed to be going to pull up the legs—I mean the spuds—and move at one point, I believe, but don't ask me."

"Pull up? What for?"

"I don't know. Mr. Nolan's been pretty acid, from what I hear."

"Yes. He was putting on the old sea dog act with me just now. Talking about being the law here."

"What?"

"Honest to God. You know—'clap the yellow-bellied scum in irons, Mister Mate.' "

Guggendorf laughed.

"Damn nearly. Seriously, what do you suppose the drill is on that, doc? Is he the law in our little triangle of paradise?"

"Oh my God, I don't know, Larry. I suppose technically he might be, since we're outside territorial waters. But it seems just damn silly. It doesn't arise. We're not under the

Naval Discipline Act. Or are we? He must've been mad because some stores or something he wanted didn't come."

"Well, maybe."

Gainer got rid of the chewing gum. "How you been getting on with the fellows?"

"Fine. Good chaps." Guggendorf took off his glasses and sat on the stool polishing them. "Get on with them very well. They're unusual men, aren't they?"

Gainer looked at him, then reflectively at the deck. "Finest men you ever saw. They're the last category of men I know, except steel riggers, who put in a full day's work. They work in miserable conditions, they put up with monotony, they sleep in bunks four to a cabin, eat canned food for weeks and they slog it out like hell.

"These men are a special breed of people. Look, a floorman works twelve hours on and has twelve hours off. He eats a meal before he goes on and a meal when he comes off. That leaves him ten hours. He has to wash up and shave. This gives him about an hour free time. The rest of the time he sleeps. He sleeps eight hours and he needs it. He just has time to come off, have a meal, a wash and fall into bed. He works two weeks on without a day's break and a week ashore.

"Boat time's a man's own time. That means as soon as he gets into the boat to go ashore, it's his own time. A hundred miles odd to the base means a fourteen-hour trip. After a fourteen-hour trip in a rough sea to get back to the rig, a man puts on his hard hat and works for twelve hours.

"They're very rugged men. The old roughnecks who bit the neck off a whisky bottle and then worked twelve hours—these you see no more. But the offshore men are the same kind."

Gainer stopped, slightly embarrassed by his own advocacy.

"Why do they do it?" the doctor said.

Gainer grinned. He thought of his own love of the game and the milieu, the mystique by which it held him. "Difficult to explain. The pay is not all that. It's harder all the time to find drilling crews. They're getting fewer and fewer, anyway, the real ones. You watch 'em up on the derrick floor and you'll see what I mean. A driller soon knows whether he's got four men or a *team*. Hell, I talk too much."

"I don't go much on Lockwood."

"Well . . ." They exchanged a glance.

"Always bellyaching about something."

"Sure," Gainer said. "He hasn't got enough work to do. They're the people who cause you the trouble on an offshore rig, the ones who haven't got enough to do." He picked up his gloves and hard hat, shut the locker and went out.

He walked over to the hatch and went below, looking for Jackson, the second driller. The ladder descended over the long steel tank full of clay-coloured liquid mud—not natural mud but the special and highly complex drilling fluid with solids in suspension—which would be pumped down inside the pipe during the drilling and forced up again between the pipe and the wall of the hole, lining the hole and carrying the fragments of rock cuttings which the bit had drilled out from the bottom. The mud was the lifeblood of the drilling process.

On the deck below, mud had spilled over and slopped everywhere over the rubber flooring. The mud pumps which would keep the mud circulating were not working. Gainer went through the compartment but didn't find Jackson. He went up on deck again towards the after end of the platform where Briggs and his crew were working on the temporary scaffolding in 'the slot' directly beneath the derrick.

The base of the great triangular platform had a notched cut in it—the slot—over which stood the derrick, the void of the notch allowing the drilling to be done into the sea. Anybody standing on this scaffolding could therefore look straight up, through the temporary gaps in the working floor of the derrick above, into the framework of the derrick rising directly overhead. The guidelines which ran from the derrick above into the sea beneath indicated the line the drilling would take when it began.

"Hey, Larry, you old son of a gun." Jackson was supervising the work. "I didn't know you were off the other day. How was it?"

"All right, Jacko. Everything okay?"

"Boy, oh boy. If I had the wings of an a–an–gel."

Jackson was boyish, slightly built, with cheek muscles like apples and brown curly hair. He had a gap between his two front teeth. He was years younger than Gainer or Nolan but an experienced driller and had worked from Lake Maracaibo to the Persian Gulf. Gainer liked his boyish charm, his chuckling good humour and juvenile spirits. The entirely natural way Jackson treated everybody as equals made him popular, though there was a harebrained and practical joker side to him which had given him a wild reputation.

"The redhead in the base office asked me to give you a message," Gainer said. "She made me promise. She said, 'Tell him one Wednesday in two from the twenty-fifth. He'll understand.' Whatever that means."

Jackson grinned. "Thanks, boy."

71

Briggs was swearing over the casing which had to be fitted over the complete system of BOP valves, etcetera and then filled with oil to protect it on the sea bed.

"Oh, Mr. Jackson." Somebody shuffled up behind. It was Quidd, Nolan's clerk.

Quidd was small, with a knotted red face and raw wrists. He had large damp-looking nostrils. His hard hat was much too big and came too low over his eyes so that he seemed to be looking out, hot, sore and ratlike, from some recess.

Quidd was loathed by the men. He was Nolan's spy and snooper and also, in an incidental way, operated the radio, which seemed an incongruous skill in him. He moved about on thick rubber-soled boots and had a darting sort of energy. He never mixed with the rest of the crew or had meals with them—collecting his food and eating it somewhere by himself—and rarely went ashore. He despised the others with a monstrous scorn which was part of his curious inner intensity. He was alien to the oilmen's world and lived for Nolan with a fierce protectiveness. Inexhaustible, on his feet at all hours, looking after Nolan's clothes and cabin, serving him like a slavey in the mess, he looked as if he rarely changed his clothes and often slept in them.

"Mr. Jackson." He was thumbing his greasy notebook. "Mr. Nolan wants to know why there was a delay cementing the twenty-inch pipe?" Quidd spoke with his lower lip. It was the only part of his face that moved.

Briggs looked as if he were going to blow up. Jackson looked at Briggs and chuckled. But Briggs gagged it back. Jackson said, "The casing suspension head wouldn't mate up with the running tool."

Briggs interposed threateningly, "And if you come creepin' round here, you little bleeder——"

"You touch me! I'll tell Mr. Nolan!" Quidd backed off.

"——I'll push your face in."

"You touch me! I'll report you to Mr. Nolan." One eye cocked up, Quidd wrote rapidly. Jackson laughed.

"Mr. Nolan says he wants to know when you latch on the BOP."

Briggs said, "I'll tell him!"

Quidd turned to Gainer. "Mr. Nolan wants to know where the power swivel is." This was an item which Nolan had put in for some months before, a refinement, not strictly necessary for the drilling; though with it they would work faster.

"As far as I know, it's still on order."

"It's not with these stores?"

"Why don't you go and see?"

"Mr. Nolan told me to ask you."

72

"Well it isn't."

"Did you chase it up when you were ashore?"

Gainer didn't answer.

"You didn't make inquiries? Mr. Nolan's been asking for it especially."

"Sure, I asked everybody including the doorman but nobody had seen it." Quidd made Gainer sick.

"I'll tell Mr. Nolan." Quidd wrote in his book; he repeated the words 'including the doorman' aloud for Gainer's benefit.

Gainer turned away; but Jackson had gone. Gainer was exasperated but squashed it. He knew that these constant inquisitions, Nolan's hounding of the crew for every lapse or small delay, had some of the men like Briggs in a murderous state.

He went back to the main deck. He leaned on the rail, watching the supply boat unloading.

The breeze freshened and it came on a light blow. The supply boat put out extra fenders. The sea changed colour to a deeper green; there were white crests to the horizon. An empty Swedish cargo steamer daubed with red lead came up, riding high out of the water. She passed half a mile off, showing her screw. Not long after, a small black tramp, swirling smoke, went slowly past on the other side. They could see the men on the bridge scanning them with their glasses.

Joe Havenga, the Negro cathead man * came up to where Gainer was talking to one of the floormen. "Say, boss, could I have a word with you?"

Gainer stepped aside and Joe lowered his voice confidentially.

"You heard what happened, boss? Mist' Nolan tell you?"

"Tell me what, Joe?"

"Seems we wasn't usin' the sonar 'fore we set down here."

"You're right. Nobody understands that damned sonar machine since Vaisey left. What about it?"

"Well, boss—" Joe looked embarrassed. "'Seems there's somethin'—I dunno—somethin' down there, boss—ol' sunken somethin'."

Gainer waited for more and Joe nodded. "Yessir. An' it looks like it's und'neath Mist' Mack."

"What does?" Gainer said. "What do you mean? What's the joke, Joe?"

"Cross my heart 'n wish to die," Joe's cheerful face was serious; he spoke softly. "They seen some bits o' wood 'n

---

* The cathead man has charge of a rope, or *cat line*, which he coils around a winch (the *cat head*) which is really a protruding end of the main drum hoist, and hoists whatever is attached to the other end—mostly drill pipe.

stuff floatin' up—the boys in the boat there—and we got 'em fished out. I reckon we must've broken up that stuff, whatever 'tis, when we spudded in. Or maybe that ole twenty-inch pipe an' then the G and A done it, I dunno."

"When was this?"

"First thing this mornin'. We got that ole TV camera down to take a look. I reckon there was too much mud to see much but there's somethin' down there, Mist' Gainer. It looked like an ole steel plate an' locker or somethin' or a bulkhead or somethin' with rivets in it."

Gainer scanned his face. Joe looked serious.

"I'm telling you the truth, boss. An' you know what that is? I seen too many o' them things to make a mistake. That's mighty like a bit of ole navy boat, Mist' Gainer. Yessir, Mist' Gainer. I seen 'em aplenty, I busted them things apart, boss, when I was workin' in the breakin' yard. We used to break up them ole navy boats, destroyers 'n cruisers and li'l craft an' they had them lockers on deck an' all—an' sho' as I'm tellin' you the truth, boss, that's one of 'em down there right now."

"Who was with you, I mean when you used the TV?"

"Mist' Nolan, sir. That's all."

Gainer looked at Joe. "Nobody looked since?"

"I can't tell you. I dunno, sir. Mist' Nolan was down at Spud three bit later on and we was all told to hold everything and all the work stopped and the boat shoved off. Seemed like we was pullin' out 'cause you know Mist' Nolan, he don't stop for nothin', an' we had the ole diesel goin' awhile. Then it was changed and we jest carried on again."

Gainer looked around in search of Jackson. He couldn't see him. "All right, Joe. Let's go and have a look now."

"Yessir."

They turned together, walked across the deck and went up the ladder to the control room. The electrician was working on the control connection which had failed. The TV set was housed at the end of the control panel. The camera, lowered on guidelines to the sea bed, could pan in an almost complete circle right or left and tilt 190 degrees.

Gainer switched on. In a few seconds, the screen became dimly illuminated, a fuzzy grey. They could make nothing out. Gainer adjusted focus and definition. Still nothing.

"That mud—that's worse'n this mornin'," Joe said. "Mist' Nolan made a mark here, boss—you see dis mark—that's where we seen this wreckage." There was a fibre pen mark on the set casing on a bearing of 075 on the dial.

Gainer switched on another light, peered into the screen, then manipulated the controls which moved the camera forward a few feet. But it was no better. He had known mud to block the light of a 1,000 watt bulb six inches from the camera.

"No good, Joe." He switched off.

Joe said, "I tell you Mist' Gainer, that's part of some boat down there. Maybe there was some destroyer boat or somethin' got sunk here in the war and there's some magazine down there."

"And maybe there's just old rusty iron, Joe."

"Yessir. But we're getting off-a here, boss, ain't we?" Joe was quiet and serious; he wasn't scared. "We better shift right off-a here, Mist' Gainer. Yessir."

Gainer found Jackson by the port spud. Jackson had heard about the wreckage below but didn't seem worried and laughed as if the whole thing contributed to his private entertainment.

"Is it right that we were starting to move, then Nolan changed his mind?" Gainer said.

"Yup. Looked like it anyway." Jackson was still grinning. "Got ready for lowering. He started working the motors on Spud three for a bit. Then we all turned to again."

"What do you make of it?"

"Oh, God, I just kept my wine-red nose out of it, boy. Say, I just got some mail. Did you hear about the Jap girl and the golfer?" He laughed again. He didn't care.

"Where is he?"

"Well, he's coming up to the third tee, see, when——"

"Nolan, you chump!"

"Oh! Nolan? How do I know? Listen, there's this short-arse old boy going round with the caddy and they get to the third tee——"

"Sure. Later."

It was getting dark. The breeze had dropped again. Gainer crossed the main deck between the racked pipe and stores to Nolan's office. It was empty. Nolan had a cubicle cabin next door.

Gainer knocked and turned the knob but the door was locked. He waited for Nolan to open. Nothing happened. Maybe Nolan was asleep? It seemed unlikely—and Gainer thought it didn't matter if he was. He knocked again. "I'd like a word. This is Gainer." No answer. The jalousie was up inside the window and there was no light. He couldn't be there.

He went searching but Nolan wasn't to be found. Quidd, in the galley, didn't know where he was, for once. There was no response when he knocked at the cabin again. Gainer felt curiously uncomfortable. He believed Nolan was inside. But why in the dark?

Behind him, the deck crew were rigging lights. The big arcs were on over the derrick floor and the pipe racks and the cranes still working supplies. The lights shone on the sea. Four of the drilling crew who would soon be at work on the rotary table were at early dinner in the mess.

Gainer felt baffled. He went restlessly aft again. Jackson and Briggs were now supervising a larger group of the crew preparing to lower the BOP into place, the final preparatory stage before drilling began.

Gainer looked on unseeingly. What was Nolan up to? He went back and knocked at the cabin once more.

"Come in." Gainer turned the knob. Nolan was sitting on the bunk. There was only the light from the open door and through the slats in the jalousie. Nolan reached out and switched on the bunkside light.

He looked washed out and his hair was somewhat rumpled. Perhaps he had been asleep? Gainer noticed some cards were laid out in a game of patience on the flap under the jalousie. The glow through the slats might have been enough to see by. But why in hell did you play patience with the light out? The cubicle was untidy. There were a few pictures torn from magazines stuck to the walls; the Taj Mahal, a blonde with a big bosom.

"What is it?" Nolan said. Gainer realized that there had been a moment's pause since he had entered. Nolan didn't seem put out by it.

"I've been trying to get sight of the mudline and see what's down there."

Nolan didn't say anything. He got to his feet, buttoning his shirt and wetting his lips. His movements seemed slow. He bent and glanced at himself in the tiny glass. He kept his back turned to Gainer and Gainer had a fleeting impression that he was getting a grip on himself.

"Seems we didn't take a sonar sounding and we're straddling some sort of wreckage down there."

No answer.

"Joe Havenga says you both saw it. If that's so, the sooner we move the better, don't you think?"

Nolan stripped a bar of gum and began chewing. He screwed the paper into a twist, dropped it. He was still turned away from Gainer. He started brushing his hair.

"BOP stack down yet?"

"It's about ready," Gainer said. "So what?"

Nolan put on his dark glasses.

"You aren't going to put it down here?" Gainer said.

76

"No?"

"But you've seen for yourself——"

"Do you think I'm going to sit down, waste three or four days retrieving the G and A and dismantling the rest of the stuff we've just put down, then shift location, jet another thirty-inch and get this whole structure set up again for the hell of it? We've had two modifications since we ran the twenty-inch. It took them two goddamn hours to fit the suspension head to the universal running tool. You think I'm doing that again?" He turned around. He looked his usual self. "Not a chance. I'd be obliged if you'd get the stack latched on right now and start making hole fast."

"But, hell, it's asking for trouble. Say there's a load of explosive down there?"

"Suppose there ain't? Have you seen any? Havenga didn't. I didn't. Do you expect me to pull out for fairy tales of the North Sea?" Gainer wondered why he hadn't noticed Nolan's slight impediment on sibilants before.

"The debris alone is reason enough if you ask me."

"Yeah, but I'm not asking you."

"There are forty-two men on this platform, Gene, and if you don't give a damn about the——"

"I've got orders to drill, Mr. Gainer, and I'm goddamn going to drill. I'm in control of the situation. If it interests you, I've just had a new string of messages from the Company insisting that we keep right on drilling—'with utmost urgency' they call it, that's the sort of language they're using. And they want downtime cut to nothing, see—and that's what I'm going to do."

Gainer said, "Then why did you want to lower on Spud three this morning?"

Nolan threw him a half-scared, half-startled look. Gainer saw he had hit a nerve. At that moment, Ransome, the engineer, appeared in the open doorway and Nolan turned to him.

"The prime movers," Ransome said. "I've got a hairline crack in the casing of Number One fuel pump, chief. Been on the blink for some time as you know."

"What's your answer?"

"Have to change the pump. Luckily we've got a spare."

Nolan gritted his teeth. "All right, but for Christ's sake move it fast."

Ransome didn't look too pleased at this reception. He was wiping his hands on cotton waste. "We had to raise on Spud three again."

Nolan looked at him without speaking.

"She's been sinking. Very slowly. Couple of inches at a

time. But the movement's there. I don't know if it's still the soft bottom. Loo's like it."

Nolan was chewing. He said, "Keep me in touch. If it starts going again, I want to know right away. See? Right away."

Ransome nodded and went. Gainer waited till he was out of earshot. Nolan had collected up the cards and was snapping the edges with his thumb—a small release of tension.

"If these people get to hear what's down there on the bottom, there's going to be a row; you know that?"

"That's what they're hot going to hear, ain't it?"

"But good God, it doesn't make any sort of sense! It's bad enough to have this trouble with the spud sinking. We could take a list and never get back again. You want to shut your eyes to reason. We have to do one thing—send for tugs and move off. If you think that supply boat can move us, you're crazy. And you know we have to shift or you wouldn't have started to lower this morning."

Nolan snapped round. "Yeah? It so happens that we can't lower on Spud three."

"What?"

"You heard me."

"But you started to, this morning."

"I *tried* to. I *failed* to."

"I don't get it."

"The spud will go down but the gearing jams in reverse. You can't lower on Spud three without risking a major breakdown and I'm here to drill, Gainer, with the tools I've got. Now goddamn it, do *you* see?"

Gainer stared at him.

The spindles of the two main gearings on Spud three, obviously damaged in the past before Contram had acquired the platform, had been giving trouble for many months. At times they had difficulty when they had been hoisting the legs to shift the drilling location and occasionally when jacking the platform up the legs, though not—since the load of the platform was not resting on the legs then—when lowering the legs to the sea bed. Yet the trouble had been sporadic; and they had dealt with it as a fault they had to live with until a refit could be carried out. They had had specialists out to examine it—but the answer was always a refit. As a result of the conflict in Contram, the refit had been postponed; and this situation was the price.

But listening to Nolan now, Gainer realized something further. Nolan had made a long inspection of the gearing after they had moved from the last hole and must have learned the extent of the trouble. He had spent five hours on the gearing of the spud with one more specialist engineer flown out from shore. Nolan had said nothing afterwards. When Gainer and Ransome had wanted to know what the engineer had said, he had put them off.

"You knew there was a chance we wouldn't be able to move down that spud, Nolan, didn't you?"

"The BOP's about latched on. You'd better get making hole, Mr. Gainer."

"Didn't you?"

"Don't shout at me, Gainer!"

"Do you expect me to drill in these conditions?"

"Why not? I don't need to shift from here. I can sink wells in all directions. I can drill a six-well pattern—eight wells!—ten wells! I can drill you wells eight feet apart! I'll have you drilling the bottom out of the whole goddamn North Sea, Mr. Gainer, before you're finished!"

Gainer stood staring at Nolan's face. Nolan was snapping the cards with a loud clacking noise. Gainer turned and slammed out.

6

THE platform blazed like a lighted ship at sea. It was half past one in the morning. The arcs swung in the night wind. High up, a red light burned on top of the derrick and below it other lights sketched the framework of braces against the dark.

The diesel engines were working and over their thudding and the faint swish of the sea there was the sound of steel fiddles and wire accordions playing in excruciating musical cadences—the sounds of the brake on the drilling drum—as if the imprisoned spirits of all the machines under the sea were squeaking and screeching and tunefully beseeching release.

Gainer shut the door of his cabin behind him and took off his hard hat. He was tired and uneasy. Guggendorf was reading in his bunk. A plugged-in electric boiler on the floor was beginning to boil.

"Hey, doc, the workers keep you awake?"

"Have you struck oil yet?"

"We're piping it straight to the tankers."

Guggendorf laid his open book on his chest and looked down from the upper berth. "You know what Jackson told me?"

Gainer sighed. "Yes, I can guess. We can't do anything about it."

"But isn't it dangerous?"

Gainer sat down and began taking off his heavy drilling boots. "Maybe." He was still shaken at Nolan's outburst. And he didn't want to spread the disturbing knowledge about the gearing. They had begun drilling. Gainer had stayed on the rotary long past his tour, going over the drilling programme. He was too tired for a lot of explanations.

Guggendorf swung his legs over the edge of his bunk and dropped to the deck. "Cocoa for the working man." He unplugged the electric pot. "Want some?" The doctor was a great beverage taker.

"All right."

"Or would you prefer Horlicks?" he added earnestly. He

bent searching among the cluster of tins in the bottom of his locker.

"Anything you say." Gainer took off his second boot, zipped his overalls and got out of them. He washed up, cleaned his teeth and pulled on clean pajamas. As he finished, the doctor handed him a steaming cup. "What's this?"

"Vitabol. Terrific stuff. Lead in your pencil. Here, needs sugar."

They sat down and sipped.

"*Is* it dangerous?" the doctor said.

"Probably. We're taking a chance. Nolan thinks he knows what he's doing."

"What was the matter with him tonight? He came into the mess. I thought he looked edgy."

"Boy, you know he's a queer bird."

"Is he?"

Gainer hesitated. Should he say? "He was holed up in his cabin tonight. Locked in. Didn't answer. Seemed to be in the dark, too."

"Probably sleeping. You've known him for years, haven't you?"

Gainer sipped the hot sweet liquid. "Used to be a terrific hell raiser. Even the old oilmen, the ones who'd seen the rough days, reckoned he was one of the red hot gamblers and a mad drunk. He'd do anything. Over the top stuff. I mean, he was a nut. They used to be scared of him—and those roughnecks didn't scare easily. You could feel it coming on with him, when he wasn't drinking I mean—a sort of brooding calm. You felt there was some terrific pressure under the surface. I don't know whether you've noticed it, perhaps you haven't seen enough of him yet. You used to get a sense of impending violence. You noticed that?"

The doctor shook his head. "Can't say I have."

"Well, maybe I've got a wrong slant on him, I don't know. He used to have another side, apart from his drilling—admirable. I mean, he was what they called a good guy. You know?

"There was one episode down in Colombia. We were working north of Elcasto; it was a new field and we were drilling hard to small pockets of oil. We'd been down there for a year living in huts about five miles from Fuentes, a big run-down village they called a town. We used to drive in once a week, get drunk, maybe lay a woman. There was a little girl who used to come out with her old man selling vegetables to the camp cook. She was very pretty, about twelve years old, cheerful, a good kid.

"I don't know how, but Nolan got to know that the local

police chief was hanging around the child, trying to make her. The police chief wore a shiny leather belt and a revolver in a holster. It was no business of Nolan's but Nolan warned him off. Then he must have caught him with the kid. He beat him up.

"The police chief was mortally humiliated. Everybody could see he was biding his time to shoot Nolan. It was a hell of a situation. We expected Nolan to get it every day. We told him but he refused to listen, was furious with us. He used to drive into Fuentes and get blind drunk. We used to send some of the men in after him. The police chief never touched him. He was waiting for some chosen occasion. He had it all worked out. He was all ready for Nolan.

"Then Nolan unexpectedly caught him with the child again. The police chief pulled his gun, Nolan got it away from him and shot him dead.

"There was a tremendous row. The Company used high pressure. The local authorities accepted self-defense. Then the political opposition in Bogota heard about it and raised all bejesus for the Company."

"What happened to Nolan?"

"The Company knew that he was one driller in a million. They shipped him out to Borneo. Couple of years later he was back in South America."

They finished the drink.

"You kept hearing about him—crazy episodes," Gainer went on. "He was drilling in Bolivia, in the Bermejo field, and he used to drive into Santos on Saturday nights, commandeer a tram with some of his pals, load it with crates of whiskey, start it up and throw the handle away and drive round the town for hours whooping and hollering and shooting off pistols. They had to cut the town current off twice to stop him.

"Then once up in Peru, near Lobitos, he took the fire engine out and had the town in convulsions and the riot squad and mounted police galloping after him for three hours—miracle he didn't kill somebody. That sort of thing. It was legendary."

Guggendorf was grinning. "I bet it was."

"I wasn't with him continuously, of course. I used to see him at intervals when we were in the field together, you know, drill together for six months or a year then go somewhere else in different directions—the usual thing. I remember there was one period when he became—well, sort of uncertain of himself. You know, it was the sort of thing that struck you—Nolan the wild boy suddenly faltering."

"How long did that last?"

"Don't know. I was with him four or five months then. He still had pretty wild moments. But he seemed to be holding himself back. He seemed to be scared of something. I'd never thought of Nolan being scared or even moderate before—and it had *me* scared a bit, you know, doc?"

Guggendorf nodded.

"The next time I came across him he had picked up. He was sure of himself again. Very sure. He used to turn out in white overalls on the rig. You know, a driller in pure white —boy! He wears 'em now sometimes. You seen him?"

The doctor nodded again.

"It was after this that he started getting a reputation for being ruthless. He's always been a tough driver—and boy he can drive—but that was when he started screwing 'em on every job he had."

"Did he have Quidd with him then?"

"No. Don't know where he picked Quidd up. Quidd treats him like a kid sometimes."

"Yes. Quidd's a special sort of rat-slave."

"Loves Nolan—worships him. It's a strange set up."

"Nolan have women?" the doctor said.

"Oh sure. Always has. Of course he always picked the wrong women. And he couldn't help spending big on them. Hell, you know what oilmen are. But you took the gaudiest, the ritziest, the brassiest overblown peroxide diggers in the joint and you could reckon as a certainty that Nolan would make a beeline for them. He loved 'em. He never had any judgement about 'em. They rode him for every cent he had and he spent his money on 'em like water. You know how it happens with some men who've knocked around. He'd knocked around, God knows, but he believed every word they said. He thought they were beautiful. He thought they were the classiest gals you could lay hands on. He was blind to the bitch in them."

"You mean he still is?"

Gainer paused. He looked at the deckhead. "Doc, I don't know. I honestly don't know. Maybe all I've been telling you is misleading. He used to be like that—but we—ll, Nolan's a changed man, you know? There's no doubt about it. He doesn't drink any more, of course, but it's not simply that. He's not the old wild boy. No. He's not Nolan the nut any more. There's something different about him but he's not that."

"Different?"

"Well, you know, he's looked kind of strained a couple of times. Perhaps it's because I haven't seen him for a couple of years, or there haven't been any stories about him. He dropped out of sight, you know."

"Where'd he go?"

"Dunno. All I know is he wasn't drilling. You'd have heard about him."

"Perhaps he was in jail? Or he turned tram driver."

Gainer chuckled. "Could be."

"I don't think he likes me much," Guggendorf said. "But at least he doesn't trouble to hide it."

"No?" Gainer yawned. He got up. "Let's get some sleep, doc."

Lockwood, the geologist, sat in the deserted mess room with his suede shoes on the table, reading Adam. The cooks had cleared away the table after the midnight meal and gone. All the fluorescent strips were on, lighting the room with shadowless death-white light—the still-crumby tables, the racks of dog-eared, loose magazines, the silent TV set.

The door opened letting in the musical screeches of the brake. Quidd came in. Lockwood looked up. "Hello, I ssay. You're up plate. Always on the go, arn–twee? I musstt–ssay I don't know where o nearth you get the energy. It's really exhausst–ting."

The sibilants hissed whistling from his speech, the dentals stuck out like spikes. It was a vicious, supercilious, malingering voice.

Quidd gave him a bare glance, shuffling busily across the room. It was not clear whether he really saw Lockwood. He halted in the middle of the room, looking around, taking everything in. He seemed to be snuffing the air. He conveyed that this was how he preferred the place. Empty. His lips moved. "The bastards . . . the sons of bitches."

"What, Quidd, you muttering to yourself again? Really won't do. You must have a fine old conversation with yourself all bloody day. I sympathize, 'zmatter of fact. It t'isn texactly a social club, this bloody platt–form. I mean, look a titt. They're all everlastingly a–sleep. But ceaselessly! Here have I been wot'ching the bloody TV—I muss tssay I've rarely ssee namore frighttful crummy bit of old *vieux jeu*, simply sickmaking—an dnott a bloody ssoul has there been in thiss place for an hour. I mean if we had some educated types on board ——." He impatiently tossed Adam on the table. "I must have read this thing fif–teen times if I've ready twunce."

Quidd was moving towards the swing doors to the galley. Lockwood watched him from the table. One of the door leaves stuck open and he could see Quidd in the clean bare galley. He got up, lit a cigarette, stood lounging in the doorway.

"I mean, don'tt we all know itt, there's a bloody lack of amenit*j*es on board. You'd think you'd may kupp for itt by a little—well, bloody drollery, wouldn't you. Honestly though. There are ssome people you can't be friendly with. I mean, I think Gainer is an awful tough—terrible tough. I mean hussky, yess but terrible. Jackson. Well, now I *aask* you? Is itt possible? Absolutely un–conscious. But isn't itt true? They're all absolutely I mean hunks. *Hon*estly." He nasalised the hunks.

Quidd shuffled rapidly about the galley, preparing Nolan's early morning tray.

"I said to Jackson the firstt day, I said, 'You call me Vivian and I'll call you what?' I mean, a civilised bloody exchange. And you know whatt he ssaid? He ssaid 'Okay, Vi'. You know, Vi, in thattt ssmartt ssttupid way. Thoughtt it was di–*vine*–ly funny. Hilariouss."

Quidd had collected a pot, cup and spoon. He produced a key, unlocked a cupboard and took out an opened tin of orange juice. He poured a glassful, put the tin back and relocked the cupboard.

Lockwood leaned against the doorjamb, one hand on hip. He watched Quidd sullenly.

"When are we going to get a proper mail service on this bastard platt–form? I'm missing important tletters." The tone had become more nasal and vicious.

Quidd didn't take any more notice than before.

"Yes and when are we getting some decent bunks?"

No answer.

"You could be a bit more chumsy, you little stinker. Might pay you."

Quidd was reaching for the cocoa.

"You and your bloody old man."

Quidd whipped round. He faced Lockwood, scuttled forward. "You ain't fit to crawl to him. You ain't fit to crawl to his feet! Not to his *feet!*"—he jerked the open tin of cocoa into Lockwood's face. Lockwood recoiled, his eyes full of cocoa powder. He was coughing and spluttering.

Quidd had turned his back. "The bastards . . . The sons of bitches!"

Bradford stepped over the pipe underneath the No Smoking sign on the lower deck and walked across to the opening in the partition. He was wearing greasy overalls, a blue peaked cap and rubber boots.

The partitioned space enclosed a small air compression unit, a work bench with tools, another bench with the mud balance, funnels, hydrometers, viscosimeters and a litter of other apparatus and test kits. There were further mud instruments on shelves and floor; mud-testing cabinets, a sand tester, filter presses and containers of special ingredients for the mud stacked along the partition itself.

Now that they were drilling there was a great deal of noise on this lower deck. The diesel power units were situated forward on the same level and the mud pumps were working.

Behind the steel partition Bradford was alone. He wished there was a door but there was only a mud-daubed tarpaulin half hitched up over the opening.

He stepped to the farther corner, took out a packet of cigarettes and lit up. He dragged on the cigarette hungrily, cupping it in his hand. Once or twice he turned and glanced at the doorway. Trouble was that the hatch from the upper deck came down at that point. The time was one-thirty a.m. but there were seven or eight of the crew about.

The end of the cigarette glowed in his palm. He took a last drag, pinched it off. The end died in the mud with a tiny hiss. He put his foot on it to disperse the trace. He kept the smoke in his lungs for a moment, then expelled it.

He tucked the butt into the packet and put it away. He stood leaning against the bulkhead. Harrison, the night mud man would be down in half an hour. Bradford was rearranging the watches to give himself the leeway he needed. He ached for more of the cigarette. He ached for Judy. Inwardly he groaned.

He was still unsettled. He had been lying in his bunk this morning thinking about Judy. There was no damn privacy on this job. He had been thinking of her naked under the white fur coat he had bought her; maybe with long black stockings too, up to the top of her thighs, and the narrow suspender belt she wore sometimes. Suspender clips back and front. Black high-heeled shoes. With ankle straps. Yes, with ankle straps. Sexy ankle straps. He could see her putting up a foot on the chair to fix one. The coat fell open.

Bradford cleared his throat. His hands felt clammy. He had paid £2,000 for the coat out of the £3,000 Ambrose had advanced. She'd been marvellous. He wanted her to make love in it. She'd let him do so much, then rolled away, said he was crushing it. Then just to give him the bite she had dropped it and trailed it after her out to the bathroom, laughing over her shoulder.

It was on the bathroom floor when he went in. Just lying there like that. She had nothing on but the black shoes. Pushing her buttocks against the washbasin he told her he wouldn't crush it. He pleaded. She put it on again and held it round him with both arms while he did it standing.

Bradford swallowed. Have to see her soon. She was marvellous. Judy baby, in that coat again. Soon.

Somebody came down the ladder from the hatch. Bradford started forward, looking earnestly at the clip board hanging up. Whoever it was disappeared aft. He relaxed. Silly. No bloody privacy on this bloody rig. Last time he'd work in these conditions. He'd be the boss pusher and have the boss house. He'd buy Judy some of that heavy silk underwear, get her to . . . oh Judy, Jesus . . . kill it . . . kill it.

He buttoned the flap of his pocket over the cigarettes and went to the bench. He bent down looking at the counterweight of the mud balance. The mud balance consisted of a graduated bar with a cylindrical cup at one end, a sliding rider and a counterweight at the other end. It balanced by a knife edge on an upright stem rising from a circular base screwed to the bench.

This small, simple instrument was the safety gauge for the entire drilling. You filled the cup with mud and it told the density of the mud or drilling fluid with which the drilling was being done. A mistake or misjudgement in this density could produce disaster. The long column of mud being forced down the hole by the pumps was the only thing that would keep down any gas, oil or water there was below. If the weight of the mud were misjudged, the column might be unable to hold down gas or oil pressing up from the underground structure—often with immense force—and there would be a blowout. Blowout preventers could sometimes not be shut in time. A blowout could mean fire, explosion—the death of the platform.

Bradford bent down examining the smooth outer casing of the counterweight and the cup. He knew exactly what he had to do to upset the calibration and falsify the instrument so that it would give inaccurate information. He could even make it look like a manufacturing fault in case they came across it. Easy.

At that, there might be nothing to come across. "A final job," Ambrose had said. "No more Mister Mack." Bradford had pretty well come around to it. In the end Ambrose and Harry had been talking as if he had agreed to a final job. Funny how you got used to the idea. Harry kept saying it would make things less risky in the long run. They wouldn't have a chance to find the evidence. It had sounded crazy at the time. But he saw it now.

When he had mentioned the mud balance, they had asked

what if somebody else checked it? A simple routine check with water would show it had been tampered with.

Bradford had smiled. That was all right, he had told them. They didn't know Harrison. Harrison, his Number Two, had been a mud man for thirty-three years. Never put a foot wrong. After thirty-three years he didn't believe anything could happen to him. He wasn't going to do any checking. Ambrose said, "You'll have to keep Mr. Harrison sweet, won't you?" Ambrose could say a thing like that and give you the willies.

Bradford turned away from the bench. He hadn't yet, in fact, made up his mind exactly what he was going to do. He was the expert. It was his decision. They'd all said so. He was in a position of power.

It was a little foretaste of how things were going to be when he was boss pusher in Mexico. He'd have 'em screwed there. He'd get Judy to drive out to the drilling sometimes in her smart clothes. They'd all see who he was then. A girl like that didn't pick a half-wit. She could get any man she wanted. He'd have her meet Ambrose and Harry. On the other hand, no . . . The idea wasn't really pleasing.

He went through the doorway and climbed up on the walkway along the mud tank, looking into the tank. The liquid buff-coloured mud was swirling gently. At moments it looked like fine stretched silk. At the starboard pump Bradford jumped down and watched the big horizontal piston-plunger visible through the inspection window moving back and forth, driving the liquid mud through the system into the well hole.

He straightened up, glancing round. Nobody about. He crossed the few steps to the next compartment. There was a steel door marked in red DANGER KEEP OUT. The steel bulkhead alongside was marked *No Storage Along This Partition*.

Bradford took out the key he was making and put it into the lock. He stood turning it gently, feeling the lock action. The key wasn't quite there, would not yet turn it. He took it out, looked at it closely, then tried it again. He stood fiddling, gauging where it had to be modified.

Something snapped him alert. He palmed the key, stepped away from the door. Somebody was beyond the end of the mud tank. Bradford sprang to the mud pump and stood, hands on knees, apparently absorbed in observing it.

"Hi, Brad. How's the duck soup? You're on late, boy." It was Jackson.

"Just finishing."

88

"Yuh. A woman's work is never done, as the actress said to the bishop." Jackson laughed.

Bradford scanned his face. Jackson hadn't seen anything. Close call. Jackson must be the night driller. Bradford managed to laugh too.

"Get any mail?" Jackson said.

"One from the wife. You?"

"Letter from Shorty Young. You remember Shorty? Remind me to tell you about the Jap girl and the golfer. Bushada!" Laughing he turned away. "G'night."

"Goodnight." Bradford watched him disappear up the hatch. It was all right; Jackson hadn't noticed. It showed how you had to watch it.

Beyond the pump he saw Harrison shuffle into the partitioned space. He went over. Harrison was reading the mud log. He looked up at Bradford over the top of his glasses. "Okeydoke?"

"Everything okay," Bradford said.

"Right. Cheerybye."

"Goodnight, Jim." Bradford climbed to the upper deck. Cheerybye! Silly old sod; he could imagine her look if he said Cheerybye to Judy one night. A mud man for thirty-three years. Just about his mark, poor bleeder.

On deck it was a fine night. The breeze came fresh off the sea. The moon was out. Two ships were moving to the north. The lights of Argo 1 blinked brightly on the horizon.

Bradford headed towards his dormitory. On the way he glanced back. One of the night drilling crew was sitting on the stool by the draw works console feeding off with the brake in his hand. The square steel pipe of the kelly turning above the rotary table glinted in the light of the arcs. Jackson was standing to one side looking at the record book. He was on duty all right.

Bradford continued along the deck. The door of Nolan's office was open and the light was on. Nolan was sitting at the desk alternately writing on a pad and consulting a thick book alongside.

As Bradford reached the dormitory block, Quidd came out of the galley carrying a billycan. He ignored Bradford, carried the billycan to Nolan's office and went in. He took off the lid, poured the scalding cocoa into a cup. He put it down at Nolan's elbow.

"Wait!" He turned with sugar and spoon, put three spoonfuls in. "Drink it while it's hot."

Nolan glanced at it. "Okay." Quidd was still stirring it solicitously.

"Go on. Drink it now." Quidd withdrew the spoon. His

89

sore, ratlike eyes rested on Nolan with devotion. Nolan dropped the ballpoint, took the cup. "Okay. Go to bed."

Quidd didn't move. He didn't even want thanks. He said "Drink it now."

"I'll drink it."

"More in the billy."

"I won't need it."

Quidd stood watching him drink. "Those bastards! Those bastards. Won't leave you alone."

There was a pause while Nolan sipped.

"Coding a message, ain't you?"

"Uh-huh."

"What's it about?"

Nolan looked at him. "We can't lower on Spud three without jamming the gearing. Maybe we could force it. I reckon we could get down a way but we'd jam it into a major dockyard repair job for sure. I guess they have to know this. I guess I need to get clearance on this situation, see? Don't I, Quidd?" Quidd was nodding. "It ain't going to stop us drilling, though, eh? We're going to drill till we hit the pay sand, yeah. But maybe they want a conference on this thing."

"You talking about Mr. Stoneman?"

"Yeah."

"You take care of yourself! Those bastards!"

Pause.

"You're going ashore to Belle, I know?"

"Check."

"Spendin' on her. A highbred shiverin', skinny, fancy little dog costin' three hundred pounds . . . (his voice quavered) three hu–u–nd–red pounds. Holy Mother!"

"She has to have dough, Quidd."

"The sons of bitches!"

"The gal needs the blue chips."

"Ain't it how you keep her for yourself? Ain't it?"

"I ever tell you she's half French?"

"Fat, hard-case digger from Atlantic City." But then Quidd grinned wide, showing discoloured teeth.

Nolan didn't say anything. Quidd dropped his voice. "But you're all right with her, ain't you? Ain't you? Look at me! Answer me! You're all right with her. You're safe. You're great!"

"Yeah. You know how it is, Quidd, don't you?"

"I know."

"I'll have to get the big bonus on this job."

"She's a hook, ain't she? You gotta have her. Different hook to me."

No answer.

"Those bastards! They don't take care of you."

"You take care of me, Quidd, eh?"

"I'll take care of you."

The group of men stood round the mess room bulletin board reading the notices. The board was covered with old notices left there dog-eared and thumb-marked. Quidd had marked the latest with red crosses.

The top one was headed GLOVES. It said, "I observe some floormen and roughnecks are wearing loose-cuffed gloves on duty. This is STRICTLY FORBIDDEN. All gloves must be tight-fitting. This order will not be repeated."

" 'I observe!' " Briggs said. "Old sore-arse again."

"Listen to this one." This was Sutherland, the head derrickman, who had come back on board with the relief tour. "Final warning," he read. "Crew of this rig are losing far too many hand tools. Searching for tools wastes valuable time. Further losses will not be tolerated. F.S.Nolan."

"You know what the S stands for, don't you, Chalky?"

"Aye." Chalky White, 5 feet 4 inches, was one of the floormen who worked on the rotary. He had once been in a circus and his great social assets were a three-card trick which had the high gloss of professionalism, and a fake strong-arm act. He was irrepressibly cheerful. His great friend was Joe Havenga.

"If they put enough tools on board, you wouldn't have to go looking for them all the time," Briggs said. He glanced at Willis standing next to him. Willis continuing to read, nodded with tight lips.

"Here's another. MUD HOSE. The safety chain on the mud hose was left unattached today. There is no excuse for this negligence. If it happens again SOMEBODY is going to get his pay docked." It was also signed F.S.Nolan.

"How about us stickin' up a notice about the grub?" White put on an affected voice, "Dear Pusher, Crew will no tolerate any more bleedin' beans on toast or your ropey steak."

"Yes, why not?"

"I've about tadd this rhubarb bloody jam for breakfastt." They turned. It was Lockwood behind them. "Why can't we have honey or Mar—mite?" He passed on out. They turned back.

"It's Quidd keeps running to Nolan telling him the tale."

"Course it is. Scribblin' in his bloody book. I saw him spot that hose chain."

"He nurses the maintenance expense record as if it was his money."

"I'll gut that little weasel one day," Sutherland said with

sudden intensity. He was a tall young man with a high-bridged nose and thick black hair, a good-looking face. His tone made White look at him sharply.

Willis said to Briggs, I've got two new men again on this tour—with the compliments of Mr. Barker, our so-called shore Superintendent. Where he picked some of 'em up, I don't know. What with this lot"—he gestured disgustedly at the notices.

"I've had my bellyful," Briggs said.

"Here." Sutherland reached forward with a stub of pencil and wrote 'Push it' across the bottom of the Final Warning.

". . . or some divine Mar—mite, lambie—pie," Chalky said imitating Lockwood and they all roared, moving out of the mess.

On the far side of the room, the door to the galley opened silently. Quidd came out. He stood on tip-toe sniffing the air; his large nostrils fluttered open and shut. Then he went quickly to the bulletin board, read the pencilled phrase.

For a flash, as he stood stretched up reading, he expressed a concentrated intensity of rage. He snatched the notice off the pin, folded it and put it in his pocket. His lips moved silently. He waited a moment, fingering the paper in his pocket, then went out onto the deck.

The day was windless with high clouds to the north. The sea was a flat calm and the frontiers of its different-coloured zones were visible on its surface like the shapes of lost headlands and peninsulas. High above, a jet airliner drew its straight, white mark across the sky.

Gainer was just waiting to take his turn of duty at the rotary table. They were about to make a connection—fitting * a new length of drill pipe to the top of the string being drilled into the sea bed. The kelly, the square steel pipe hanging from the hook in the derrick with the whole string of drill pipe suspended from it in the hole, had now sunk almost completely through the rotary table. The kelly had drilled down as far as it could and more pipe now had to be fitted to it and drilled down in turn. This was repeated throughout the drilling process.

The driller at the draw works console pushed back his stool and pressed a buzzer. He cleared away a few encumbrances around him and made an entry in his notebook. They were drilling fast and penetration was excellent.

Joe Havenga appeared with three floormen in overalls and hard hats as the driller stopped the rotary movement of the

---

* Termed "stabbing in."

table. They began hosing down the slippery rubber flooring. The driller put in the motor again and the great travelling block and hook above began to rise slowly and smoothly up into the derrick, drawing the kelly squeaking and steaming up through the rotary in the floor.

One of the floormen hosed it down, removing the drilling mud. As soon as it was completely withdrawn the driller stopped, lowered everything in again, then slowly pulled it up afresh. Joe stood marking the kelly with chalk every yard. The top of the drill pipe itself, yellowed with mud, appeared through the table. Two floormen moved forward and threw a steel clamp **, like a deep steel corset, into the hole. It closed tight around the top of the pipe and jammed there with handles protruding, holding the drill pipe in place in the rotary table.

The men moved back and hauled forward the two big steel tongs that hung on cables at waist height, horizontal to the floor. They were now going to "break out" and unscrew the kelly from the pipe, so as to be able to add more pipe on top. This was the heavy work of drilling; the men heaving at the massive gear, shouldering the tongs, lifting the slip—all in quick movements without a pause.

Joe clamped his pair of tongs—the backup tongs—to the pipe below the kelly and threw his weight against them. The other man clamped his pair—the breakout tongs—to the kelly and held them. The driller threw in the motor. The steel cable that attached to the breakout tongs snapped taut. The motor revved. The kelly and pipe were screwed hard together and the screw joint would not give.

Gainer glanced up and saw that Nolan had come up the steps on to the derrick floor. Gainer raised an eyebrow. Nolan was wearing his all-white outfit.

The driller put in the motor again. It thudded heavily. The steel hawser on the tongs vibrated under the strain. One of the floormen stepped cautiously back. Joe was still bearing against the backup tongs. Then the screw grip of the joint gave, the breakout tongs swung. Immediately, Joe heaved his tongs aside and the rotary table was revolving clockwise, unscrewing pipe from kelly.

As the kelly and pipe separated, the men stood back. The liquid mud welled out. The mud pump had been shut off and the outflow subsided in a few seconds. Lending a hand, Gainer stepped forward and helped Joe and the other two men push the kelly, now hanging free on the hook, to one side.

** Called a *slip*.

Here the new length—or joint—of pipe was waiting, its top emerging from a hole * in the derrick floor.

The fourth floorman had coiled a chain, called the spinning chain, round this new pipe. Power applied to the chain would spin the pipe and screw it into the kelly held poised above it.

They hauled the kelly over to the pipe. Gainer glanced at the driller and at the same moment saw the tangle of wire cable which had been kicked there from somewhere and lay around the length of chain running across the floor.

His warning shout was drowned by the driller putting the motor in hard. The chain snapped taut. The wire tangle flew upwards. Nolan threw himself bodily forward, knocking Joe Havenga staggering aside. The cable slashed the air a foot above Nolan's head and zig-zagged madly.

Gainer was motionless. The driller jammed the motor to a stop. Nolan and Joe were sprawled on the derrick floor, the others gaping at them.

Gainer jumped forward but Nolan waved him off. "Okay, okay!" He sat up, picked up his dark glasses. He looked around at Joe. Joe was getting to his feet, obviously still baffled.

Gainer kept saying to himself: he saved Joe. He saved him. The wire could have cut Nolan's head off.

"You all right?"

"Okay."

Nolan was adjusting his glasses. He looked down at his white overalls, now smudged with grease and mud. He didn't seem concerned about it.

Suddenly he exploded. "Who brought that goddamn cable to this floor? Who brought it here? Jackson's in charge? Where's Jackson? Why isn't Jackson here? Give me that notebook. Quidd! Quidd! Get Quidd here at once. I'll get to the bottom of this by Jesus." He screamed, "Quidd! Get Quidd!"

There was a big game of stud poker going on in the mess room. Men coming in for food found themselves confined at one of the long tables, the rest of the space being occupied by the gamblers and their financial backers. The game had started hours earlier among men off duty and had gradually grown. In the last half hour it had begun to turn noisy.

The sound of voices carried over to the port side of the main deck where Gainer was standing with the doctor and

---

* The mouse-hole. Not to be confused with the rat-hole, which is also a hole in the derrick floor, but sheathed, in which the kelly stands when it is not being used.

Joe Havenga. It was a mild night with intermittent moon-light.

"They seem to be workin' it up, boss," Joe said, grinning.

"Sounds like a good session."

"I think Mist' Jackson feelin' pretty good. He's been doin' all right. When he gets goin' dere's noth'n'll stop'm." He chuckled.

There was a brief silence.

Joe said, "Is this true we ain't gettin' any more men?"

"Yes, Joe. The Company, as they put it so elegantly, is 'having to shave costs', so it's cutting the size of the crew. That's the word, anyway."

"That's no good, Mist' Gainer."

"Well, we're having to give reasons for every extra high item," Gainer said.

Joe digested this. Then he said, "I'll jest go 'n have a look at that game, sir."

Gainer and the doctor moved off a little down the deck. The doctor was munching biscuits. "We're kicking up a lot more noise, aren't we?"

"Drilling much faster. Nolan's raised the pump pressure to 2,300 psi."

"That a lot?"

"Hell, man—it's capacity! Besides that, he's loaded the bit for all it can take. We drilled the last hole with about 27,000 pounds. Know how much we got on this bit? 50,000 pounds!"

"Wow!"

"Nolan couldn't get a power swivel, so we're going hell for leather without it."

"Risky?"

"Nolan says its okay with that weight on the bit. Maybe it is. I never drilled this fast before. But are we making hole!"

"All in the interest of saving the Company costs and getting there first, I take it?"

"Right. But you can't satisfy the Company that easily. Now they're bellyaching about Nolan drilling another deviated hole."

The doctor said, "Even I know straight hole is cheaper."

"Sure. What they don't know is that Nolan's aiming to slant the hole so damn close to the Atlas's territory next door that it won't make any difference."

"What for?"

"The data looks good and he reckons he can get away with it."

They were interrupted by a wrangle of voices from the direction of the mess. Jackson came stumbling up, laughing helplessly. "Poor old Whispering Bill Wallis . . . s' like taking milk from baby . . . Out of mouth o' sabes 'n bucklings . . . Bushada! Say d'you hear—Oh my God—(more laughter) . . . the Jap . . ." He was drunk.

Gainer knew that if Nolan saw him there would be a convulsive scene. Nolan had a mania about no liquor on board and no smoking except in the mess. The crew's belongings were regularly searched for liquor when they came aboard—one of the things they were constantly complaining about.

Jackson lurched and grabbed Gainer's arm with a laugh.

"Ole Shorty Young. You remembsh—orty, doncha?"

"Better get to your bunk, Jacko," the doctor said. Gainer wondered where he had got the stuff.

"Why'n hell sh'd I?——" Jackson started arguing with the doctor that he was sober. Gainer noticed that Joe Havenga had followed Jackson out. It appeared that Jackson, who had somehow got himself drunk alone, had started baiting some of the men in the poker game, insisted on joining in, had won to begin with but then began fooling and disrupted the game. There had nearly been a fight—and Willis was keeping back a couple of roustabouts who wanted to come after Jackson now.

Gainer saw that it was the idiotic sort of incident that could suddenly develop into something ugly that they would all regret. Be all right ashore but not on a platform. Jackson had fastened on the doctor and was making a noise.

Across the deck a figure showed against the light in the doorway of Nolan's office and came out. Gainer thought it was Quidd. "For Christ's sake shut up, Jacko. Clear off to your cabin." He gripped Jackson's arm.

"What's matter, ol' Larry, boy?"

Glancing back, Gainer saw that it was Nolan, not Quidd. Nolan disappeared behind the pipe rack on the deck, coming their way.

"Shut up—here's Nolan."

"Whooza—frayda Nola . . . Whohoo!" Jackson whooped again. Gainer caught a glance from Joe as Joe moved in.

"I'm sorry Mist' Jackson." Joe's eyes gave a roll. One big black hand closed round Jackson's mouth, the other jerked Jackson's arm into the middle of his back. With a heave Joe forced Jackson towards the hatch. They covered three steps. Jackson struggled. Joe changed his grip and lifted him. They reached the hatch as Nolan rounded the stacked pipe.

"All yours," the doctor muttered and disappeared after them.

Gainer leant against the rail, watching the distant lights of a ship. He heard Nolan stop a few paces away, then approach again.

Nolan came up, hands in his pockets. He was wearing his dark glasses. Gainer nodded a greeting. "Nice night." He hoped it sounded natural.

"Yeah." Quiet, very mild tone.

Had he seen anything? "Plenty of shipping round here." Gainer nodded towards the lights.

Nolan didn't say anything. Gainer thought; Can I move off? Then Nolan said, "I'd appreciate your opinion on a point, Mr. Gainer."

Gainer looked at him with mild surprise. Nolan was standing scratching his neck. His brow was furrowed. He raised his hand and adjusted his glasses and Gainer thought there was something slightly unusual in his manner. The shadow of the crane partly hid Nolan's face but Gainer had the same impression as before in Nolan's cabin that Nolan was trying to keep himself in hand.

"Certainly. What about?"

"Could we go to my office?"

"All right."

They crossed the deck, Gainer asking himself if Nolan *had* noticed Jackson and was preparing some blast. In the office, Nolan shut the door, motioned Gainer to a chair. He sat on the desk stool. He wet his lips a couple of times. The change in his manner was accentuated. He was quiet, almost hesitant. He reached for a packet of gum. He seemed for a moment as if he didn't know how to come to the point. He held the gum out.

"Gum?"

"Thanks." Gainer shook his head. He noticed that Nolan's face was slightly contorted. Nolan had a little difficulty stripping the paper from a bar of gum. He folded the bar deliberately into his mouth. He had a slight hand tremor.

Gainer felt uncomfortable. A glass was tinkling somewhere with the drilling vibration. He wanted to move it, stop the nervous ting-ting-ting.

"What's on your mind?"

Nolan said, "Do you seem to feel we're listing, Mr. Gainer?"

"We're what?" It was a small, cold shock. Gainer stopped moving. He looked at Nolan. He knew he hadn't misheard.

"Listing."

"No. There's the inclinometer if you have any doubt. Have you looked at it?"

"Yeah," Nolan said. "Yeah. It's—it's okay. I reckon I—It's okay." He held out the packet again. "Have some gum?"

Gainer reached out. He concentrated on extracting the slim bar. His eyes flicked up at Nolan. He took the gum and unwrapped it and chewed. There was a brief silence.

"You play draughts, Larry?" Nolan said.

"Draughts? Haven't played for years."

Nolan adjusted his glasses. "I was going to say how about a game?"

"Fine. Why not?" He paused. "You mean now?"

"Yeah." There was a tiny edge of eagerness in Nolan's voice. "How about it. There's a game called Fox and Geese. You know that?"

"Hell, it's years since . . ." Faint recollection of a puerile boyhood game stirred in his memory. The whole episode shouted hideous incongruity.

"I'll show you," Nolan got up quickly and went to the door. "Get the things."

Gainer could hear him opening and shutting drawers in the cabin next door. He sat very still, waiting for Nolan's return.

7

It began to drizzle at dawn. Nolan was on deck early. Gainer came up and found him discussing the deviation of the hole with Willis. Nolan was entirely his usual self.

He had ordered the helicopter for 0930 hours to go ashore to the Company. He spent nearly an hour going around talking to Bradford, Ransome and others, and wasn't ready on time. Gainer went around with him. Nolan was aggressive, sarcastic—unchanged.

He finally took off in the helicopter at 0955. For once, there was a Company car free at the dockside depot and Nolan caught the fast train to London. At 1450 he was in the lift at Contram travelling up to Stoneman's floor. Stoneman wasn't back from lunch at the Guildhall.

Nolan went down and made war politely on some of the specialists on lower floors. He didn't waste any strength. They were going to be bombed from directly overhead by Stoneman, when he had said his piece. At 3:45 Margie Field located him on the third floor and summoned him up.

She showed Nolan into the Chairman's office. Nolan was not wearing his dark glasses. Meldreth and Stoneman were sitting together at the desk facing him as he came in, talking to another man who had his back to the door. They broke off as Nolan came down the room.

"Come in, come in." Stoneman extended a hand and said to the man, "This is Mr. Nolan, our Tool Pusher on Mister Mack. Now you can hear at first hand. How are you, Nolan?"

"Great, thanks."

"This is John Julius, our lawyer."

Nolan and Julius nodded to each other. Nolan didn't like lawyers. Julius, who was about forty, was short and very dark, with a heavy blue shaving area and a white tie. He had been going over the legal situation with Stoneman and Meldreth, telling them that the pressure was piling up, since the Dutch who had filed a further suit, had obtained a preliminary decision in chambers which was going to tell considerably in their favor later. Contram must counterattack. An extremely costly and complex action was building up. They would need a further conference with senior counsel without delay. Stoneman did not think it necessary to explain any of this to Nolan.

"Sit down, Mr. Nolan," Stoneman said. "Anderson is coming up in a moment. We had your coded report about the state of the gearing." He turned to Julius. "They've got a mechanical failure which would mean a major refit to rectify. Since they can continue operating, it's academic—doesn't arise. But I wanted you to be here, John, when I told Mr. Nolan (he turned back to Nolan) that there is ab—so—lutely no question of our interrupting operations to bring the platform into dock. Absolutely none. It is out of the question."

Julius shook his head in support.

Nolan's brow was furrowed. He fingered his dark glasses in his breast pocket. "We have this soft bottom condition where we are operating now; the thing will have to be done and— All I'm saying is that if we had to pull out, we couldn't do it —maybe we couldn't get down at all. And anyway it would involve a dockside repair job,"

"We know that. You've reported it," Stoneman snapped.

Nolan hesitated. "It's dangerous—plenty."

"Dangerous?" Stoneman narrowed his eyes.

"We could list over—the way they lost Mister Gus 1 and that Trans-Gulf unit."

"We are not playing table tennis, Nolan." Stoneman's tone was icy. "We all know the risks we have to take in this business. Don't we?"

"I mean——"

"Don't we?"

"Well, sure, but——"

"This is a new line from you, Nolan. I'm surprised."

"Line—it's not a line. I just mentioned it." Nolan spoke rapidly, nervously, as if he were anxious to efface an impression. He rapidly pulled the dark glasses from his pocket and flipped them on. "Let's forget it, forget it."

Meldreth was watching him. He had the impression that Nolan found it too low in the deep armchair. He would have to struggle to get out of it. Nolan seemed to feel trapped. He was fidgety but trying not to fidget. He looked very uncomfortable.

Nolan's attitude to Stoneman was one almost of fear and respect. Stoneman, of course, had found him and given him the job. But it struck Meldreth that there was some other element in the relationship—something of the mysteriousness in which Stoneman managed to involve other people.

"Anyway, you are supposed to be self-supporting," Meldreth said. "Can't you do the repair yourself?"

"No sir. We'd have to dock," Nolan said. "This is a full-scale engineering job." (Meldreth knew this already, of course.)

"Yes. In other words, a three-months lay-off," Stoneman said. "Possibly four, in the state of the market." He caught an eloquent confirmatory shrug from Julius. "Naturally, it's ridiculous—naturally! We might as well throw our hands in. We can't afford a *day's* loss! Mr. Nolan, you were put in there to drill—and we expect you to waste no time!"

"Yes, sir."

Meldreth was thinking what Moreno and company would make of the gearing failure if they found out. They would certainly press it as a reason for giving up; but Moreno wouldn't stop at that. Meldreth could see him spreading alarm among the men, starting a strike, raising a lot of hooh-ha about safety regulations. He took a fresh cigar from the box and cut it carefully. He had signed all the documents for the purchase of Mister Mack.

"No question otherwise," he said.

Julian said to Stoneman, "I think it is important for Mr. Nolan to understand the legal position. If we strike oil first, Mr. Nolan, we shall be in possession. You have heard the old adage about possession being nine points of the law. Well, it is still true in some cases. It will be very much more difficult for anybody to contest our rights when we have struck oil."

"And there's this other thing, John." Stoneman leaned eagerly towards the lawyer. "There will be no proration *."

"Yes. This is very important."

"When we make a strike, we're going to sit on it. We are going to keep quiet until we have three or four wells down —then give it the gun, produce hard, flat-out, all we can."

"Right."

"It will be time enough to talk proration when Atlas move over and start drilling next door—if we haven't won the claim by then."

Nolan said, "If Atlas make a strike, they are going to pipe

* Proration (Hideous word) means that where two or more companies drill down into an oilfield extending under their adjoining lands, they restrict the amount of oil they take instead of taking all they can. This is to maintain the pressure of the underground gas which drives the oil to the outlets (the drill-holes) and thus allow the maximum quantity of oil to be extracted from the field as a whole. Under the Law of Capture, and before the State proration laws in America, a ruthless operator could so reduce the gas pressure that his neighbour was left without enough to bring his oil to the well.

the stuff away, make out the well-head's farther off. Put the production platform a couple of miles away."

"True."

"You won't find much pressure and you won't get much help on proration from them."

"I know it. And all this, Mr. Nolan, is why we can't afford to waste any time; and why we *must* make a strike first."

Meldreth's glance went up. Miss Field had put her head in the door. "Mr. Moreno on the phone, Mr. Stoneman. I told him you were in conference but he said to interrupt."

Stoneman got up. He stepped through into his office and shut the door. Julius produced a cigarette case, which he did not offer to Nolan, lit up and began going through the papers in his briefcase. Meldreth was studying documents on his desk. Apparently neither of them wanted to say anything while Stoneman was out of the room. Nolan sat in the deep armchair.

Stoneman's muffled voice in the next office began to rise and presently he was shouting. Julius glanced awkwardly up at Meldreth. Meldreth's eyes were fixed unwaveringly on his papers. He might have been stone deaf.

Stoneman was obviously having a blazing row with Moreno. They could only hear a few words. ". . . am keeping you informed! . . ." and a shouted "bloody sabotage!" Meldreth's and Julius's pretended absorption with their papers became ludicrous. They sat motionless. The minutes passed. The shouting went on. Nolan uncrossed his legs, shifted.

Then Stoneman's voice stopped. After a longish silence, the door opened and Stoneman came in again. The leathery folds of his face looked petrified. He sat down. He was seething with cold anger but keeping possession of himself. Julius, who had stuffed his papers away, said in an unnaturally quiet voice, "I must go," and got up. "There was the other thing."

Stoneman said, "Leave us a minute, Nolan, if you please."

"I have a list of things to raise," Nolan said.

"In a moment."

Nolan persisted, "We need the telex hookup. Keep asking. Can't go on relying on radio."

Stoneman looked at Meldreth. "Hasn't it been done yet?"

"Applied for. JB's always handled the Post Office. The PO are talking about priorities for people who are drilling in British concessions."

Stoneman said to Nolan, "Wait in the secretary's office. Anderson is coming up."

Nolan got up and went out.

Julius said, "Lavaca Tools are threatening to issue a writ. I was talking to Rogers. It would be bad if they did. They are undoubtedly ganging up."

"Moreno's crowd is getting at them. I'll let you know what to do."

"Sooner the better."

Stoneman rapped, "Do I keep you waiting for decisions?"

Julius twitched up one corner of his mouth with irritation but let it pass. Damn well working off his bad temper, he thought. He nodded and went.

When he had gone, Meldreth pushed back his chair and crossed to the window. He longed to be able to walk straight out like Julius but knew he couldn't. He knew that Stoneman was going to ask him to do something dangerous and unscrupulous. He did not want to hear what Moreno had said. He didn't want to hear anything. He wanted to go to Reine; he wanted to take her in the Rolls and hide his fear against her breast—no longer lusting after her but a frightened old man awed by the happy and confident young creature whom he met gratefully now with love in his heart.

"Walter." Meldreth flinched. He remained facing the window, waiting for the next lash.

"Get on to Union Finance. We want £900,000 for two months, against the Danish bonds and the platform."

"The Danish bonds have been——"

"Don't argue."

"Without the Board's consent, it would be——"

Stoneman's voice was not unkind. "You must do as I say."

Quidd sat down on the mattress and reached for the pair of Nolan's socks he was darning. The door of the radio hut was locked. He was snug. He was safe. Quidd always locked himself in now while Nolan was ashore. The sons of bitches!

Quidd nominally had a bunk in one of the crew dormitories but he had long since jammed a shapeless mattress into the radio hut and slept there with the window shut, never making up the bed and hardly ever, it seemed, changing the sheets.

Across the hut was the desk, radio key, transmitter, and receiver with the fixed connections and switches. This and the narrow path to the bed were the two clear spaces. The rest of the hut was cluttered with Nolan's suitcases, hanging windbreakers, waterproofs, rubber boots, brooms, a stepladder and accumulated junk reaching up the bulkheads.

There was a pile of gummy medicine bottles and boxes by the bed, dusty cardboard cartons, two broken chairs, a broken lamp, a radio set that didn't work, mattress ticking and empty files.

Quidd didn't mind the disorder. He was safe in the knowledge that Nolan's cabin and office were cleared and neat. Nothing useless there, nothing in the way, everything scrubbed, scraped, polished, laid out.

Quidd licked the darning wool to a point, threaded the needle. He looked round. Barricade the door too? That bastard Sutherland. No. He would trust.

He caught a glimpse of his face in the glass. It was the first time he had seen it for days. He could go three days without needing a shave. When he did shave, Quidd saw his face without taking it in. Now he saw his short faintly reddish curly hair. Parted in the middle. Always parted in the middle since birth. Aunt Felicia had said he had been born with it. That was why they had named him Leon.

His eyes switched to the cardboard boot box of belongings on the floor, the only possession of his own, besides his clothes, in the hut. A letter there from Aunt Felicia. He had noticed it again this morning when he had looked at the holy card. It had come six months before. He hadn't opened it. He had turned it round, looking at it. But he hadn't opened it. Never opened letters. They lay in the cardboard box. Like bombs.

He was feeling thirsty. Could do with a cup of tea. It would have to wait. He only went out late—when the bastards were asleep.

He darned Nolan's sock.

He knew exactly what Mr. Nolan was doing now. He was with Belle. Quidd wasn't jealous of Belle. She was on the receiving end. He had told Mr. Nolan so. Mr. Nolan wouldn't admit it. But Quidd knew he knew it was true.

He knew where they were now, too. They were in the nightclub. He was spending on her, throwing money away on her. She was made up to kill. Quidd could see her. Her peroxide hair, her big figure. Her eyebrows were thin, painted on, like the feelers of insects. She was poison.

She was going to make a scene at the nightclub. Mr. Nolan was going to say she was damn right. They'd paid, hadn't they? They expected service. She had to be poison to people. She had to make scenes. Maybe she thought Mr. Nolan liked it. She was like the others—the bastards. But she'd stuck by Mr. Nolan. It was because she was on the receiving end. They were *all* on the receiving end. The sons of bitches.

Quidd took the other sock. He moistened his lips. He was safe.

Twelve hours after Nolan got back to Mister Mack, they had a 'twist-off'—a major drilling mishap—with the drill string broken far down the hole.

It was four o'clock in the morning and the rotary started to spin faster. The hands on the torque recorder and the weight indicator and mud pressure dials slacked off. The driller at the console braked, jumped up, called out to Jackson and stopped the motor. Jackson came over, they tried a turn or two while he watched the dials.

"Oh Christ, a fish," Jackson said.

They called Nolan. He was sleeping heavily and they had difficulty in waking him, but when he came he was furious and slanged Jackson in front of everybody.

Jackson didn't take it very seriously. "Look up the log and you'll see I made a note about the tool marks on some of the new pipe." (He hadn't made a note or seen any tool marks; but tool marks *could* show where pipe was weaker and might break under strain).

"Get Quidd! Give me the goddamn driller's notebook. A fishing job now! Holy God—of all the goddamn set of incompetent bastards." But a twist-off is not foreseeable and Quidd was going to have a hard time finding a culprit.

They pulled the string of pipe above the break and began the laborious process of fishing for the part still in the hole, one of the most maddening, worrying, nerve-racking and frustrating tasks in a driller's life.

After his first outburst, Nolan became incisive, unhurried —the supreme professional. He studied the break at length, went over the drilling records which gave size of bit and the heavy pipe above it, the drilling speed, mud pressure and so on, examined all the instruments, made a careful analysis of the situation. They had a conference—Nolan, Gainer, Willis and Bradford.

It soon appeared that it was not a simple twist-off with the broken section free in the hole. Mud circulation had stopped and—probably as a consequence—somewhere below the break there had been a cave-in* and the pipe was stuck. The break was in a bad place, had left a heavy weight of pipe and drill collar below and it was a deviated hole. Gainer saw grimly that they were in for it.

Gainer was feeling edgy and miserable, but for a different reason. Nolan had come back from the London visit saying he had seen Margie in a nightclub off Piccadilly the night before. She had been "with some American guy," he said, without making a point of it; and Gainer hadn't asked more.

But he had visions of Mike Welsh or one of the other Americans she knew giving her a good time, pursuing her.

* Cave-in. When the side of the hole caves in and grips the drill string.

105

There was no prospect of his getting to London himself; and even if he did, it would again only be for a brief spell that wouldn't resolve anything.

And, of course, he saw that her glamour, her special magic seemed, by the very contrast of this male life that he hung on to and wanted, all the more appealing. Sometimes, as now, they seemed irreconcilable! She existed for him as an ideal—an ideal bound up with the atmosphere she created, with her expensive and neglected clothes, a sort of hard, joking defensive comradeship, her amusing willingness to get canned occasionally, the interior of her flat and so on.

There were moments when she had a sort of mongrel charm, a child-like candour. And she belonged, he thought, somehow to the stage, to a certain life of the stage anyway— he saw her as the ideal of the 1935 musical comedy chorus girl—especially in her joking acceptance of the toughness in life—but so much prettier, so much smarter than the real ones must have been. Her occasional panic-stricken looks, her frank smile, even the slimness of her bare little arm—all these were Margie in this adorable and unrivalled way.

Obviously one of the men round her was going to be decisive before long. Soon there was going to be a new turn in her life—and she would disappear.

What could he do?

"What's the matter?" the doctor said.

"Oh, nothing."

"Here—have some Juvenate. Lead in your pencil. Terrific!"

They had failed after forty-eight hours to get the fish. They had engaged a Bowen overshot* but all their endeavors to pull or back off sections of the stuck pipe had come to nothing. They ran wash pipe—a large pipe over the sunken drill string—to wash it over with mud and help release it, all this entailing heavy, exhausting work, constantly pulling pipe and equipment engaged in the hole, running in new tools and pulling them again and beginning afresh.

Every fresh step involved study, consultation, careful thought; yet for all the deliberation, the sense of urgency grew constantly since, apart from the loss of time, conditions at the bottom of the hole would be deteriorating. Once Nolan had a screaming fit at Bradford who wasn't ready with the required mud mixture. Everybody knew that if they failed to recover the fish and couldn't cement it over and rebore satis-

---

* Bowen overshot. A specialized fishing tool which is lowered over broken pipe to engage it and allow it to be pulled. If the fish still remains stuck, the overshot can be released for something else to be tried.

factorily, they might have to abandon the hole completely—
all the time and labour and cost thrown away.

Nolan was at the rotary table day and night directing operations, full of resources, tireless, sarcastic, restlessly on edge,
holding himself down. Quidd, grotesque in an ankle-length
camouflage cape, brought him cups of cocoa and warm
clothes. Gainer and Joe Havenga watched engrossed while
Nolan produced half a dozen dodges to make the fish come
(which had Gainer silent with admiration) but which failed,
too.

The third afternoon after the twist-off, a little mist came
up. They worked late into the night at the fish. They had finished another washover and Nolan was using a rotary jar to
free the stuck pipe by striking it heavy blows. They were
going to continue the jarring for several hours more.

At three a.m. Nolan left Jackson and Willis in charge to
get some sleep. The night was black and mist was showing
under the arcs. Jackson was on the rig floor with Chalky
White and Sutherland, the derrickman, telling dirty stories.
Willis had temporarily gone below. The jarring string was
being monotonously lowered and pulled.

Presently White looked up at the mist. "Hope we're not
comin' in for a load o' fog."

Jackson laughed. "In November, you idiot?"

"Why not?"

"Well it ain't the month, boy. Not at sea. Spring and summer if you like but not now."

"No joke? They was talkin' about it in the mess tonight."

" 'Sright," Sutherland said.

"Well, there's nothing doing."

"I been lookin' up at that old foghorn and thinking of ships
loomin' up like, with a bloody great blare—bloody great liners, you know. 'Alf the chaps believe it, you know, Jacko."

"It's true, I'll bet you," Sutherland added.

"Oh my God—wonderful idea!—let's let the damn thing
off." Jackson roared with laughter. "Terrific!"

"What?"

"Nolan would raise blue murder."

"We'll go down and tell him!" Jackson was dancing at the
idea. "He'll swallow it."

"You can go, Jacko."

"You scared little bastard."

"I'll go," Sutherland said.

"No, hell, he'd get up. I'll go."

"Let him get well asleep first."

They waited, scarcely able to contain their nervous, expect-
ant joy. Sutherland and White became more and more enthu-

107

siastic. Sutherland made some cocoa but Jackson didn't want any. When Willis returned they told him. He didn't look approving but didn't say anything.

At five o'clock, Jackson said, "Okay, Chalky, here we go." He went down the steps from the drilling floor and crossed the deck to Nolan's cabin. Watching him from under the derrick, they saw him pausing at the door for a moment, suppressing his mirth. Then he knocked on the door and put his head in.

After a moment, a light came on. Jackson apparently had a brief exchange, then withdrew. He shut the door after him. The cabin light stayed on as he came back grimacing towards the derrick, then went out again.

Jackson came up the steps spluttering.

"What'd he say?"

"Oh God," Jackson could hardly speak for laughing. "He sort of boggled up and you could hear his eyes popping. 'Yes, who is it, Elmer?' He called me Elmer! I don't think he could even see. 'Oh, Mr. Nolan, this is Jackson,' I said. 'We've got a bit of fog out. I reckon we ought to blow the foghorn for safety's sake. Never know.' He still trying to see me. 'Okay Mr. Janson,' he says—*Janson*. 'Carry on. Call me if it gets worse.' So here we go, Chalky, boy."

There was a switch in the dog house, the small cubicle near the derrick floor which housed some of the drilling instruments and a mike. He made a flourish with his hand and threw the switch over.

The terrific blare of the foghorn sounded out into the night from above. Jackson's face was illuminated with joy. The deafening blast—on and off at intervals—woke most of the sleeping men on the platform. They listened for a second or two, identified it, turned over in their bunks, cursing and thinking this was the end of sleep.

Jackson was holding on to one of the derrick uprights for support. White and Sutherland were also laughing noiselessly. Willis kept out of it but Harrison and half a dozen others drifted out and looked round puzzled, then joined in the joke. Jackson let the horn rip for twenty minutes, then Willis persuaded him to turn it off.

At dawn the weather was still heavily overcast. The platform stirred into other activity. In the mess at breakfast, Jackson kept a straight face answering questions about the fog.

"It went that-a-way," he jerked a thumb over his shoulder. "We scared it, boy."

He kept nudging White and saying in an undertone that they had to wait for Nolan. Five minutes later, Nolan came in. He sat down at the other end of the table. Quidd serviced him as usual. There was the usual hubbub of voices and clatter of dishes. Nolan started to eat. He stirred his coffee and took a sip.

"Fog cleared pretty fast," Nolan said.

The general noise noticeably diminished as most of those at the table realized that Nolan was the one man on board who didn't know about the foghorn joke. Or if he knew, he was playing for trouble. There was a slight pause.

"We blew it off," Jackson said—and laughed. White gave an unnaturally loud and obviously uncontrollable hoot. Nolan cut some bacon, ate it. He buttered a piece of toast. He looked around. "Yeah?"

Jackson, Sutherland and White were convulsed.

"What's so funny?" Nolan said.

Another pause. "What Jacko—just said, that's all," White managed.

Some of the others at the table were grinning openly. Eyes were going from Nolan to the three. Nolan went on quietly eating. He took another sip of coffee. As he was putting the cup down, he seemed to catch a look from Quidd. There was a flash of communication between them. Nolan had abruptly sensed that he was the butt of the joke. His expression changed.

The men at the table became interested in their plates or other things. They stopped grinning, one or two got up. The atmosphere became electric—unnoticed only by Jackson, White and Sutherland who were wiping their eyes.

"I said what's so funny, Mr. Janson?"

This produced another outburst from Jackson. White had his head on his arms on the table.

"Mu—mu—who?" Jackson weakly cooed.

"Can't we all enjoy it, Mr. Janson?" Nolan snarled.

Jackson roared again.

Suddenly Nolan jumped to his feet, knocking his chair over. "You goddamn son of a bitch, you wiseass twist-off professional——" He was screaming. "What d'you think you've got to laugh at? Clear out of here! Get out. Quidd! Quidd!" He snatched up his plate and hurled it backhand at Jackson. It skimmed Jackson's head, remnants of food flying, and crashed into the bulletin board on the far bulkhead.

"Wh-at—?" Jackson sputtered, only half realizing what had happened.

Nolan grabbed the coffee pot. Hot coffee slopped on the table. A man opposite jumped back. Quidd caught Nolan's arm.

"Mr. Nolan—urgent for Mr. Nolan," a voice said over the intercom. "Mr. Nolan wanted in the control room."

Men had pushed back their chairs from the table. One or two were grousing. Nolan was shaking with fury, staring at Jackson and the other two.

"Ransome calling Mr. Nolan. Mr. Nolan wanted in control room. Urgent."

Quidd said something and Nolan looked round at him. A group of the men who were stubbing out cigarettes and leaving the mess took Jackson and the others out with them. Nolan looked round at the chair Quidd had righted and sat down. He pulled out his dark glasses, flipped them on. He sat staring at nothing. His jaw muscles tightened as he clenched and unclenched his teeth.

"Where is Mr. Nolan? Will Mr. Nolan please come to the control room?"

Nolan made an effort, got to his feet. At that moment, Gainer looked in. "Gene, can you come quick, please?"

Nolan went to the door.

"Spud three's going," Gainer said.

Nolan fingered his glasses, looking left and right across the platform as if he were judging the situation. They ran across the deck up the steps. Ransome was in the control room by the panel.

"She's going down an inch a minute," Ransome said excitedly. "Damn near an inch a minute. Look at it. I'm giving her leg all the time."

They looked out of the window. The jacking gear was working, hauling the platform up the leg. On the panel, the spud recorder dials showed that the leg was sinking. Ransome was having to jack the platform up the leg at the same speed to keep it level. They stood watching the dials. Momentarily, the needles wavered, then began moving again.

Ransome was stretching his mouth with tension.

There was a grinding which abruptly increased in volume; then the jacking motion became spasmodic. Their eyes went to the gearing.

"She's jamming."

"For Christ's sake, give her the juice," Nolan shouted. Ransome jumped to the smaller switchboard and threw in the auxiliary power unit. The jacking nevertheless jolted to a halt. They all stood still, trying to sense the beginning of the list. The smell of burning electric connections drifted in.

"We're going over!"

The leg was still sinking.

"Jesus."

"Ring the general alarm."

The floor of the control room vibrated, there was a crash from the top deck; loose equipment began to slide. Gainer reached for the alarm and turned it on—and at the same moment the jacking began to respond again. He flung around. Outside, he could see the great gear wheels turning slowly in the racked outer framework of the leg.

Ransome shouted, "Easing up, chief."

The dial needles were stationary. The leg had stopped sinking. They stood watching the dials. Gainer glanced at Nolan's face. He could not see Nolan's eyes behind the glasses. He knew that if the movement began again they were practically helpless.

8

BRADFORD walked quickly through the main mud compartment. He had been waiting for an hour for the opportunity and was keyed up. The men had called for a midnight meal in the mess and there had consequently been a certain amount of coming and going. His rubber boots thudded audibly on the deck since the diesels were not working. But he had to look as if he were on duty in case he were seen or had to answer a sudden summons to the derrick floor. They were still fishing and were calling for mud circulation at intervals.

Bradford paused at the starboard mud pump. He couldn't see anybody coming. He was about to step forward then looked back. He thought he caught a quick movement in the next compartment; he waited but it was nothing.

He crossed to the steel door, took his key and tried it in the lock. He had already knocked out the deckhead light so that if anyone came down the hatch he would be invisible in the shadow. The key turned. He had to shoulder the door hard to open it. He removed the key and slipped inside.

Standing in the dark, he pushed the heavy door shut, locked it behind him and stood still listening. There was a faint smell which he couldn't identify.

He took out his torch and passed it round. An empty space on the bulkhead facing him was painted in red EXPLOSIVES DANGER NO WELDING. It was a small wedge-shaped compartment about twelve feet long and ten feet across at its broadest, opposite the door. The floor was clear and the rest of the bulkhead space was fitted with storage racks, many of them empty.

The torch picked out a long, thin, metal cylinder perforated lengthwise with eight holes. The holes looked like gun nozzles. It was a gun perforator—a multi-barrelled gun which the driller lowered to the bottom of a hole and fired bullets from into the rock to help the flow of oil. More guns packed in boxes and back-off shots * were stacked alongside with cartons of bullets and charges.

---

* Fishing tool used with explosive.

Bradford walked around flashing the torch. There were large basket-bound carboys of hydrochloric acid on lower racks and the floor. On other racks were explosive disintegrators and fuse material. Farther on, bedded down in two deep bins filled with sawdust and shavings, were two containers marked DANGER GELATINE DYNAMITE. The lid of one had been taken off and loosely replaced. Bradford leaned over and lifted it. The container held six cartridges, each the size of a thick candle, cushioned in sawdust.

Bradford put the lid back. He stood with the torch beam on the containers. He felt the pride of accomplishment in getting access to the compartment. Now he had everything set. He was going to make a final job of it all right.

He wanted a cigarette. He fingered the packet in his pocket but dared not light one. No danger from the explosives; but the smell of tobacco would persist in this confined space and he couldn't risk it.

He put the torch over the remaining bins. He would have to connect up some fuse system when the time came; and there was, he knew, an electric time fuse on the perforator guns which could be set at an interval of hours. It would have to be carefully timed—a precision job.

Bradford was sure he could get Parrish, the Sikorsky pilot, to play. Parrish was fed up with Nolan, he was monumentally fed up with Mister Mack. Bradford had been drawing him out lately, though you never drew Parrish far. A cocky bastard, Parrish. He liked himself. Walked with his back arched in and his backside sticking out as if he owned the place. Parrish was inshore with the helicopter now. Bradford believed he only wanted to stay in the job until his end-of-the-month pay.

Bradford hoped Ambrose or Raymond weren't going to approach him. Parrish wouldn't wear it. Bradford had told them to leave him alone, leave it to him. He knew Parrish; he knew how to handle him. Ambrose hadn't looked too convinced. But they obviously didn't want to bring anyone else in if they could help it. Still, Raymond might try something with Parrish. It was unnerving.

Raymond had been the great pal, "Good old Brad"ing him. Perhaps they thought he would be too scared to go after them if it didn't come off as planned? They had better not make a mistake there. He wasn't going to let Judy go. He had thought about it too much now—the new life, Mexico, the money and her. It had become a reality which he was already half enjoying.

The circle of torchlight on the floor at his feet made him think of the light from the shaded lamp with her lying on the bed in her black nylon chemise against the white rumpled bedclothes. Lying on her back, one thigh crooked over the other. "You can take it off." She knew he was going to break the straps, tear it. He always wanted her to be wearing something. The time he had snapped her beads, gripping them in his teeth. That had been in the bathroom, too.

Bradford wished he had one of those big snifters of brandy Raymond was so fond of handing out. Right here and now. And one of the fat cigars. That was for later; not much longer now. They'd be laughing. They'd have a big American car with leather seats. Wide leather seats. It was another thing she was marvellous at, making love on the car seat. She always knew when he said, "Let's just go for a ride, dear."

Sometimes he chose the country, a lane, sometimes they stopped in a darkish street, put the lights out. Once or twice in the summer she'd dared him and he had pulled up while it was still light and people about, on a public car park once, and they'd had it. For kicks, she had said. Marvellous, she'd been. Marvellous.

He clenched his teeth, forced his mind away from her. He felt he must have a cigarette. His mouth was salivering with the need for tobacco. Suppose he waved his arms after a few puffs to disperse the smoke? Wouldn't do.

Twisting his finger, he searched for a corner of nail to gnaw. This existence was soon going to change. There would be real opportunities with Atlas, they'd said—the top money class. That was for him. The top money.

Outside, there were voices and movement. Bradford snapped off the torch. Two or three men were near the door. He thought he recognized Willis's voice but couldn't make out the others. They might be looking for him. They came closer, then seemed to be at the door.

Bradford stood motionless. He felt a prickle of sweat on top of his head. Had they seen the torch-light under the door? He imagined them standing outside, speaking in whispers, watching the crack under the door.

Suddenly he was screwed up. Suppose Nolan was going to try to loosen the fish by detonating a charge near it—a common technique—and they were coming in for the explosive?

There was nowhere to hide. He was locked in. Bradford's mouth stretched, drawing the tendons of his neck. He hardly breathed. There was a jolt on the door. Somebody outside said "Take it easy."

Silence. Then the voices passed on.

Bradford waited in the dark. Presently he heard the muffled and muzzy sounds of something over the intercom. He shaded the torch with his fingers, went to the door and unlocked it. He hauled the heavy door open an inch or two and looked out. Nobody. He went through, pressed in the shadow locking the door behind him. The next minute as he was walking through the mud compartment, White came out of the partitioned area.

"Oh Brad, lookin' for you. We're going to start her up."

"I got diarrhea."

"What?" White looked at him.

"I said, I can't help it, I got diarrhea."

"Eh? What of it?" The look more puzzled.

"Nothing—nothing." Bradford felt the prickling on his head again. Damned fool, giving excuses before they'd been asked for! And to White! He groped for some way to carry it off but could not think of anything.

White went up the hatch. He looked back before he disappeared. Bradford fingered the key in his pocket. Okay, okay. Take it easy. Okay, Judy. Okay.

Quidd had somehow found out about the foghorn joke. As tale-bearer and Nolan's snooper, he could not learn the facts directly but had evidently overheard enough to put together what had occurred.

Nolan called Jackson to his office for an explanation. Jackson tried to throw it off lightheartedly. Nolan was coldly sarcastic but no more. On the whole, Jacko chuckled afterwards it had gone off pretty well.

But Guggendorf decided that Quidd must have found out something more. About eleven o'clock on the morning after he had seen Jackson, Nolan rang for the doctor to come to his cabin. He was in a T-shirt, a pair of greasy overall slacks, wiping his arms after washing. He had just come from the derrick floor where he and Gainer had again spent most of the night on the fishing.

"Doc, I'm starting up a new thing, a tour of inspection. Take a look-see at this whole goddamn platform—main deck, crew quarters, galley and so on. Same below. You'd better come along."

"Me?" Apart from anything else, it seemed an odd moment to choose. Nolan looked all in, and apparently they were no nearer getting the fish.

"You're supposed to be in charge of health on this rig, I thought?"

"Yes, but I mean, this inspection. You mean for rats or something?"

"Maybe. From now on we're having an inspection as often as I say we need it. As a regular thing. Safety regulations, cleanliness, order, maintenance—the works."

"You mean a sort of Pusher's rounds? Like the navy?"

115

"Yeah. Why not? Like the navy. Yeah—sure. Like the navy," Nolan said. He called out for Quidd and told him to fetch Willis. As Quidd was going, he called after him, "And Joe Havenga too. Doc, get a torch. We'll start in five minutes."

The doctor felt that there was something behind it. He couldn't fathom what it was. "I have a couple of men coming along to the sick bay," he said.

"They'll wait."

There was a small delay while Willis was located and told, and Quidd collected an inspection book to note any deficiencies they came across. Nolan was impatient.

The doctor felt the absurdity of the scene as they marched across the deck—Quidd leading, then Nolan, the doctor and Willis, all, except Joe Havenga behind, with torches in naval fashion. Jackson was going up the steps to the derrick floor and the doctor caught his gawk, then his look of hilarity. Jackson started marking time, lifting his knees high, and whipped an invisible telescope under his arm.

They started with the main deck, quickly passed round the working gear, pipe racks, stacked material, put their heads in to the mud lab. They walked straight past the radio hut, examined the shale shaker—Nolan stopping from time to time to ask a question which Willis usually answered. Once Quidd made a note in his book when the answer wasn't satisfactory.

Next they went through the crew's dormitories, washplace, the galley and mess room. The men stared. At Nolan's orders, Quidd shone his torch under bunks, into corners, pulled out pairs of boots, dirty towels, old gloves, paperback books, socks and so on—discarded junk stuffed away out of sight. While Quidd directed the torch beam, Nolan peered behind stoves, into cupboard and storage space, making comments where things were dirty.

The cooks were busy. One of them lifted the lid from a big pan, dipped a ladle below the cloud of steam and solemnly held it out full of butter beans. The doctor nodded with equal solemnity. Behind Nolan's back, the men winked at each other. The doctor wondered for a moment if Nolan was going to play the thing to the limit and ask the men how they liked the grub. But they went through without it.

As they reached the lower deck, the doctor saw Jackson about to turn into the alleyway behind the mud tank. Jackson saw them and after a pause, evidently decided he had no time to do whatever he was going to and turned away, making the small ladder to the deck above. His expression was one of humourous boyish embarrassment.

Nolan and the others were moving out towards the tank.

The doctor saw Jackson go fast up the ladder. Quidd didn't appear to have noticed. What was Jackson doing? He was supposed to be on duty fishing at the rotary table. After the foghorn row, there could only be some urgent and overriding reason for his rushing down here.

The mud pumps and diesels were momentarily stopped. The inspection party went past the chemical storage tank, through the mud-mixing compartment and the partitioned space where Harrison was on duty into the main mud compartment. There was a walkway along the main mud tank.

"Why don't these damn lights work here?" Nolan was irritatedly working a dead switch. The narrow alleyway between the mud tank and the bulkhead dividing off the engine room was one of the darkest areas on the deck. Quidd headed along it flashing his torch. There was a scattering of discarded material lying about.

"Look at this! Dirty as hell down here. Get it cleared up, Willis."

Quidd was searching with the torchlight near the dry mud bin which jutted out at the end at an angle. They all stopped and looked on. Out of the corner of his eye, the doctor saw Joe Havenga edging to one side. Quidd had found a mud rake and was poking it into the dark space.

The doctor moved to place himself between them but Nolan shifted and prevented him. The doctor caught the glint of a bottle and Joe trying to kick something over it. Quidd made a sudden movement and Joe must have thought he was seen. There was a loud clatter. Empty beer bottles and a bottle of whisky rolled out under Joe's feet. Quidd gave a sort of bark.

"What the hell's this?" Nolan said. All the torches were on the bottles rolling down the deck. Joe was motionless, looking at them in great dismay.

"I said what's this!" Nolan yelled. "Whose is this? Who brought this goddamn liquor aboard?"

Quidd had jumped forward and was pulling away a set of driller's overalls from the hiding place, then a windbreaker, stiff with mud, which had been packed over the stock of liquor hidden carefully between the dry mud bin and the bulkhead.

"Here." Quinn shone the torch in. There was a thicket of beer bottles and two more bottles of whisky.

"Well for Christ's sake! Howdya like that? Howdya like that? Who brought this liquor aboard this rig? What were you doing there, Havenga? Was it you? That's who it was, it was you, wasn't it?"

"Nosir—ah—" Joe looked crestfallen.

117

Quidd had darted aside, picked up the overalls and was running the torch over them.

"Now you know why there aren't any goddamn lights here, don't you?" Nolan was yelling. "Now you know!"

Quidd held out the overalls, pointing to the inked initials inside the collar. Nolan didn't get it for a moment. Then he bawled, "Send for Mr. Jackson. Get Jackson here at once."

Quidd went himself. Jackson came down grinning and gangling, moving his head from side to side, trying to carry it off. Nolan was fingering his dark glasses. "You bring this liquor on board, Mr. Jackson?"

"Uh—that is——"

"Did you?"

"It must have slipped into my suitcase."

"While the fog was up, is that it?"

"Yup." Jackson laughed—but defensively.

Nolan screamed, "While the fog was up and while you were twisting off, you goddam drunk! You think I'm having drunks aboard his rig? Give me that stuff, Quidd!"

Quidd handed him a bottle.

"I don't allow any goddam liquor on this rig. Do you hear? *Any* liquor! Do you damn well hear, Jackson?" He lifted the full bottle and smashed it to the deck. Willis, Joe and the doctor stepped sharply back. Nolan grabbed another bottle from Quidd, smashed it to the deck, and a third. "Any goddamn liquor, d'you hear? Toss the rest over the side, Quidd —now!"

He stood, out of breath, hunched forward. He lifted a hand, fingering the dark glasses.

Jackson shrugged sheepishly, trying to put a face on it; then abruptly he turned and walked away and went up the ladder.

They had failed to bring up the fish. They were sleepless and exhausted. Their nerves were on edge. They had tried everything they knew. The broken string of drill pipe with the bit at the end was clamped fast in the long hole curving under the sea bed. At one point in their struggle, Gainer had lost the overshot with which they were trying to recover the fish. Nolan had retrieved it. They had found it difficult to get alignment with the end of the broken drill string and the curved hole and limited the length of the fish they had been able to wash over at one time.

It was ten o'clock in the morning. They were on the rig floor and had just had another conference with Bradford about the mud they had been using. From the beginning, Nolan had maintained that over-sanding of the mud had been one of the original causes of the caving; but Bradford hadn't been able to give any satisfactory explanation.*

"Okay," Nolan said, dismissing Bradford.

The weather had turned cold and windy. A sea was running and the elevation of the platform left them exposed. Nolan crossed over to the strip of protective canvas they had rigged up at one side of the derrick floor. He seemed personally involved in the drilling, Gainer thought, bound up himself with its success or failure. Gainer went over.

"What are you going to do, Gene?"

"I don't know."

"Plug and rebore?" **

Nolan shifted irritably—obviously reluctant to throw away all the time and labour they had expended.

On the rig floor before them, the men were still hard at work. Once more they were pulling up the drill string with the last, useless, ineffective fishing tool at the end. They were still a team, but they were slogged out.

Joe Havenga was hosing oil and mud from underfoot. Briggs, at the console, was raising and lowering the hook and elevators which were pulling the string of pipe and fishing tool from the blocked hole. Chalky White and two other floormen were working the break-out and back-up tongs, then shouldering aside the 120-foot length or "stands" of steel pipe *** hanging from the elevators and standing them in the derrick.

High up in the derrick, Sutherland, the derrickman was reaching far out, like an acrobat, from his tiny platform, the fourble board, to unclamp the pipe from the elevators, haul it towards himself and rack it in the "fingerboard," as White and the men below swung in the bottom end and stood it down. Sutherland was held by a single safety strap across the front of his platform.

The stands of pipe, each weighing three-quarters of a ton, bent outward under their own weight as they stood racked in

* Drilling mud is meant, among other things, to line the sides of the hole so that they do not collapse (cave in) or let water or gas seep through.

** When a fish cannot be recovered, the hole is "plugged back" with cement to a suitable geological formation and a new inclined hole is started and drilled alongside but away from the abandoned hole.

*** Known as fourbles. A fourble is four lengths or "joints" of thirty-foot drill pipe screwed together. Pulling pipe in fourbles means fewer joints to break out and less time lost in hoisting the drilling string. Single and double joints are called singles and doubles, three joints together is a tribble.

rows. The floormen worked with scarcely a pause, in a rapid back-breaking sequence.

Haul over tongs, kick hose from hole, kick slip into hole to clamp on pipe, snap on tongs, bear against them, release as driller gives a quick pull to break the joint, swing tongs away, kick hose into hole, shoulder released pipe over to stand, reach for elevators coming down on the next stand, clamp elevators to pipe in hole, haul out slip, kick in hose, pause while stand of pipe is hauled aloft, swing in tongs, kick out hose—over and over for thousands of feet of pipe.

Briggs barely flipped a glance up at Sutherland. A second after the elevators were off, he had the travelling block and hook falling at express speed. He braked it inches above the floormen's heads. By the time the men had latched the next stand on, the diesels were going and hoisting the stand aloft. Each 120-foot stand of pipe was being drawn out of the hole, broken out and racked in the derrick inside a minute.

"If you're going to rebore, we're not rich in drill collar," Gainer said.

"I know it!" Nolan turned restlessly away. Gainer wondered if he had reported their plight to the Company.

Turning, he saw Quidd come up the ladder to the rig floor. Quidd approached. One of the floormen was hosing the stacked pipe, the other watching the block and elevators dropping fast. The next moment, the man sprang back as the elevators dropped past their usual point and hit the derrick floor two feet from Quidd. The floor shook under the impact.

Luckily, only the elevators' two long steel arms and attached clamp had hit. Briggs at the console immediately drew them up again six feet above the floor.

"What in Jesus do you reckon you're doing?" Nolan said.

"Maybe the clutch slipped," Briggs said pugnaciously. "We done so many round trips on this damned fishing job, I wouldn't wonder."

Nolan was white. "That was deliberate, Briggs."

"Are you accusing me of serious negligence, Mr. Nolan?"

"You're goddamn right, I am."

Briggs blocked the brake. He left the console and walked across towards Nolan. He was a big thick-chested man.

"I've just had about enough of this. You withdraw that accusation, Nolan, or you're going to get the bloody consequences."

"Shut your trap, you slob! You're about as much good as a sheep's spout on a butcher's board." Something in Nolan's manner seemed to deter Briggs.

"I'm not standing any more of it—sweating our guts out day and night. You can't get the fish. Why don't you throw it up? We're short-handed—bloody inspection parties nosing where they've no business—I been drilling for thirty years and I never seen anything like it."

"Well, you're seeing it now and you can start learning fast."

"There's notices on the board that'd get you a strike on your hands with some crews."

"Yeah? I noticed some of your drawings on them, you dumb bastard. Like the ones you draw on lavatory walls." Nolan was taut with scorn. The constant defacing of the bulletin board notices infuriated him.

Briggs opened his mouth silently.

"You ought to sign 'em," Nolan snarled.

"You're going to get a strike with this crew too, don't worry. That little weasel of yours snooping round."

"So maybe your clutch just slipped to kill him off just now? That's what it looked like to me."

"Mr. Nolan, I am bloody well—"

"Don't you bloody me, Briggs! Get off this floor and stay off till I tell you to get to work again."

"If you think you can get away with this, Nolan, you're mistaken. What's wrong with this rig? Why did we start that list again the other day? There's soft bottom here, ain't there? Why not admit it? I've been told there's other things and we ought to be pulling out."

"Sure, you've been told, you punk. Have you got any more secondhand rumours? Maybe somebody told you how to get the fish up and you can pass it on? You been drilling for thirty years and you can't handle a goddamn brake yet. Well, Mr. Wiseass Briggs, until you're put in charge, I'm giving the orders around here and you can get off this rig floor, you crap-faced dope, right now!"

Briggs stood glaring for a moment, then stepped back. "Okay. You want trouble." He swung round and walked off.

White went over to the draw works console and took the brake. Nolan crossed restlessly to the far side and back again, adjusting his dark glasses.

Quidd waited a minute, then went up. He had a radio message in his hand. Nolan took it, read it slowly. His lips tightened. He stood looking at the message. He crossed over and handed it to Gainer. Gainer read it.

We have inside report that Atlas have struck highly promising pay zone which they intend exploiting top speed stop Atlas further awaiting new semi-submerged deepwater platform which will operate three wells simultaneously stop this now on way to your area stop meanwhile Atlas intend using

121

*this in court to press legal claim stop imperative therefore
you make utmost repeat utmost efforts to achieve successful
strike stop give reasons why your situation report is overdue
stop what is your present drilling depth and formation reply
forthwith signed Stoneman.*

It did not sound good, Gainer thought. The last part about
the situation report confirmed that Nolan had not reported
their fishing breakdown.

He glanced up at Nolan. Nolan was watching White at the
console. Suddenly Nolan exploded, "For Jesus Christ's sake
get it moving there. You think we've got all damn day and
night? Get Willis up here. Keep that goddamn pipe moving! I
want action, for Jee—sus Cuhrist! Do you hear? *Action!*" He
was screaming. The tired men were moving over the rig floor
at the double.

Jackson was drunk and happy.

He picked up the canvas bag with deliberate loving care,
put his shoulder to the steel door and pushed it open. He
lurched inside—the bag zig-zagged. He made a grab for the
door edge and recovered, holding the bag out safely. He was
laughing softly to himself.

He put the bag on the floor, pushed the door to and locked
it. Dimly he registered the smoothness of Bradford's key in
the lock. It recalled his own deftness in helping himself to it
and redoubled his laughter. He stood leaning against the door
in the dark, laughing.

He wrestled a torch out of his pocket. EXPLOSIVES
DANGER NO WELDING leapt out from the bulkhead.
Jackson's eyebrows mockingly rose. Laughing, he lurched,
reached out wildly sideways, found nothing. The torchlight
flew up, he nearly fell; his hand grasped support and he clung
to it, given up to mirth.

Good ol' Brad. Never miss his key. What a place for the
hooch! Never find it here. Nev' in thous' years.

He steadied himself, gazed at the rack he was holding and
placed the torch on the lower shelf so that it shone out into
the compartment. He reached to the small emergency light
and switched it on. All ri', all ri'—Nobody'd see.

He bent down swaying and managed to zip the canvas bag.
Bottles clicked. The bag was full. It was nearly all whisky.
His cap fell off. He reached for it, missed, got it, flipped it on
askew, flipped it again. He was softly chuckling ho-ho-ho.

He groped round in the bag, extracted a half-empty bottle.
As he was straightening up gripping it, he pitched forward off
balance and charged across the compartment. He stumbled,

122

hit the far rack and went over holding the bottle high. He sat holding the bottle, back against the rack, laughing. He unscrewed the cap, took a drink, dropped his jaw, took another.

Nursing the bottle, he looked round the compartment. He recapped the whisky. With great deliberation he put the bottle down and got to his feet. Holding the racks, he went round. He started to laugh again. He lurched sideways, staggered several steps, nearly fell, clutched the nearest rack.

He hung into the rack, laughing, looking at the back-off shots and detonators.

"Bam-bam-bam!"

He swayed on, slipped, grabbed the edge of the bin, gazed swaying down at the dynamite. His mouth rounded in mock awe. "Yowie!"

He zig-zagged back to the canvas bag and dragged it over to the bins. He extracted two bottles of whisky. He stood over the bins. Now his laughter was silent. He steadied himself, reached out, holding a bottle over the cartridges. Then he jabbed it downward, standing the bottle end-up in the sawdust. He pressed on it, working it round, boring it into the sawdust and shavings. He flipped up the shavings, covering the bottletop.

"Zowie!" He stood swaying, contemplating the bin.

"Find it now, yol' bastard." More laughter. He brought up the second bottle. It slipped in his fingers. He made a grab, juggling with it until his hand knocked it sideways. It dropped just inside the bin. Jackson laughed. He buried it in the sawdust too.

He went back and pulled the bag across to the farthest rack. Slipping and lurching, he lifted it in, pushed it to the back, scrabbled some boxes of cartridges in front.

He stood up, reeled towards the dynamite bin, slipped as he reached it and fell. He hauled himself upright, locked his elbows over the edge, gazed at the containers.

"Whezz my drink?"

He looked muzzily round, managed to steady himself long enough to see the bottle, pulled himself up on the bin and went crabwise, clinging to the racks. Reaching for support, he pulled down a reel of detonating wire and smaller objects.

"Sshh!" Finger to lips, he stood looking down trying to see what had fallen. He stepped forward, tripped on the wire and fell full length. He lay sprawled.

Presently he saw something on the floor near him. He fixed it, managed to focus. The whisky bottle. He reached out and got somebody's hand round it. He hoisted himself on elbow, took a swig. He spluttered, laughing. He stood the bottle down. It fell over and rolled. His elbow slipped on the floor and he flopped and lay still—out.

Abruptly everything went right.

In a final attempt, without hope, without even anger, Nolan dislodged the fish at four o'clock in the morning and they brought it incredulously up. Four hours later, the helicopter, which had been delayed ashore, arrived with gear they had ordered. Nolan threw off his exhaustion as if he had only missed half a night's sleep—driving the drilling on again with a sort of mad renewed energy.

Day after day, Mister Mack drilled deeper under the sea. The relief tours came and went. The weather turned cold and the winter wind struck through to the bone. The sea got up. Rain lashed the platform. Day by day Nolan climbed to the top of the derrick with binoculars to watch Argo 1—standing hunched into the wind and rain as if some demon were on his back.

But the supply boat failed to return. They had lost some high-grade pipe of the sort they were now using, in an earlier hole and had not been replenished and, as a consequence, were now running out of it for the drill string. The drilling at high speed was putting a tremendous twist on the string. The rotary table on the floor of the rig was spinning eight full turns before the bit at the bottom began to turn.

Nolan urged the work on faster and faster. Gainer watched him becoming increasingly keyed up as they emptied the rack of high-grade pipe joints. He screamed at the smallest check.

"Why don't you send them another blast?" Gainer said. But Nolan was evasive. Gainer waited until Nolan was asleep one afternoon after night work and sent off a hot message demanding the pipe forthwith. He kept back the carbon copy and told Quidd he need not log it. Quidd took it without objecting. When Nolan turned out a couple of hours later, Gainer said nothing to him about it.

After dark it was pitch black beyond the lights and bitter cold. The men on the rotary table were muffled to their ears. Gainer came up the steps. Joe Havenga was moving pipe up the ramp with the catline.

"What's this, Joe?" Gainer said.

"For the string, Mist' Gainer."

"You've got it balled up, Joe, that's the wrong pipe. We're using the ASC—thicker walled."

"Yussir. I know, sir. Mist' Nolan, he said this what we gonna use in the string now. We ain't got no more d'oder, sir."

"But we'll have another twist-off."

124

"Ah doan know that, sir. You bedder see Mist' Nolan, sir."

Gainer went down. There were lights in Nolan's office. Nolan was sitting at the desk studying the casing and bit programme tables. He had his dark glasses on.

Gainer sensed something odd. He tried to take the thing casually. "Oh Gene, seems they're going to use some of the old pipe in the string."

"Yeah. What of it?" Under the surface, Nolan snapped taut. He looked as if he knew he was taking a risk but wasn't going to admit it.

"Hell, it's asking for another twist-off."

"Yeah? You breaking out for tool pusher?" *

Gainer thought it was best just to grin.

"I happen to have knocked the rotary speed off, if you'd trouble to look," Nolan said. "That's Grade D pipe and I know what I'm doing. See?"

The rotary had hardly slackened more than a few revs, Gainer knew. Maybe Nolan could get away with it; there was a risk.

Nolan adjusted his dark glasses. "I'm not being stopped by any goddamn drill pipe, see? I'm in control of the situation. I've never been beaten yet, for God's sake. I'm going to get oil on this job or I'm going to drill so many holes the goddamn sea'll run out."

He jumped up from the desk. He started running back and forth in the tiny office. "You know something? Uh? Maybe you don't. I'll tell you. I never quit yet—never quit a field yet without it was voluntarily. Never quit yet. You know that. And I got gas or oil where the other guys said there was noth'n. Dry holes. Noth'n. Just dry holes, boy. Yeah. But I got it."

The tension in him was rising. "Yeah!" he said. "Yeah! We got soft bottom, ain't it so? Ain't it so, Gainer? We got a fish, didn't we? We got a goddamn lousy bellyaching sonofabitch no-good crew and a lousier supply outfit; but by Jesus we're gonna get oil, we're gonna get oil if it takes us all to Kingdom Come! Goddamn it, Mr. Gainer!"

Gainer gave a nod, looked away. He felt extremely uncomfortable. It was too damned awkward. It was nutty talk. Didn't make sense. It was like the Fox and Geese game.

He moved to the door. "Sure. Absolutely. You're right—well, goodnight, Gene." He stepped out, escaped, moving across the deck under the lights, mentally shrinking in expectation of Nolan's voice calling him back.

---

* Break out. Driller's slang for promotion. i.e. "He broke out as pusher for Gulf."

The brake was wailing on the drum like lost women wailing to the wind. Higher up, there were other voices of the wind through the derrick, moaning and gabbling, hooing and talking mad, fast past the wires and braces, muttering in low, stark, raving madness. Loonies and junkies were climbing the derrick in the night. Then iron bagpipes screamed from the drum and the mutterers up in the derrick were asking who?

The arch lights were swinging. All around, the vast invisible presence of the sea moved, hissed faintly, a fine high curling hiss of foam blowing fine off the waves. Insanity gabbling around the corner of the mud lab. The muttering whispers came to him from all sides. Gainer hunched his shoulders, heading for the mess room—lights and the crew.

Gainer was off duty next morning. He slept late, till after nine, got up and had a shower. The temperature had risen but it was still windy on deck. He dressed and went into the mess for breakfast.

The mess was deserted. Pete, the second cook, put a plateful of good crisp bacon and fried eggs, crinkly brown at the edges, in front of him. Gainer ate with appetite. Breakfast was the meal of the day he enjoyed best. Pete brought his coffee.

"Good grub, Pete. Good as mother's own."

Pete grinned. "Well, thanks." He folded his arms and stood watching Gainer eat, as if he were enjoying it himself. Gainer had noticed other cooks do the same. Pete was a little dark-haired man about thirty. He was obviously pleased at the praise.

"Who'd be a cook—all kicks and no meals, eh, Pete?"

"Oh, well," Pete grinned.

"Couldn't get oil without this, boy."

Pete wiped his hands with his rag. "You got enough coffee there?"

"Yuh."

Pete went back to the galley. Gainer thought Pete was a good chap.

He reached over the grease-thumbed stencilled sheet on the table giving the overnight radio news bulletin, which Quidd produced daily in spite of the TV. He propped it up, buttering his toast, and reading. Nothing much. An American space shot. Floods in India. Death of a boxing champ. There was an item about another rig setting up in the North Sea—but it was miles away, right out of their area. Weather forecast bad.

He poured himself more coffee, taking it easy. There was a blast of wind and the door banged open. Gainer looked round. It was Quidd. He came in.

126

"Mr. Nolan wants you. In the office."

"Right." There was something in the summons, if not in the manner of it, that sounded a warning. What was the mood now? Gainer thrust back the recollection of the uneasy scene of the night before.

Quidd stood there. "Mr. Nolan said now."

"Yuh. Right now." Gainer stirred his coffee. He took his time. He stirred it thoroughly, picked it up and sipped. The coffee was hot and good. He put the cup back in the saucer, stirred again.

He could hear Quidd breathing behind him.

"Mr. Nolan's waiting," Quidd said.

"I heard you," Gainer said, not turning. They would have to do something about Quidd, Gainer thought. One of the men was going to take care of the bastard one day. That was certain. Gainer wished him luck, whoever it was. Sutherland was after him, he had heard.

He took another drink of coffee. Quidd breathed at his back. Without having to look, Gainer could see the damp nostrils, Quidd's hot offended eyes.

He finished the cup, pushed his chair back. Quidd led the way. Nolan was standing at the office door. He stepped back inside as Gainer came up. Gainer saw that Nolan was still tensely screwed up.

"You send a radio message to the Company yesterday, Mr. Gainer?"

So this was it. Gainer nodded. "Yes, I did."

"There's no copy on file and you told Quidd not to log it."

"I've got the copy. I guessed you wouldn't care to know——"

"Who gave you authority to send radio signals over my head?"

Gainer said, "You know yourself it's a damned scandal they haven't delivered the pipe, we——"

"*I* decide what's a scandal on this rig, Mr. Gainer." Distractedly, Nolan's hand was searching the desk for his dark glasses, patting papers, shifting files.

"That's why I signed it with my name. They'd know it was my complaint."

"Your complaint! For God's sake." Nolan's voice rose but he was checking it. He was visibly holding himself down. "Who's in goddamn charge here?"

"All right—hell—you are. I'm not contesting it. I'm not even interested. But we're supposed to be drilling flat out and we need the pipe. I send a signal for it. So who's murdering who? Talk sense, man!"

"Sure talk sense! Sense! Only the Company don't think you

127

do, Gainer. There's only one sort of sense around here and I talk it, see? *I talk it!* You don't and Jackson don't. I talk the only sense that's talked on this whole, entire rig, Mr. Gainer, on this whole goddamn entire rig and get that through your head!"

Gainer was staring at him. Sweat was out on Nolan's face. There was a faint frightened look in his eyes, very faint and frightened. Urgently he searched for his dark glasses, turned and saw them on the shelf behind, flipped them on. His hand was shaking. He snatched up a radio form from the desk.

Inform driller Gainer tone his uncoded radio message yesterday unacceptable stop report circumstances stop did message have your authority stop if not why was it sent stop reply to above by pilot's hand message.

"And here's another," Nolan said.

Henceforth you will keep strict radio silence till further orders stop Atlas have code and are monitoring signed Stoneman.

Nolan looked up. "That make sense, Mr. Gainer?"

9

IT came on to rain in mid-afternoon. The wind drove the rain in hard stinging sheets across the platform. The rain hit the sea like needles. The sound was needles shaking in ten billion envelopes.

Gainer was on the derrick floor. The canvas shield did not give much protection. He pulled open the door of the dog house cubicle and went in to consult the four-channel recorder.* They were approaching a point when they were going to run a multiple shot recorder to give them the latest angle of inclination and its direction, and Nolan always wanted to be present at these moments.

Gainer made a mental note, went outside and sent the cat-head man for Nolan. The man came back saying he couldn't find him. Gainer put out a call on the loudspeaker. Then Joe Havenga, who had been off duty, came up to the rotary table.

"Mist' Nolan up the derrick, sir."

Gainer hadn't seen him go up. He went down to the main deck, walked out beyond the pipe racks and looked up. Nolan was at the top of the derrick on the highest platform, outlined against the sky, looking out with raised binoculars towards Argo 1. His trousers and coat were snapping in the wind. He scanned the horizon to the north and south then moved back on Argo 1 again.

There was something crazily disturbing in it—in his stance, in his figure in the streaming wind. Nolan riding the crosstrees . . .

What was going on out there? Was he really seeing something unusual? Gainer sang out to Frank on the table to go easy, went quickly to his cabin for his glasses. He crossed the deck and climbed the ladder to the helicopter platform.

On the top, he had to crouch in the wind. The Sikorsky was roped down. Gainer edged against one of the supports

---

* An instrument in a metal case, looking something like a seismograph which records details such as hook load and weight on the bit, pump pressure, rotary torque, rate of penetration, etc., to give a neat accurate record of the drilling operations.

for the safety netting. Seen in its extent, the sea was much rougher than he had thought.

He lifted the glasses and focused on Argo 1 which suddenly seemed at a great distance. He could see two helicopters, one hovering over the platform and one turning in the air nearby lifting some gear. There was a big boat standing off the port side and a smaller boat at the platform itself.

Gainer couldn't make out what they were doing. Men were getting into the boat alongside. He could see more in the big boat standing off. Apparently they were keeping this boat away because the rough sea made it risky to move it close to the platform.

Gainer studied the boats again. There were a good number of men in the bigger one. The smaller boat seemed to be transferring men to it from the platform. There were obviously more men involved than an ordinary crew relief. Gainer watched. Why were they pulling men out of Argo 1?

He remembered Stoneman's radio message about the new Atlas rig on the way. But they were obviously not going to bring it out in this blow. He scanned the sea. There was only one black-hulled cargo boat wallowing away through the white crests.

It looked like a weather shutdown. Argo 1 were getting the men away while they could, leaving a skeleton crew.

He dropped the glasses on the sling round his neck. Nolan must have seen and understood it. He crouched, looking out over the sea. The wind was getting stronger. He felt sharply uneasy.

He went down. Nolan came down the derrick about ten minutes later. He looked numb from the wind. He didn't say anything. He was quiet.

"We're about ready to run a multiple shot," Gainer said.

Nolan went over to the dog house and pushed the door open. Gainer followed him in. Nolan stood there a moment, uncertainly. He looked in an absent way at the four-channel recorder. He leant both arms on the machine's case, staring at the roll of graph paper marked with the mechanical pen scratches and the driller's explanatory notes. Gainer unhooked the clip board with the directional data and glanced at the figures. He looked up. Nolan was still staring absently at the recorder chart.

"You want to run the multiple shot?"

Nolan looked up. "Uh? Yeah. Sure."

Gainer put his head out and called the orders to Frank. He let the door swing to again.

"What's doing on Argo 1?"

Nolan looked at him. His brow furrowed. He looked sad,

lonely and scared. Somehow, he usually looked scared when he didn't have his dark glasses on, Gainer thought.

"Yeah. What's going on?" Nolan said.

"Are they pulling out?"

"Maybe."

"They're taking most of the men off."

Nolan didn't answer. Of course he knows, Gainer thought; he's seen more than I have; he damn well knows. Why doesn't he say?

He said, "Stoneman said they are into a good pay zone. Why would they take the crew off when it's so good?"

Nolan didn't look at him.

"Looks like a weather shutdown, doesn't it, Gene?"

Nolan said, "Yeah. Yeah, could be."

Frank put his head in the door for Gainer. "You ready, boss?"

"Okay, coming," Gainer said. He went to go out, then turned. "You hear the weather forecast?"

Nolan flicked a glance up, nodded.

"They put out another bulletin at two o'clock. Warning to shipping."

Gainer paused. "What are you reckoning to do, Gene?"

For a second there was a trapped look, a faint glimmer of fear and appeal in Nolan's eyes; he didn't answer.

"Mr. Gainer—" The door opened in Gainer's hand.

"Okay." Gainer glanced back at Nolan again; then went out.

The wind had increased by midnight.

The lights made the darkness of the night deeper. They could see the white foam of the sea in the dark and the high lash of spray round the platform's legs.

As Gainer was coming out of the heads, Joe Havenga came across the desk. "Say, Mist' Gainer, what they doin' out there on that ole Atlas rig?"

"I don't know. What?"

"Well, some of the boys seen you and Mist' Nolan look'n out there and they was look'n too and they's sayin' that they pulling out on account of this here bad weather. That right, boss?"

"Maybe. Looks as if they can't operate when it gets rough. We got the edge on them there, Joe, eh?"

Joe chuckled uncertainly. "Yassir." He didn't look convinced. Gainer didn't particularly want to convince him; but it sounded as if there were enough rumours going round among the crew without encouraging them by explanations.

"That right we gettin' down drillin' into gas now, Mist' Gainer?"

"That's right. We've just hit gas." It was high-pressure gas and Joe was going to know anyway. "Be shutting in for production before you know."

"Yassir." Joe gave another unconvinced chuckle.

"Well, I'm going to turn in. Goodnight, Joe."

"Goodnight, sir."

Gainer walked across the deck. There was a light in Nolan's cabin but the door was shut. Gainer skirted the racked pipe. He was trying to keep his mind off Nolan and the confrontation he felt was looming up. He was tired and yet unexpectedly on edge. Their situation was obviously worsening and he felt a crisis was coming on. Everything was made more precarious by Nolan's uncertainty—the quick and baffling transitions up and down from abrupt fury to the strange wordless moods, and then again to the driving inexhaustible energy.

The sea below was making a lot of noise and the wind howled past the derrick brace wires. He stepped over some coiled hose, turning towards his cabin, anticipating the doctor's night greeting with one of his lead-in-your-pencil beverages. Two nights before, the doctor had produced a new one he had kept in reserve called Actijuce. Gainer grinned.

"Mr. Gainer." Quidd came hurrying up behind him. "Mr. Nolan would like to see you."

Gainer groaned inwardly. "All right."

He turned back, knocked at the cabin door and went in. Nolan was sitting at the wall flap. He looked round. He had his dark glasses on. Gainer noticed that there was nothing on the wall flap.

"Larry, c'mon in. Take a seat." He reached out and pulled forward a stool. His manner was slightly nervous, anxious.

"Thanks." Gainer sat down, hoping it wasn't going to be long.

"Uh—you care for a snack—sandwich? Anything to eat?"

"Hell, I'm too tired."

"We'll get it sent in."

"Thanks all the same."

"Sure. Okay." Nolan cast about, searching the shelf with quick fingers, found a packet of gum.

"Say, Larry, how about a game? How about seeing how good you are, eh? You reckon you could do any good? Uh? C'mon now." His fingernails were scratching at the packet of gum, trying to break open the tight wrapping skin. Momentarily he lifted a hand and adjusted his dark glasses. "Uh? You wanta? How about it?"

Gainer realized that he was sitting tense. He wanted to get up and go, do anything rather than sit playing this crazy game. "I'm knocked out, Gene. Another time."

"No—c'mon now. C'mon." Nolan spoke urgently. "One game now, uh? One game." C'mon."

Gainer said, "You get Quidd in, he'll play with you."

"He does! He does!—" Abruptly Nolan checked himself. Gainer could see him screwing down his enormous excitement. Quietly Nolan said, "He's gone to bed now. Like you to play. One game, Larry." Very quietly.

"All right."

Nolan was on his feet. He pulled open the drawer under the bunk, searched in it, pushed it back and pulled open the one below. He was scrabbling among the clothes and other things in the drawer, failing to find the board and men.

He pulled the things from the drawer, jumbling them indiscriminately, spilling them out. He jumped up, snapped open a suitcase on the floor, didn't find them. He was in a silent panic. He threw the door open. It banged in the wind. Gainer heard him noisily searching the office next door.

Nolan came back. "Can't find them." He kept twitching his dark glasses. He bent down again at the jumbled contents of the drawer, suddenly gave a laugh. "Here all the time." He pulled the box of draughts from the back of the drawer, stuffed the spilled things in again. "Good. Good," he said.

He shut the door, put the board on the flap and emptied out the draughtsmen. He took the packet of gum.

"You use this?" Gainer watched him concentrating his attention on his hand to stop it shaking. Nolan's jaw muscles clenched and unclenched. He put the packet down beside the draughts board.

"You to p—play, Larry."

Jesus, Gainer was saying to himself. Jesus.

"You hear, L—Larry? You to play."

Bradford closed his extended fingers round the cigarette, taking a long draw. He glanced over his shoulder at the door space. A lot of noise tonight. The wind and the sea outside were adding a sort of high thresh to the sound of the diesels.

Bradford couldn't understand where the key had gone. He knew he hadn't lost it. It was simply mislaid; but he couldn't find it. He had probably taken it out with the other contents of his pockets and inadvertently put it down somewhere. But where? He had never kept it among the things in his locker, so it wasn't there.

He drew on the cigarette again, looking towards the workbench. But he had already searched the benches and the

133

shelves of the partitioned area and the mud lab on the deck above. A dozen times he had reached into the space by the compressor and felt the empty bracket on which he had hung it.

It was a bloody nuisance. He could start making another key; but it had taken him time. And he wanted to get moving now. He was going to give Mister Mack the works. They had begun to drill into a gas zone, which might help the works arrive.

He had been talking to Parrish. The weather was turning bad. He could tell Parrish didn't want to hang about much longer either. There were a lot of rumours going round. They were supposed to be taking the men off the Atlas rig. Atlas looked after you. Atlas were going to look after him, once he'd done this job. Mexico, the big pay. Judy. Parrish was going to play; he felt confident of that. Parrish had to play.

Bradford took a last pull at the cigarette, pinched it out. He went to the door and looked round. All clear. The wind was howling beyond the hatch. There was a smell of burning oil from the engine room.

He moved over to the steel cabinet where he kept the pH meter * and the chloride test kit * and which he now kept padlocked. He unlocked it and took out the two small electric detonators he had stripped from one of the connections for the perforator guns. He plugged in the soldering iron and looked over his shoulder. He pulled open the deep bench drawer ready to sweep the detonators in, in case he were interrupted. Then he took the coil of fuse wire, adjusting it to the connection he had made.

He stood working at the bench, occasionally glancing over his shoulder.

Then he jolted at the bells ringing through the compartment. He snapped round.

There was smoke beyond. It was the general alarm.

All over the platform the men were startled by the alarm. Most of them were asleep since it was two hours before dawn and only Bradford, the drilling crew and the engine room watch were on duty.

They turned out of their bunks in confusion. Only a few remembered what they had to do, though every man was supposed to know his emergency station. Nobody understood what had happened.

They threw on their clothes and made for the open deck. By the time the first groups had got out, Willis and others

---

* Instrument and chemical kit for testing the degree of acidity or alkalinity and determining the chloride content of drilling fluid.

were shouting to them to go to their stations. An engineer ran up the hatch from below.

"Bloody fire—where's the fire party?"

"Fire party?——"

"Nolan's down there."

Gainer and Willis headed down the hatch together, followed by half a dozen others. There was some smoke in the lower deck compartments coming from the far end by the engine room. They ran past the mud tank—then saw Nolan in the thickest of the smoke battering an upturned fire extinguisher on the deck, vainly trying to make it work. Smoke was belching out of a big waste drum two feet away. Nolan's eyes were streaming. He was in his pants, barefoot. He kept lifting the extinguisher and hitting it on the deck.

As Gainer turned for the engine room, Ransome and the second engineer ran out pushing a trolley foam pump.

"Get back!"

Everybody recoiled. They turned the nozzle to the bin and foam shot out. In a few moments, the bin and surrounding deck were snowed under.

They made a search of the lower deck but found nothing more burning. How the waste in the bin had ignited, nobody seemed to know. The engineer on watch had not left the engine room for an hour or more. Bradford had been checking over his chloride test kit, he said, and hadn't seen anybody.

Gainer thought Bradford seemed pretty shaken by the fire. He kept looking at Nolan and wetting his lips.

Quidd had discovered the fire and rushed to Nolan who had rung the alarm. Quidd had apparently been going around. Gainer caught a quizzical look and a quick grin from Jackson.

"Snooping, the little bastard," Jackson whispered.

Gainer gave him a long look.

Nolan was brisk but silent. Gainer could see the anger working under the surface; but Nolan was fully in control. The earlier mood had passed. Nolan called the doctor and Willis and they spent about twenty minutes going round both decks. Then Nolan broadcast a general return to quarters. The men trooped across the windy deck, a good many crowding into the mess calling for early breakfast.

A heavy sea ran all morning with the wind still strong.

At two o'clock in the afternoon, the alarm bells rang again. Before the men could move far, the bells stopped. The men looked at each other. Nolan's voice came over the loudspeaker.

"All crew on deck. All crew turn out on top deck at once. Crew on top deck at once."

"That's this in aid of?" The men who had been sleeping after night work were grousing.

"The bloody navy, lad."

Nolan was standing on the steps to the control room. He had a microphone in his hand. The men gathered, facing him, in the space between the stacked rows of drill pipe and on either side. The wind ruffled hair, flapped their jackets and overalls.

Nolan lifted the mike.

"There was a fire on board this morning. Maybe some of you guys didn't know that. Well, I'm telling you. It was started in a waste bin on the lower deck and I am now conducting an inquiry to find out who was responsible. I want to make it clear to you—all of you—that I am going to find out who this wonderful smart guy was. I am going to find this smart aleck oilman who wants to start a fire—and when I find him, believe me, I am going to see he gets the bum's rush out of every drilling I can plaster his name on."

He paused, looking round sarcastically.

"I hope I don't have to tell you oilmen, you veteran oilmen, what fire means. Do I? We are now, moreover, drilling in a gas zone—I said *we are drilling through high-pressure gas.* Maybe this doesn't strike any of you fine oilmen as relevant? But to get it right on the line, I called you up here so that nobody need think he's going to get away with this goddamn negligence.

"That is not all. The general alarm this morning and the general alarm I have just rung, show that there is no goddamn fire organisation on this rig.

"I suppose nobody has been so gracious as to read the fire notices on the bulletin board. If they have, it didn't appear in your brilliant performance this morning. I was practically putting out the goddamn fire myself, singlehanded, before any of you professional oilmen could stir out of your beauty sleep. If it had been for you, we might have burnt out."

He looked round. They weren't liking it. Briggs would have made trouble, all right, Gainer thought. It was lucky Briggs wasn't there. Briggs had gone ashore with the last tour and hadn't returned. He had been replaced by a new man named Sowerby, a tall thin dry stick who, if he had any resentments, kept them to himself.

"It may come as news to you," Nolan was saying, "I say it may be *news* to you, that every man on this rig has a fire station. You know what a fire station is? That's someplace *you* have to be. It may come as a further surprise that every

136

man has an emergency duty. If you gentlemen will be so good as to look at the bulletin board you are so keen on defacing, you will find it all set out there."

The men were shifting. There were exasperated expressions. Some were muttering to their neighbors. Rain began to come down in gusty sweeps.

Nolan raised his voice. "I am going to give you gentlemen some further information. Every man on this rig is under formal obligation to do emergency duty. If you have not read the Company's notice to this effect on the board, I can warmly recommend it. I can also promise you that I intend seeing that obligation carried out in full. Absolutely in full. In future I am going to ring the general alarm as often as I see fit, until every man on this platform goes to his station at the double. *At the double!*"

A protesting voice called out, "Aye, aye, sir!" Gainer grinned in spite of himself. The rain came down harder.

"Yeah," Nolan said. "A little naval discipline wouldn't be bad on this rig, at that. Not bad at all. It so happens, however, that I have my own methods of getting work carried on efficiently and—"

More shouts of interruption.

"Okay. Okay. Do I hear some of you want to complain? I will only point out that I have so far been considerate enough —the word is considerate—not to give you any fire drill. *Any* fire drill. The law makes it obligatory. You know that? I have been relying on your common sense. I see this confidence has been misplaced. So now you know who you have to thank. That is all."

There were more shouts—but they were lost in the wind. The rain was lashing the platform.

"What about getting us off here out of this lousy weather?"

"Yes, what about that?"

"I said that is all!" Nolan bawled.

There was a vague movement as if some were going to argue; but it broke up. They were all wet. They began to disperse.

"I'll be damned."

"Where does he think he is?"

Gainer watched Nolan. Nolan had handed the mike to the electrician. He was standing with the rain pouring off him, watching the men moving away. The doctor came past Gainer, hunching into his collar, his hair dripping.

"He wouldn't have got away with that if it hadn't been for this rain," the doctor said.

There was a fierce gust of wind. Gainer felt the salt spray

on his lips. He looked over the side. Another lash from the sea spattered him.

Jackson was sitting on the iron ladder slung like a ship's gangway underneath the platform to the sea. He was on the halfway landing and he was soaked. The spray kept showering over him. Every few moments a green waved raised itself and shattered against the ladder under his feet. Jackson gripped the handrail and half rose, recoiling against the ladder behind him.

He had a thick fishing line in one hand. He jerked it with sharp pulls of his forearm. He was chuckling to himself. He heaved in the fishing line, swung the triple hook and weight at one end and launched it outward. The splash was not visible in the general turmoil below. Jackson hauled on the line. He jerked his arm, trying to pass the line over the piece of flotsam which was appearing momentarily just below the surface.

"Jacko! Come up here, you damn fool!" Gainer checked himself at the top of the ladder, sprayed by a wave which had soaked Jackson again. Jackson had plainly not heard him.

Jackson flicked the line. Apparently the hook caught somewhere below. He gave a mighty heave, half rising on the step. A drum appeared spinning on the foam. Then the hook slipped and it sank back out of sight.

Gainer went down the ladder. "Come up here, Jackson! What the hell do you think you're doing?"

Another wave showered them both. Gainer noticed that it was dirty water. "Jacko! You'll get knocked off, you bloody fool."

Jackson heard him and turned. He gave a whoop and a laugh, jerking up his arm with the line again.

Gainer saw that he was drunk. Jackson slipped, grabbed for the rail, hung for a few seconds as if he were going down, then pulled himself upright. He laughed soundlessly, looking up at Gainer. Gainer watched the sea for an opportunity, went down the remaining steps. He grabbed Jackson's arm.

"What the hell do you think you're up to, Jacko? Come up out of this."

"Hey, Larry—Larry—look a' here, boy. Want to hook this."

"Leave the damn thing or you'll be in with it. What do you think's in it, gold nuggets or something?"

"That's an old depth-charge or a mine, boy. Yowie!"

"What?"

Jackson had flipped the line again and hauled in. The hook caught for a moment then slipped off.

"Wait till I get it up on deck an' show Nolan!" Jackson roared with laughter.

"You're crazy, that's an oil drum or something. Now leave the damn thing alone and come up from here."

"Whoop—nearly had her that time."

The drum had sunk again.

"You think a depth-charg'd float, you nut!" Gainer shouted.

"This one's doing all right."

"It's an oil drum. Now cut this out and come up."

"You see that ol' rust, boy? Maybe we'll only get a teeny weeny bang. Every man at his emergency station. Zowie!"

Gainer got an armlock round his neck. "Cut it out, Jacko or I'll make it rough."

He saw the wave coming and hung on with both hands, arms round Jackson. The sea carried over them. They came out gasping. Jackson had lost the line.

"Yah—there she goes." He pointed to the water. The drum or whatever it was, was visible just below the surface, in a deep trough. It was rusty and greenish with marine growth. Could it be something from the wreckage below?

Spray showered them again. "Now come on, Jacko. Get up there!"

Laughing and spluttering, Jackson went up with him.

"And for Christ's sake, get to your cabin before Nolan sees you."

10

THE weather was thickening. There were big seas and the wind continued to blow strongly. The weather bulletins forecast heavy gales.

The drilling went on. They had drilled through a zone of high-pressure gas pushing upward at 8,000 pounds a square inch—enough to blow everything out of the well if they lost control.

They were holding the gas down with the heavily weighted mud which they watched for the smallest change. The mud, a compound of chemicals and other materials, was being pumped down the hole and kept in circulation by the mud pumps. The hydrostatic pressure of this column of dense mud in the hold was holding the gas far below in place.

The supply boat arrived but could not come alongside because of the heavy sea. They watched it pitching and rolling uncomfortably a few cables away. Nolan put the helicopter up and at considerable risk managed to bring a few items inboard; but they couldn't handle the pipe and after the boat had been standing by for twenty-four hours, they turned out at daylight and found that she had gone back.

Gainer was on the rotary table till two in the afternoon. He came off numbed by the wind. He threw his gloves down, took off his boots and unzipped his overalls. The doctor came in, dishevelled from crossing the deck. He used his weight shutting the door.

"Whew, blowing like mad. Seems worse."

"Uh-huh."

"What we going to do, Larry?"

"Do?"

"I mean, if this keeps up, we won't be able to get anybody off, will we?"

Gainer sat down, peeled off a sock. "Looks not."

"That's not so good, is it?" The doctor took off his jacket, hung it up. "I mean—makes you feel pretty helpless since the boat sheered off, doesn't it?"

"We're still drilling, if it's any comfort."

"Well, that makes me feel better straight away."

"I thought it would."

"We still in the gas?"

"No, we're through that. Into another formation."

"Is that really high pressure for gas, Larry, eight thousand psi?" *

"Boy, is it! All you can do is hope we don't get a blowout. Then you can hope again that if we do, it blows clean."

"Meaning?"

"Meaning it's just nice clean wholesome gas and not blowing up any quartz or fragments to strike a spark on metal and have us sitting over a nice winter's fire."

"I see." Guggendorf looked thoughtful. "Isn't this the sort of situation then, if I've understood the thing, when you'd start casing and cementing?" * *

"You pushing for driller, doc?"

"No, but isn't it?"

"Nolan reckons we can hold it with the mud. So we could normally. You can hold fifteen thousand psi with mud—pretty well anything if you're heavy and deep enough. Trouble is, things aren't normal. Anyway it would be hell to try to run casing in this weather. You'd have to stand back all the pipe in the derrick—and that would be murder in this wind. Be asking for a smash. Casing's a specialist job and Nolan won't wait anyway, says we have to go on."

The doctor sat down. There was a pause. He said, "What happens if we start having trouble with the leg?"

Gainer peeled off the other sock. "I don't know."

"Come off it, Larry. What's going to happen?"

"It doesn't make any sense, doc. Nolan's had a row with Willis and says he's in control of the situation and we're not shutting down."

"But holy Joe, what does he think it's going to do to him? He can even stay behind with Quidd if he wants. Honest, Larry, I'm no oilman but it seems to me this situation is asking for trouble."

Gainer didn't supply the answer.

"Isn't it?"

"Sure it is."

"Then can't we do something?"

"Ring up the Company and say you resign." Then at the doctor's protesting look, he added. "I'm going to see Nolan. But—" He didn't finish.

---

* Pounds per square inch.

** Lining the hole with cement.

Nolan was asleep and Quidd said couldn't be woken up. The jalousie was raised.

Gainer stood there outside the cabin. The brake on the drum screeched into the wind. The afternoon was dark and gloomy. Heavy cloud covered the sky and it looked as if night were falling prematurely. He could hear the thuds of water below against the legs of the platform. There was nothing visible on the sea. The wind, Gainer felt, added to the isolation. The sea seemed vast and menacing, empty of succour. There were probably ships enough, just out of sight. But they seemed infinitely far off.

He put his head down and crossed the deck to the mess. Joe Havenga, Ransome and three others were having a meal before turning in. A few other men off duty sat round the room, talking and reading. The TV was going as usual—a cooking program; nobody watched. The set was always just left on.

Gainer sat at the end of the table. One group was talking with some animation. He didn't want to be drawn into the discussion. Pete served him. Pete had caught the general mood and wanted to talk; but Gainer put him off and Pete didn't like it. Gainer cursed inwardly. Frank, who was at the other table, kept getting up and looking out of the door. Gainer wondered how much the crew knew about the damaged spud.

He finished the meal. A couple of men came in and started a game of table tennis on the spare table behind. The chock-chock of the ball, the bickering and arguing among the group and the interminable buzz of talk from the TV—why was there always so much damned yack-yack?—got on his nerves. He got up and searched among the pile of magazines in the racks; but they were old and torn and he had read most of them.

He went out on deck. Evening was coming on. He went around the pipe rack and saw that the jalousie at Nolan's window was down. He went over. Nolan was in the office.

As he opened the door, Nolan made a grab at the flying papers on the desk.

"Sorry," Gainer pulled the door to behind him. "Gene, this is getting too rough. We've got to pull the string off the bottom, clear the service stuff off the deck, lay the pipe and shut down."

Nolan picked up a sheet of paper from the floor. He looked up at Gainer. "Yeah?"

"Be reasonable. If we get trouble, we're not going to be able to get off."

"Who's talking about getting off? Nobody's getting off."

Nolan's manner was moderation itself. He even looked good-tempered.

"All right. And suppose Spud three starts sinking again? You've got forty-two men here. How do you propose to evacuate them?"

"I seem to have heard this before, Mr. Gainer. We haven't run into any dire catastrophe. Meantime, we've been drilling and we're certainly going right on drilling. This platform is designed as an all-weather job and it was never intended otherwise. If you think we were sent out here to pull up and run when the weather got a little choppy, why, then, Mr. Gainer, you've got it wrong. Your offshore experience hasn't been extensive enough."

"Atlas have offshore experience and they've taken their men off."

"How do you know they've stopped drilling? They're probably making a hole right now—and you think I'm going to pull out and scram? No kidding!"

Gainer saw that Nolan believed it; he really believed that the Atlas rig was still drilling.

"Gene, look, have you seen some of those waves down there? Have you seen 'em? Coming against the spuds? We're in a heavy sea, Gene, and it's setting up a lot of extra strain. Certainly the platform's an all-weather job. But we're under all the strain we can stand and the point is, we're not mobile. We can't help ourselves. We sank into that soft bottom when it was flat calm. This sort of sea is bound to be working on the structure and if the spud goes again, we're going to be a write-off, Gene. A write-off."

"Yeah?"

"There's dirty water too. You know what that means?"

"Well, Admiral, what?"

"The bottom is being stirred up."

Nolan looked down at the desk. He smiled patiently. "My instructions are clear. I have been told not to shut down. Furthermore, Mr. Gainer, you have my assurance that even if the company suggested it, I would not shut down this rig. I am out here to get oil and oil I will get."

A flurry of rain lashed the window. They could hear the wind outside.

Gainer was losing his temper. "It's a crazy, damned, irresponsible risk and you know it is."

"You getting scared?"

"I'm not scared. I'm just trying to make sense."

"You don't impress me."

"You want to lose this rig?"

The door opened with a great gust and the papers went

flying again. Willis was in the doorway. "Somebody firing rockets or something out there."

The dark afternoon sky was declining to dusk. It was raining hard. Willie led across to the far side.

"Shot up over there. A sort of rocket."

The sea was bigger, it seemed to Gainer. The white tops were blowing off in continuous spray but the body of the waves was now massive. High moving banks of water were surging towards the platform.

They couldn't see anything. They scanned the sea and the darkening sky. Chalky White came up behind in his hard hat and gloves. "I saw it myself. A rocket," he shouted.

"Are you on the table?" Nolan shouted—and when White nodded, "Then damn well get back on it!"

Nobody could see anything. They stood hunching against the weather. Nolan turned away.

"There it goes again."

They watched the red rocket rise into the air about two miles away and burst into a brief flare.

"That's a distress flare." They stood looking out, bent against the wind and rain.

"See anything?"

"Not a thing."

Then they all glimpsed it at the same moment, a green and white sailing boat, probably sizeable but looking small in the high sea, its mast gone and with something trailing over the side. It lurched helplessly in the waves, the cabin roof swinging madly from side to side, then was gone from view in a trough. It was going to pass two or three miles from Mister Mack.

"Switch on the rig lights," Nolan shouted.

Gainer ran for his binoculars. When he got back, Quidd had brought Nolan's. The arcs were on. The boat kept disappearing from view, bobbing up again.

"Can't see anybody."

"Yeah—there he is."

A figure in blue appeared in the stern. The boat sank in a trough again. The moment after, another rocket started up but fizzled and fell.

Nolan turned to Quidd. "Get Parrish." Then to Willis, "Get some men up on the Sikorsky, ready to let her go."

Parrish came up. He had already seen the boat from forward.

"Can you get 'em out and get back?" Nolan said.

"I reckon so," Parrish said.

"And *get back,* I said."

"Yes."

144

"Then get moving."

Frank and Joe Havenga went with him.

Fifteen minutes later, everybody was on deck watching the helicopter take off. The boat was more difficult to see. They watched the Sikorsky. Its ladder was hanging, blowing out. It circled the boat several times, then hovered. They saw Frank go down with the ladder between his legs like a seaman. The helicopter dipped. Its distance from the platform increased rapidly. Then Joe went down.

Gainer and Nolan watched. Some of the crew also had binoculars. The helicopter, which had risen, dipped again and they saw two figures get on the ladder. The bottom one held the ladder while the first started climbing, then started up too. The ladder swung out in the wind. The top climber kept stopping. They made it very slowly.

"That's Joe," Gainer said. The two reached the top and climbed in. The helicopter banked, having evidently lost some distance with the boat while the two climbed up, and dipped again. After a while they made out Frank trying to climb with somebody over his back.

"The guy seems knocked out or something."

Frank was in difficulty trying to get up the swaying ladder with the man. About a third of the way up, he stopped. The helicopter banked again and came towards Mister Mack with the two hanging on to the ladder. It hovered over the landing platform and dipped to put Frank and the man down. Frank dropped about two feet, staggered but kept his feet, holding the man over his back.

Parrish came down to land and the crew moved in, ducking, to moor the aircraft; but another hard gust made Parrish gun the motor and soar again. It took three attempts to get the helicopter down and moored. Parrish and the other passengers got out. Parrish stayed, checking and tightening the moorings. Gainer and Nolan were standing in the shelter of the deckhouse. Quidd had brought Nolan an oilskin.

The first of the rescued pair was a man of about forty-five in a T-shirt and khaki trousers, unconscious with burnt hands and face. Frank and two others carried him to the sick bay. Then Joe came down the ladder ahead of the other passenger —a girl.

Joe threw a raincoat over her shoulders and helped her down to the main deck. She was barefoot and looked half drowned. Her fair hair, soaked and knotted, blew across her face. Her lips and nose were blue. She was shivering. She took a few steps. Then she sat ungracefully, with her head hanging, turned away—and was sick.

Gainer glanced at Nolan. Nolan was looking at her with

145

no indulgence. Joe and the men didn't seem to know what to do. They stood looking down at her.

"Get her to the sick bay," Nolan rapped out. "Tell the doctor. Quidd!"

Nolan flipped up his coat collar and headed into the wind across the deck. He went up the steps to the derrick floor, pulled open the door of the doghouse. It slammed to behind him like a rifle shot.

Bradford was sitting between the racks of stores in the storeroom, waiting for Parrish to come back. Parrish did duty as assistant storekeeper when he wasn't flying. The electric light was on.

Bradford examined the reddish pulpy ends of his fingers. He was sick with worry. The key had gone—definitely gone. And now he believed it had been found and taken. He couldn't have merely mislaid it. Wasn't possible. He would have come across it by now. He had searched everywhere. Somebody had discovered it. He thought it was Quidd.

He thought of Quidd quietly padding round the mud deck while he had been wiring up the detonators. That creeping Jesus. Bradford could murder him. If they hadn't had the fire, Quidd would have seen him. Perhaps *had* seen him. Every time he thought of it, Bradford felt the sweat prickling at the top of his head.

He wet his lips. Were Quidd and Nolan playing him along? Waiting for him to go a step further? Had they been watching him on the sly all along?

He longed for a cigarette. But Parrish didn't like him to smoke in the storeroom. He mustn't get Parrish's back up now, whatever happened.

The ideal course would be to wait, to try to find out if they knew. But he couldn't do that. He had had the willies yesterday, watching them trying to get the Sikorsky moored, thinking they weren't going to be able to—and Parrish would take off for the shore. Parrish had had enough of Mister Mack. Once he got ashore, he wasn't coming back—and there wouldn't be a hope of getting a new pilot to play right off.

He couldn't back out now either. That was what worried him still more, thinking about Ambrose and Harry and what they could do to Judy. They had given him £3,000. He remembered their faces. They weren't going to accept any excuses. They expected action and no delay.

And they had made it clear that they would be very unhappy if he changed his mind. Very unhappy. We understand each other, they had said, don't we, Mr. Bradford? They wouldn't stop at mixing Judy up in it. Atlas wouldn't stop at

146

anything. You wouldn't be able to get away from Ambrose and Harry. Atlas were bastards.

He studied the bitten nails again. He was going to revert to the mud balance. He would fix the calibration so that it gave the wrong weight of mud and hope for a blow-out or a major smash. But he had to do it *tonight;* and he had to persuade Parrish tonight to go with him—that was the thing.

He dare not delay any longer. Because if he didn't get away with Parrish now, Nolan was going to send the helicopter ashore with the couple they had picked up from the boat—and that would be that. Chalky White had heard the doctor talking about hospital, which meant sending Parrish in with him.

He *had* to have a smoke. He got up and went into the cross alley at the back of the storeroom. Standing in the far corner, he lit a half-smoked cigarette and drew the smoke in deeply. He was stabbing the butt out on his boot sole when the door went.

He closed his fingers around it, shrinking at the small burn, and thrust his hand into his pocket. He could hear Parrish at the other end of the storeroom. Quickly he fanned the air two or three times, then went forward.

"Hullo. Thought you'd gone." Parrish looked faintly curious. "Been admiring the stock?"

Bradford cursed his luck. Parrish had been touchy and unreceptive all day. "Yes. Nice line in whipstock ribs." He forced a laugh.

Parrish tossed a mutilated magazine on to the table and sat down. He had dead white translucent skin and black hair receding from the front of his head, and a dark shaving area. He had a hollow-backed stance and strutted. He leaned on the table, took an apple out of his overalls and bit into it. Bradford leant against the rack opposite.

"Know what they're dishing out for dinner tonight?" Parrish said. "That bloody Irish stew."

"What—again?"

"Bits of stringy neck and a few spuds and they call it Irish stew. I tell you I'm sick to the bloody teeth of this outfit."

Bradford said, "Don't worry, the weather's worse, so the grub's going to get a damn sight worse yet."

"I'm fed up with that little bleeder Quidd, too. Snooping around here, wants to make me responsible for stores we never bloody had."

"Yep. And the rest of it. Why can't they take us off like the Atlas did theirs? We're not getting danger money, I notice."

Parrish chewed a mouthful of apple slowly. "You think it's dangerous, this?"

"Dangerous? Do I think this is dangerous? Christ, I know it is. This is a lake platform."

"Come off it."

"All right. I've worked three of them. Meant for lakes, delta drilling. Calm water."

"Look, they wouldn't be using a——"

"Wouldn't they? Not to save money? I tell you, if I get ashore, you won't see me back here. Not for love or bloody money."

Parrish bit the apple again. Bradford thought he looked more irritable than usual tonight. A cocky bastard, Parrish. Full of himself. "Besides, we're in gas pockets now, you know that?"

Parrish nodded. There was a pause.

"Some rich jobs going just now if you can get to them," Bradford said.

Parrish chewed, said nothing.

"I know where I'm going; don't you worry—and it won't be this sort of lark. I'm wasting my time here. You're wasting your time, if it comes to that. I'd clear off tomorrow if I had the chance."

Parrish gave him a long look. It wasn't very friendly. "What are you getting at, Brad?"

"Nothing. Nothing." Bradford felt the sweat at the top of his head. It was going to be tough work.

The wind began changing direction in the morning, whipping up cross seas which attacked the platform first from one side, then another. The waves crashed against the legs, throwing spray up to the deck above.

The men who could were working in oilskins and sheltering behind machinery, deck houses and pipe. The floormen on the derrick were soaked and battered by the wind since oilskins were too voluminous to work in safely. Gainer had rigged up canvas shields round the rotary table, but the wind kept tearing them away and twice in the morning they missed accidents when the canvas whipped out on to the rig floor.

The sea around them was wild. The sound of the brake was half drowned by the scream of wind through the derrick.

At ten o'clock Nolan came up to the rig floor. He was wearing a leather windbreaker and his greasy, old driller's cap, like a baseball cap with the peak pushed back. Sowerby was on the brake but Gainer was standing by. Nolan went across the floor and pulled open the doghouse door without saying a word. Gainer's look followed him.

They were stabbing in a new joint of pipe.

Frank who was on the floor shouted, "Hey, look at that!" They looked up. The travelling block, swinging above their heads in the wind, was hitting the side of the derrick, shaking the braces.

The door of the doghouse slammed as Nolan came out. Gainer flicked his head up, indicating the swinging block. Nolan gave it a glance. He turned to Sowerby. He had to shout. "Why hasn't the line been cut?"

Sowerby shouted back, "Was cut—far as I know."

"As far as you know! As far as you know. You don't make it your goddamn business to know!" Nolan was in a sudden fury. "Who was on last night! Quidd! Get Quidd!"

They had failed to cut line according to Nolan's strict program. This laid down regular intervals for discarding fifteen feet of drilling line—which carries the whole weight of the drilling—and reeling on a new working length from the reserve drum on the deck below. It was good drilling practice.

Nolan turned, watching the drilling instruments facing the console. "Where did you learn to drill—at the Horses Guards parade or maybe at Bucking-*ham* Palace, you goddamn ham!" he shouted at Sowerby. "You're working a precision instrument there! Wire line, sheaves and drum—they're precision instruments, if you don't know it and they call for treatment as such. Jee-sus Cuhrist! You run worn line—you stand to get the whole block, hook, swivel and all down on your goddamn nut and this rig smashed!"

Sowerby shouted, "I think there's trouble with the crown block."

"You think! You think! Jesus, that's the trouble, you think! That weight indicator is about as sensitive as a horse's ass.* Look at it. And you *think* there's trouble with the crown block!"

He swung on Gainer. "And why didn't our Mister Smart driller see that there's friction on the crown block?"

Gainer shouted, "Gene, this is crazy. You can't go on drilling in this."

"Yeah? Is that so? We got a little blow on, ain't we?"

"For Christ's sake, we're going to have a smash if this keeps up."

"But in the meantime, you can't see that the crown block lubricating is fouled up, besides the line not cut. This is lubri-

---

* The crown block is the system of grooved wheels (sheaves) at the top of the derrick over which the drilling line passes. If there is friction on it, the driller's weight indicator will not register properly—a dangerous thing.

cating week, by God. We lubricate once a month around here!"

Quidd touched his elbow, cutting him short. Quidd's camouflage cape was billowing round him.

"The line wasn't cut yesterday," Nolan yelled. "Get the man responsible and bring him here right away. I don't give a damn if he's sleeping. I don't give a damn where he is. Get him out."

They waited, taking what shelter they could. Sowerby and the floormen wanted to keep out of it and resumed work, laying the crown block on the floor, bringing up the cutter and sledgehammer to cut the line. Nolan watched them with a critical eye.

Quidd came back with Sutherland.

"Yeah, so it's Sutherland, our oil man. Good morning, *Mister* Sutherland." Nolan treated him with sour geniality. He didn't swear and just shouted enough to make himself heard. He wound up, "Now while Sowerby cuts the line, you go up and look at the crown block and don't come down till that fouled-up lubricating system is working perfectly. See? I mean perfectly."

Sutherland said, "I just came off."

"Yeah. Sure you did. I know that. I want that crown block lubricating system in perfect order—and in double quick time. I don't mean just grease it—I want that full pressure lubricating system in order, see? Now goddamn it, get up there!"

Gainer could see Sutherland containing himself. Gainer wanted to intervene. It was purely punitive for Nolan to send Sutherland to repair the pressure lubricator. They had stopped trying to use it long since and greased the crown block with the old-fashioned grease gun, a simple and sure method. Sutherland chewed his lip. He shot a narrow-eyed glance at Quidd. He crossed the rig floor, went behind the draw works. A minute later, he came out with a bag of tools, slung it over his shoulder and started up the derrick.

They watched him climb. He was used to it; the wind tore at him. He paused at the fourble board, chafing his hands against the cold, then went on up. He climbed out on the crow's nest platform round the top of the derrick where the crown block was housed.

Sleet came down in stinging gusts at noon. Sutherland was still up working on the crown block. They could see him stop at intervals, hunching away from the wind and sleet, blowing on his hands.

At twelve-thirty, Gainer found Nolan in the mess. Nolan liked to lunch early. "Come in," Nolan said genially.

"They've cooked a fair steak and French fries, for once. Join me."

"Thanks. I don't want any lunch."

"Say, Larry, have you noticed we never get any fish on this damned rig? How is that?"

"I don't know—and right now I don't care. Gene, if you don't bring that boy down, I'm going up there myself."

"Who?—Oh you mean Sutherland? I'd appreciate if you'd not do that. There has to be some discipline on this rig and I have to apply it. It undermines my position to have you going about calling down what I say."

"I'm not doing anything of the sort, but you know damn well that pressure lubricating system has been fouled up for months. It has *never* worked properly. We never even try to use it now. Anyway, for heaven's sake there's a way of treating the men. Don't you think we're giving them enough as it is?"

Nolan continued to look genial. "Well, well. I should have paid more attention to this humane side of your character. Yeah. Maybe I ought to make you Welfare Officer for this rig. How's that appeal to you now?"

Gainer said nothing.

"Sure. Welfare Officer. You could hold a welfare parlour a couple of times a week, Tuesdays—Thursdays. Uh?"

Pete came in. "You ready for your lunch, Mr. Gainer?"

"No thanks, Pete."

"Say, Pete," Nolan said. "You got a family problem?"

"Uh, Mr. Nolan?"

"I said you got a family problem? How's your wife feel when you're not home Saturday nights?"

"I ain't married, Mr. Nolan," Pete said.

"Well that's too bad, Pete. Too bad. Maybe it's because you got a private problem on your mind? These embarrassing little things can often be cleared up in a frank, man-to-man talk with an understanding, experienced older man."

Pete's mouth was open. He was looking blankly at Nolan.

"If you just explain the circumstances in a full and open way—in confidence, mind you—to the Welfare Officer, why, I'm sure that——"

"Oh for Christ's sake!" Gainer said. "It's not funny."

Pete, who saw that there was something further that he didn't understand, went out.

Gainer said, "I'm sending Sutherland down. I'll fix it."

Nolan grinned. "Okay, okay. If that's the way you feel. Who's stopping you? All I'm interested in is getting the system working again."

Gainer went to the door. Nolan called out, "Oh Mr. Gainer, I'm told there's a possibility of more gas tomorrow. If so, we should be going into it about six in the morning. We might add a little weight to the mud for safety's sake, just a bit before that. Get Bradford to tell me what he suggests."

"Okay."

Gainer went out. He crossed to his cabin, put on a short windbreaker jacket and gloves and pulled on a tight wool cap. He went up to the rig floor and started up the derrick. Half-way up he was gripping hard; the wind was trying to pull him off.

He went on up and reached the top. There was no shelter. Sutherland was getting what he could by crouching behind the sheaves of the block. He had stopped work from cold. He was blue. He nodded wordlessly at Gainer. Gainer put his mouth to Sutherland's ear and shouted, "Go down. I'll fix it."

Sutherland shook his head.

"Okay. What's the trouble with it?"

They worked for two hours, Sutherland mainly passing tools. Gainer cleared the rest of the six lubricating tubes, pumped up the oil and re-established something like the working flow in four. But he knew the system wasn't going to work and they would go on using the grease gun. The futility of it maddened him. When they had finished, he crouched down beside Sutherland. "Can you get down now?"

Sutherland nodded. They started down. Gainer went first. Sutherland came down slowly after him. Gainer didn't realise how numb he was till they reached the bottom. It hurt.

"Okay? You all right?"

"Thanks, Mr. Gainer," Sutherland said.

Gainer went to his cabin. He was soaked as well as frozen. The doctor turned around and Gainer saw he had been writing at the desk flap. "What the devil've you been doing?" the doctor said. "Was that you up there? What were you doing?"

"Crown block." Fumbling, Gainer began to strip. "Nolan suddenly wanted the lubricating fixed up—a thing that's never worked—so that we can drill efficiently."

The doctor put the pen down, looked at Gainer with tight lips.

"How's the patient?" Gainer said, to change the subject.

Guggendorf shuffled the papers on the flap together. "Pretty bad. We're not equipped to treat burns of that degree. He's got an internal lesion which I can't sort out. If that isn't enough, he's a mild heart case too, poor fellow."

"Conscious?"

"I'll have to take him off—if we can get off in this weather," the doctor said.

The door of the cabin was rattling in the wind. Gainer went on towelling. "Who are they? Did you find out?"

"Swedish. And do you know what—she's Axel Kellman's daughter."

"That so? That mean something?"

"Hell, Larry, the Kellman Foundation. Haven't you heard of Kellman? Swedish tycoon. Swedish Iron Corporation. Swedish Glass—wood, pulp, finance, politics. I nearly worked for him once. He runs model communities."

"Over my head, doc. She all right?"

"Yes. Except for shock. The man's a steward and cook, or was, named Lindblom. It was a fine boat apparently, the Helge. I've been writing it out for Nolan. There were three other men on board, all lost—the captain, engineer and another man, owner of the boat, who seems to have been her friend."

"What happened?"

"They had an explosion in the engine room and started a fire. Lost the engineer at once. They managed to put the fire out but were out of commission. The other two men were lost at night; they were trying to cut away the mast and gear which had gone when the boat was run down by a freighter."

"Nolan seen them?" Gainer said.

"Not yet."

Gainer said, "You'd better get them off here, doc. And when you're ashore, you have to get in to Stoneman somehow and make him see sense about us pulling out."

The weather became worse in the night. The winds, now gale force, veered against the tides, throwing up high cross seas. Spray was showering over the main deck at intervals.

Gainer woke up with the cabin light on and the doctor shaking him. "Hey, Larry. What's going on? You hear that?"

Gainer sat up, swung out of the bunk. There was the sound of motors above the wind outside.

"Isn't that the helicopter?" the doctor said.

"Sounds like it. What's the time?"

"Dunno. Nearly morning."

"What the hell are they doing? If they're going ashore they'd better take you."

As they scrambled into their clothes, the motor revved loudly, then, as if the aircraft had suddenly risen, it began to fade. They ran out.

Quidd and Nolan, half dressed, were in the middle of the deck, looking up. The dawn light was paling the sky.

The helicopter was about 150 feet above the platform and banking away. It was flying without lights, a black outline, dangling a rope. A score of other men, already up, had turned out.

Nolan swung on Gainer. "You mind telling me what's going on around here? Who sent him away?"

"I haven't sent him anywhere. I don't know what it's about."

"Jackson! Jackson! Who gave the goddamn orders for Parrish to leave?"

Jackson came down from the rig floor. He hadn't given any orders nor had anybody else. They stood about, ducking away from the spray, trying to make out what had happened. The groups of men grew larger. Somebody discovered a bracket from the Sikorsky's undercarriage by which some mooring had been attached, denoting a hasty take-off.

The helicopter had sheered off. It quickly gained altitude and became a diminishing speck. Nolan went to the rail, still looking into the gloomy grey sky. A spattering of sea water fell over him, then quickly afterwards a heavy shower of spray. They could hear him. "You goddam, no-good sonofabitch. I'll have your guts . . ."

The doctor cupped a hand at Gainer's ear. "Have we sunk or something?"

"What?"

The doctor was pointing over the side. The sea looked as if it had risen and was much closer under the platform.

As Gainer went towards Nolan, somebody behind gripped his arm. It was Harrison, the Number two mud man. He looked startled. He cupped his hand like the doctor, "Mud's falling in the tank. Pretty fast."

"What?" Gainer thought rapidly. "Gas showing on your detector?"

Harrison nodded, looking beyond. "Can't find Bradford."

Gainer turned but Nolan was coming towards them.

"Mud's falling in the tank," Gainer said.

Nolan stood stock still for ten seconds. Then he shot out, "Shut the BOP! Harrison, keep your pumps up."

Before he had finished Gainer started running along the deck. Nolan was after him. Gainer was first at the ladder to the rig floor, swung up two at a time. He shouted at Willis on the brake to stop the rotary, leapt at the hydraulic blow-out preventer control panel. He slammed down the black handle of the main switch, shutting the powerful Hydril valve over the pipe, then as Nolan came up, the handles of the three rams, blocking the pipe just below. They stood panting, watching the panel controls.

"Made it," Gainer said. "We made it." He looked at

Nolan. Nolan was getting his breath back. He said, "Get Bradford," then turned and went over to the doghouse.

Gainer called to Willis, "Bradford been up here?"

"Haven't seen him. What's happened?"

"Don't know yet. We started losing mud pressure."

The sound of the wind through the derrick and the general hiss of the sea was louder now with the diesel stopped and no shriek of the brake and Gainer and all of them suddenly felt more exposed, as if the noise had been an assurance which had now gone. After Gainer's answer there was an interval when none of them said anything. They all seemed to be taking in their situation. Then Joe Havenga went up to Gainer. "What happened, Mist' Gainer?" The others came up.

"Don't know but I can guess. Go and get Bradford, Frank, will you, or Harrison—or somebody's going to get hell soon."

The doghouse door slammed as Nolan came out. Gainer said, "What do you reckon, Gene?"

A stinging flurry of rain blew across the rig floor. The wind seemed to have increased and roared through the derrick overhead.

"We've hit low-pressure gas in this new zone—uh?" Gainer said. "That it?"

Nolan nodded. He was wearing his dark glasses. "We've been holding that high-pressure gas in the zone above okay but this new zone's porous, it's absorbing mud. So the hydrostatic pressure's gone off and the mud ain't holding the high-pressure gas any more. Where in hell is Bradford?"

Willis yelled to Harrison, who was heading along the deck buffeted by the wind. They stood waiting while the search for Bradford went on. They did not connect it with the helicopter's departure. Nolan started another prolonged angry discussion about this.

Abruptly, Joe said, "Hey, Mist' Nolan—look at that ol' sea out there!" He was pointing. They all turned.

The sea about 800 yards away seemed to be boiling. Slowly pulsating jets of water were beginning to rise, first twenty, then thirty and forty feet above the waves—the unmistakable sign of high-pressure gas escaping from below. There was no smell; but they knew that a great invisible plume of gas was beginning to rise on the wind. The boiling, combined with the movement of the waves, the great charging sides of green-veined water and foam, made it look as if heavy surf were breaking on a reef.

They looked at each other.

"Holy Jesus."

Nolan was at the rail, hunched forward, gripping the rail and staring at the erupting gas. He snapped round.

"Kill all the lights! No smoking. Stop the galley."

Willis went quickly to the doghouse where there was a microphone and loudspeaker.

"What is it—a formation fault out there?" Gainer shouted. No answer.

"Good God, is it coming over here?" Harrison said.

"Looks as if we've blocked off the gas with the BOP and it's leaking out there, huh?" Gainer said.

Nolan fingered his dark glasses.

"How in hell's it coming out of the hole?" Gainer shouted. "We have to shut in the hole and get out of this."

"Is that so?"

"What do you mean?" Gainer stared at him. "You mean you're going to try to stay on this hole with a gas leak out there?"

Nolan didn't answer.

"Gene, for Christ's sake."

Nolan said, "I don't know exactly what we're going to do. For the moment, we're staying here."

Gainer looked into the dark glasses, trying to see Nolan's eyes. The glasses were splashed with rain. "Gene, there was a rig off the Gulf, where they hit high-pressure gas at eight thousand. It wasn't even soft bottom. The gas washed the sea bed right away from under the rig and the entire rig and one-hundred-forty-foot derrick disappeared in twenty-one minutes. You mean you're——"

"You heard me, Mr. Gainer!"

11

PARRISH dropped the Sikorsky over the North Scully inlet, banked and came in to land. They had had a rough trip and the high winds and rain had not decreased over the coast.

The Contram base was still deserted except for a couple of lighted windows in the main office, a moving truck and a group of workmen at one of the wharfside buildings. The men stood watching the helicopter come down. Parrish landed and stopped the rotor.

Bradford beside him was scanning the muddy wharf, the storage area and the space round the office building. On the way in, he had wanted Parrish to fly direct to the Atlas base. Parrish had said no. Anyway, why the Atlas base? He was curious. For himself, Parrish had scarcely found it necessary to consider it. For one thing, it would destroy his pretext for leaving Mister Mack—a straightforward lie that he was simply carrying out Nolan's orders to fly in. If that wasn't accepted, if it came to pressure, he would be ready with the argument that he had realized he would never get off unless he took off when he had, and that he had a responsibility for the Sikorsky's security.

But why Atlas? After his refusal, Bradford had hedged. He had not produced any clear reason. He had kept saying that he anyway, he was bloody glad they'd seen the last of Mister Mack, that was certainly that; they'd fixed Mister Mack. It had sounded a bit stupid. Bradford was a stupid bastard, a bragger. A bit snaky too. Bradford thought he had persuaded him to leave Mr. Mack. Maybe he had helped tip the balance; but Parrish's mind had been pretty well made up already, well, going on that way. He had brought Bradford off for one thing because Bradford had been so insistent—but also because it gave him a certain support. He had given Bradford the full line about saving the Sikorsky and about Nolan's orders.

Bradford's reasons for quitting were his own look-out. Parrish wasn't interested. Didn't want to know. He had told Bradford so. He had let Bradford see, as a matter of fact, that he thought he was a louse for leaving like that. It suited his purpose. But this idea of landing at Atlas was funny. He wondered if there wasn't something more to it.

Parrish leaned over and unfastened the door on Bradford's side. Bradford was reaching back for his bag. Parrish got out himself, walked round the machine giving a visual check. He bent down tugging at the length of mooring rope still attached to the undercarriage, then dropped it. He went back and lifted out his bag.

Bradford was standing by, looking, Parrish thought, a bit edgy. "You got a car here, Ed?"

"Unless somebody's pinched it." He headed across the muddy space to the wire fence with Bradford following. Three or four cars were parked. Parrish opened a dirty buff Vauxhall, got in, pulled the choke and pressed the starter. The starter produced a faint wheeze.

"Christ, they're supposed to keep the bloody battery up." He tried again. On the third wheeze, faintest of the lot, the engine suddenly and surprisingly coughed and started. Parrish nursed it into strength. Bradford waited, then got in beside him.

"Which way you going?" Bradford said. "I reckon we ought to go around to—you know, I mean, I think we could do ourselves a lot of good. Come on, Ed, whyn't you come? It's a different set-up."

Parrish said testily, "I'm not interested in going anywhere right now except home. I've told you. I've had enough of one lot for the time being without running around to another."

"All right. Well I think—I mean, you know your own mind. Anyway, let's get out of here before Voyss or some other headache starts turning up. Will you drop me in town?"

"That's where I was going," Parrish said.

They drove out of the gate and down the bleak cobbled road towards North Scully between sheds, dumps, a factory or two, blackened areas of grass strewn with old oil drums and broken fences. The wind buffeted the car and the rain kept on. But now Bradford had thrown off his anxious look and was buoyant and talkative.

"Smoke, Ed?" He offered cigarettes. Parrish shook his head.

"By God, I'd like a nice big fat cigar right now," Bradford said. "And I'm bloody well going to have one. Soon as we get in. A fat cigar, thinking of Mr. Bloody Nolan. Am I glad to be rid of that packet. Mr. Bloody Nolan and his do this and don't do that. And that squirt, Quidd. You know I'd have murdered that little sod if I'd gone on much longer. I swear it. What a bunch! You ever see anything like it? I didn't. That's Mister Mack taken care of anyway. Won't be seeing them again. We certainly fixed that lot. Certainly did that." Bradford laughed.

Parrish gave him a quick glance. "Did?"

Bradford laughed again, then checked himself by drawing on the cigarette. He looked at Parrish with an expression of jauntiness and suppressed sarcasm but now Parrish was staring ahead at the road. Bradford waggled his head. His outstretched fingers playfully drummed the dashboard in front of him. His tongue was in his cheek. His faint reflection in the windscreen showed that he was on the edge of saying something but containing himself. He was mightily pleased with himself.

"Ah well, never mind . . ." He looked out of the window, grinning to himself.

"What?" Parrish said.

But Bradford wasn't having any. "Nothing . . . nothing," he said, still grinning. "So much for Mister Mack. What an outfit. When I think of that crowd. Good riddance, eh? What you going to do, Ed? I mean keep in touch, won't you? Must keep in touch. You're damn right, if we hadn't got off then we never would have. You could see that, couldn't you? See it coming a mile off . . ."

He kept chattering on. They reached the town. The streets were busy. Trams and buses were full of morning crowds. Bradford kept up his cheerful talk.

Parrish said, "Where do you want to go?"

"Eh? Oh drop me anywhere, Ed. Anywhere. Over there'll do. I'm going to buy myself a fat cigar and as soon as they open I'm going to have a bloody great brandy. Just to celebrate getting shot of Mister Mack. You're right, good bloody riddance to Mister Mack. What you say you're going to do, Ed? I tell you, keep in touch. Perhaps you don't feel like it straight away but there are a lot of good things going. I tell you. The pickings are about if you know where to look. Yep! The pickings are there all right!" He laughed.

Parrish pulled up at the curb. He said, "Where you going to be?"

"Uh?" Bradford was reaching for his bag in the back.

"I think you're right," Parrish said. "We ought to keep in touch. Where do I get hold of you?"

Bradford's eyes shifted. He looked at the pavement. He gave a little cough. "Well, Ed, matter of fact, I don't know. Offhand. I mean, you know—don't know what my movements are going to be. Bit unsettled. Not quite sure."

"Atlas?" Parrish watched him evenly.

"Atlas?" Bradford's jaw dropped. He swayed back, frowning at Parrish in baffled puzzlement, then quickly, reassuringly, "Oh Christ no. Oh God no. Atlas? No, no. You've got it wrong, Ed. I only said Atlas like that . . . you know . . . sort of, well, you know, thinking they'd probably be glad— first thing that came into my head really . . . oh no, not Atlas. No, no. Gulf's the thing for me, I should think. When I'm ready. I'm going to take a holiday first. Or maybe Cardinal. When the time comes. But not Atlas. Good God no. You got that wrong. Must have expressed myself badly.

"I was only thinking you might be interested for yourself. But you're dead right. Wouldn't touch 'em. No bloody fears. Not with a bargepole. No, no. You're dead right, Ed. Trouble is, I don't know what I shall be doing really and that's the honest truth. Haven't thought about it yet and s'matter of fact, to be quite honest with you, don't suppose I shall think about it yet awhile. Want a bloody rest first, after that lot."

Parrish said, "Suppose I give you my address?"

"Yuh, yuh. That's it. Right. That's it. You give me yours and I'll keep in touch. Good idea. Very good idea, Ed."

Parrish rooted round in the glove compartment, tore a strip from an old ad folder and scribbled an address. Bradford studied it. "Fine, fine, Ed. Soon as I know where I am, I'll be in touch. Thanks for everything. Hope everything turns out okay. So long, Ed." He slammed the door, stood watching the car nose into the traffic. In the driving mirror, Parrish saw him turn and walk quickly away among the crowd.

Stoneman walked slowly up and down in front of the windows of his office listening to Julius's voice. Part of his mind was taking in the lawyer's words and part was dealing with the subject which he knew Walter Meldreth was waiting to bring up.

"In other words," Julius was saying, "It's decidedly dicey. But we haven't lost as long as we keep our nerve."

Stoneman stopped pacing and snapped a look at Julius. The words, "Keep our nerve" had so suddenly echoed the thoughts in his mind about Meldreth, that it seemed almost like telepathy.

"What's the matter?" Julius said.

"Nothing." Stoneman took two steps, turned back. His look was weary and harassed. "Well, I've given you all the proof I have of what Moreno's been doing to sabotage us."

"Not enough. No good trying to pretend otherwise. We agree on that."

Stoneman drew in his beath with a hiss, a signal of reluctant admission. Their conference had been going on for nearly an hour and it was ending as he had feared.

"And we have this high-pressure gas zone which is so promising—so promising."

"And it's commercial gas, you say?"

"I said it's combustible gas. Combustible hydrocarbons. For the moment, they've drilled through it because of the promise below."

"I see."

"It's maddening, John. It's infuriating. I was told yesterday that Moreno has now won over two other members of the Board—who they are I don't know, but I expect we shall damn soon find out."

"Well, I can only repeat that if you connect Atlas with these obstructions—this sabotage, if you like—you'll discredit Moreno much more effectively. And of course you'd greatly influence the court in your favour."

Stoneman stopped at the window. He twitched the curtain to look out, then turned back. "John, this is something we must play very carefully. Very carefully indeed. You ought to know—I've not told you this so far, out of extreme caution, I have been sworn to secrecy—that Jack Neal has got hold of *more* evidence of what Moreno's been up to with Atlas——"

"Jack Neal? Do I know—? You mean the American?"

"Warren Neal, the American of our Contram Board. Always called Jack. He has a tip-off in Atlas, somebody I don't know. Anyway, he has fresh evidence of their sell-out. It includes a taped phone conversation and one document—the document bought for a high price, I may say, and without question authentic. But Neal will not give these up. He won't disclose them on his own unless we can produce further, independent, evidence. If we can do that, then he says he'll come out with them—and they would certainly be conclusive."

"Why won't he hand them over now?"

Stoneman clamped his lips together. He didn't speak for a moment. Then he said, "It's understandable. He says Moreno's too dangerous. One of Neal's firms is associated with Moreno in the chemicals field. Neal says he can't afford to wing Moreno. Too dangerous to go off half-cocked with an attack on him. If he's going to use this evidence, he's got to be sure it's going to kill Moreno. Otherwise he can't use it." He shrugged. "Understandable."

"In other words, what we need is a clincher."

"And it's what we can't get, John. We cannot get it." There was a note of desperation in his voice. Stoneman turned away.

Julius sat a moment longer, then put the papers into his

161

briefcase. He got to his feet. "The shares are beginning to move."

Stoneman emitted a sort of low groan. He turned. "What are we to do, John?"

"I don't know. I can only tell you that we may have to go into court sooner than we thought. The pressure is piling on, and I can't hold it much longer."

They shook hands in silence. As Julius went out, Meldreth came in the other door.

Meldreth held his cigar against his waistcoat. Stoneman shut the door behind Julius and turned, watching him approach. Meldreth's eyes, magnified by the glasses, looked as if they were swimming in glass bowls. Stoneman thought he was beginning to look frayed and untidy, second-rate.

He knew what Meldreth was going to say—almost the words he was going to use to say it. Meldreth was worried that Moreno and Company were going to find out about the debenture stock which he and Meldreth had issued without authority in order to finance operations. Meldreth knew he was playing the market. They had not discussed it but Meldreth did not need to be told. The report from Mister Mack that they were drilling through gas had lifted Contram shares. Meldreth knew he had used the unauthorized stock. He had explained to Meldreth that success in the field would cover them—would cover everything. They could count on the glow of success carrying them over these stock market operations. Who would want to look back too closely when the boom was on?

Stoneman walked back to the desk. Meldreth said, "Did he have any news?"

"Yes. We have a chance, Walter. If we keep our nerve."

The gas, roaring up from below, had been stopped by the blow-out preventer at the top of the drill pipe.

At first they couldn't understand how the gas had escaped from the well hole. Then Nolan had the explanation. The gas had forced its way through fissures in the cement of the surface pipe. Gainer found that they had set only 200 feet of this pipe instead of the usual 300 feet—because the formation it was sunk into had seemed very good and Nolan had been in the usual hurry to start drilling. The cement had set badly and had subsequently been loosened by the drilling work, a fairly common thing.

Having blown its way through the cracked cement, the gas had followed a natural geological fault through the loose surface sands and opened a crater about 1,000 yards from the rig. This was the crater through which the gas was now blowing into the sea and up to the surface. They could not see the gas in the air but it was there, a vast unlit gas jet. They prayed it would remain unlit. The wind for the moment was blowing it away from Mister Mack.

Nolan broadcast fire precautions. "There will be strictly no smoking by any man on board from now on. That goes for the mess, it goes for anywhere on this rig. If I catch any goddamn dope disobeying this—disobeying *any* of these orders —I'll throw him in the can. You get that? I got a compartment that'll make a honey of a can. Yeah! There are to be no naked lights. I want a check on all light switches. There's danger of the electric resistances in the cooker igniting the gas, so the galley will not provide any more cooked meals until further notice. You'll have to eat cold chow and like it."

Fifteen minutes later, the general alarm rang. When the men were assembled at their stations, Quidd and Joe Havenga went round collecting lighters and matches. The men on the top deck stood in the wind lending themselves to the process resentfully. There were angry shouts.

"Where's Nolan?"

"He's in his cabin smoking one of them cigars."

Quidd snarled at them, "Shuddup you bastards. Shuddup! You sons of bitches!"

"Let go, Chalky, I'll smash the little bleeder."

"Hold up, lad. Take it easy."

Quidd and Joe carried the confiscated lighters and matches to Nolan's office and left them there. The men were dispersed.

The sea was running high, now sending solid water over the deck from time to time. The wave tops broke against the rail. The sea continued to boil and pulsate with the gas all morning and a yellowish froth spread.

At one o'clock, Guggendorf found Gainer in the control room. "Have you seen Nolan?"

"No. Why?"

"I have to boil water. I need to sterilize things. This fellow's pretty bad."

"Well you can't do it, doc. I'm sorry. You can't risk the whole rig for one man, even if he is ill. Nolan's right there. You don't even have to ask him. I'd say the same."

"I've got a boiler with the resistance coil enclosed. Can't be any danger."

Deliberately, Gainer said. "Don't put that on, doc. I'm telling you."

"But it won't hurt——"

"Don't put it on."

The doctor's lips tightened. He looked as if he were going

to say something, then changed his mind. There was silence. It was their first disagreement.

"I hear Bradford's disappeared," the doctor said. "Is that right?"

"Yep. Seems to be."

"What is it—did he fall over the side or something?"

Gainer shrugged.

"Couldn't have been in the helicopter, could he?"

"Damned if I know."

"Do you think Parrish went off like that because he had the wind up?"

"Could be."

"Some of them are saying he went for help."

"I wouldn't think so, the way Nolan was behaving."

The doctor nodded. He looked out of the window. "That gas is a hideous sight. I can't help watching it. Look at those jets. I keep on getting the impression it's coming closer. What happens if it starts boiling up round us."

Gainer looked at him evenly. "What do you think happens, doc?"

"I think we'd have to abandon the rig and——"

"In this sea?"

A gust of wind blew in from the open door. They looked around.

"Doctor Guggendorf." It was Quidd. He looked half drowned. "Mr. Nolan's going rounds. Security inspections. Says you're to come straight off. You too, Mr. Gainer."

"Not me," Gainer said. "I don't go on his snooping tours."

"Mr. Nolan said purposely you was to come, since you ain't drilling. He said 'Since he ain't drilling.' "

Gainer felt a surge of exasperation. He and the doctor exchanged a look. The clipboards of papers hanging up were snapping and swinging in the blast. One fell.

"With torches," Quidd said. He was holding the door open. Another clipboard fell and papers flew loose.

"Let's get it over," the doctor said.

Gainer hesitated an instant more, then snatched up a torch. They went out.

Willis was waiting outside Nolan's office watching the gas. He said something to Gainer that was lost in the wind. Gainer leaned forward. "What?"

"I said looks to me it's spreading," Willis shouted.

Nolan came out with his hard hat on. He took them in with a glance. Then they headed across the deck with Quidd leading. They went down the port hatch into the mud compartment.

The usual noise of the lower deck, the chorus of sounds

that made it what it was, was silenced. The small steel compartments encumbered with idle machines now seemed places
of danger where men could be trapped. The painted grey
steel of the bulkheads no longer seemed protective and strong
but enemy. The electric lights were on, fewer in number for
some reason. The slopped mud covered the deck.

They went through the compartments. Some of the areas
of deck had not been covered and their steps echoed on the
steel plate. Quidd was busy flashing his torch into corners
and shadowy places. Nolan followed, then Willis, stolid and
serious. Gainer and the doctor were behind.

Quidd led them behind the chemical tanks. Harrison followed vaguely in the rear. They passed through to the compartment where the two switchboards and generators were
housed. Cummings, the electrician, was at the AC switchboard looking over the connections.

"You got to cut out pulling fuses down here," Nolan said.
"We don't want any monkeying with electric sparking, see?
We're taking enough risks as it is. We can't shut down everything. I want canvas rigged up over the doorways here. Your
air conditioning off?"

"Yes," Cummings said.

"I reckon it's better to keep it on if the machine's okay."

"I'll check it, Mr. Nolan."

They went on past the cement-mixing machines. Nolan followed Quidd into the small space behind the machines. Quidd
came out opening a cigarette packet. Empty. Nolan looked
on while Quidd made a note in his book. Ransome was in the
engine room. Nolan went through and stood talking to him.

Gainer said to the doctor, "Is this the lot?"

"We've got the top deck to do yet."

Gainer groaned. Abruptly there was the sound of a scuffle
beyond the doorway and Jackson's voice, "Clear off you little
—Hey, what are you going? Get out of here. Oh boy I'll
bounce you."

"Mr. Nolan! Mr. Nolan!"

Nolan looked around.

"Oh hell, it's Jacko boozing. Quick—move in there, doc,"
Gainer shouldered the doctor forward to forestall Nolan, following him up. But Nolan was already two steps ahead towards the door to the next compartment. The doctor tried to
dash past and get through first but Nolan fiercely pushed him
off.

Now they could see Jackson gripping Quidd by the scruff of
the neck and dancing in a circle repeatedly kicking his backside through the dangling camouflage cape. Jackson was
laughing and obviously enjoying it.

Nolan burst on them, grabbing Jackson. "What's going on here? Cut that out, Jackson. Cut it out!" He wrenched Jackson off, Quidd squirmed free.

Jackson swayed back, his mouth opening at first in surprise, then, unable to do anything else in the completeness of this redhanded capture, started sniggling.

Nolan had the situation in a glance. He said, "Well I'll be goddammed for a sucker." He was suffused with rage and for a few seconds unable to say anything more. Quidd had plunged into the space behind the two washing machines and they heard the inevitable clink of bottles. Rapidly Nolan ducked into the space too.

Gainer gave Jackson a grievous look. "Jacko, why oh why, for heaven's sake? Anyway, if you must, why don't you hide the stuff better?"

Jackson was still seeing the funny side. "But I was taking it lying down, boy—in my l'il corner hole. I wasn't bothering anybody."

But this time there was something vacuous in Jackson's expression which reduced Gainer's sympathy. They could hear Nolan and Quidd talking behind the washing machines and clinking the bottles. It was too damn silly, Gainer thought. Their situation was bad enough without this, without Jacko's giving Nolan another reason for one of the frightening changes of mood. Nolan's balance was too precarious as it was. He glanced at the doctor. The doctor was painfully silent.

Nolan came out, white and thin-lipped, obviously making a great effort to control himself. He had a half-empty bottle of whiskey in one hand, a beer bottle in the other. Quidd behind him had several other beer bottles.

Nolan suddenly lifted his arm and hurled the bottle of whiskey to the deck. The bottle was open and a spout of liquid which Nolan ignored spilled over him. He threw the bottle of beer after it. The bottles hit the deck near the doorway to the next compartment just as Ransome appeared in it to go through. Ransome jumped back out of the way, swore, looked in and saw Nolan.

Nolan's face was illuminated with rage. He turned, took two more bottles from Quidd behind him and smashed them furiously on the first—Willis quickly turned his head from the flying splinters—then the final one on the others. Nolan hadn't said a word. He stood under the deckhead light. His face was working very slightly. He lifted his head and touched his dark glasses.

"Mr. Jackson, I don't have drunks on my rig. I've given you fair warning."

"Okay, send me ashore," Jackson said, still happy.

"Don't worry, I'll fix you ashore, Mister. There are conditions of service on this rig, like any other. I'll see the company keeps you running, you goddamn drunk. I'll see to that all right. I'll get you run off every rig you stick your nose into, Mr. Twist-Off Jackson."

"Three cheers," Jackson said thickly. "I'll take the next boat."

"Yeah? You're being a little fast there, son. I'm still the Pusher around here and until you're off my rig, you're doing what I say." He suddenly screamed, "Now get up to top-side! Get out of my sight! Get out of my sight!"

Jackson tried a defiant salute, wobbled, turned and went out, tripped in the doorway and disappeared spluttering.

"Get that goddamn mess cleared up," Nolan stalked away and made for the ladder. They hurried after him.

It was raining on the top deck. They made for the main deckhouse. Head down, Gainer ran into Willis who had pulled up. Willis was standing there.

"What?" Gainer said, trying to catch what it was.

"Look at that." Willis was looking out at the sea.

Gainer looked round. More jets thrown up by the gas were pulsating in the sea and a new area, about 500 yards from the first, was boiling with the yellow froth.

"It's blown another crater." They were standing watching, hunched forward, holding their plastic hard hats on.

"Mr. Nolan. Mr. Nolan." Frank Curtis's voice came urgently over the loudspeaker from the doghouse. "Mr. Nolan wanted on the upper deck. We're getting some more gas blowing up here. Mr. Nolan, please."

Ahead, Nolan had stopped with Quidd alongside and was staring out at the gas. A jet rose high into the air, maintained itself waveringly for a moment, then sank. Spume was blowing continuously off the top of the waves.

Gainer went quickly up to Nolan. "That's a second crater."

"I can see what it is," Nolan shouted back. "I'm not blind."

"For Christ's sake, you waiting for one to blow right under the rig?"

"Did you ever see a gas hole before, Gainer? Do you know what it does? I'll tell you. It caves. It caves! There's a chance we're sitting on the goddamn oilfield right here and we're staying here till it caves and kills itself and then we're going to drill and we're getting oil!"

Gainer shouted, "You're crazy, Nolan. You're stark raving crazy!"

Nolan suddenly gripped Gainer by the front of his overalls. Gainer bunched up, swung his fist. They grappled, hitting each other and stumbling.

"You goddamn smart guy!" They lurched. Nolan's dark glasses fell off. Gainer flung Nolan away as Nolan threw another punch. They stood glaring at each other.

"Look here, Larry——" The doctor moved in, but Gainer shouldered him off. Then Quidd handed Nolan his glasses. Nolan took them, looking at them. He wiped them against his sleeve. He put them on, looked at Gainer. "That's not a line of talk I care for, Mr. Gainer."

"You can go to hell." Gainer turned on his heel and walked over to his cabin. He slammed the door.

He was keyed up by the stupidity of the scene, by the whole damned mad crazy situation—Nolan's wild risks, his flaring rages and unpredictable changes of mood and the impossibility of getting any rational communication through to him. Something had to be done. Something damned urgent had to be done. The situation was worsening every hour. He felt the edginess getting the better of him and hitched himself up on the back of the chair with his feet on the seat.

The doctor came in. He didn't look at Gainer. He zipped his anorak in silence and pulled it off. He looked serious.

"Cheerful little scene," Gainer said.

"Maybe it wasn't the right thing to say, Larry."

"What? Do you mean to say you're taking his side? You think he's right. Let me tell you——"

"I don't mean that he's right, Larry. You know that perfectly well. But he was worked up and you goaded him again. It was asking for it and it's just what you need to avoid. The situation is bad enough anyway."

"But doc, he's off his head. He's clear out of his mind."

"Oh damn it, Larry, I know it."

"You do? Then why——?"

"No, I don't. I take that back. I don't know. I ought not to have said it. What we have to try to do is not to make him worse. I don't say you're to blame for anything else than a sharp reaction. Natural enough, anyway."

Gainer got slowly off the chair. "You think he's mad, doc, don't you?" They had skirted this in three of four earlier discussions. They had talked round the edge of it.

"Mad—it's so easy to say, Larry. He's mad—too easy. It's a very complex state—even at its simplest."

"Oh for God's sake!" Gainer said impatiently.

"You know what he's like—sometimes he's up in the air, the next minute he's all right. At his best he's impressive, he has a strong personality. All of a sudden it fades—absolutely fades. You've seen it. He looks as if he's been rubbed out, only the vaguest outline of him left, then he's up again, irrepressibly energetic. But there are plenty of times when he's absolutely normal."

"So there are times when he's *not* normal. Isn't that it? What the hell are you afraid of, doc?"

"I'm not afraid of anything."

"Seems to me you're backing away from the facts."

"But you just can't go fooling around classing people as insane. It's not so simple."

"Okay, okay." Gainer turned impatiently, then back again. "Then what about this crazy game he wants me to play? What about that?"

"Larry it *is* crazy. It's absolutely mad." He paused. "You know something? It's a creepy kind of therapy. You know what I think? I think he learned it in a hospital somewhere. Maybe it has some association or he was told to play it when he was uneasy, to help get his tension down. It's a hold-over from something like that."

Gainer was looking at him. "But my God, doc—that's it. You've got it. You've got it. That's the answer. I told you he'd dropped out of sight for a couple of years. Nobody knew where he was. It's because he was in some institution. Nobody's ever heard what happened to Nolan. It must be it, doc."

"It could be. Possible."

"Honestly, doc, what do you think—honestly?"

The doctor considered. "Well, I tell you, he gives me the impression of trying to stay calm. I mean, in the sort of situation where he'd normally be scared as hell—I mean in something like what we're in now—because he's defending himself. He's trying to defend himself from any suspicion of being abnormal and he is overcompensating. It fits with what you say, what you've told me about him, those obsessive fits he had too. He's trying to make a big comeback, so he has to keep on what he thinks is normal behaviour. I don't know if he has been in some psychiatric ward but if so, it's probably the key.

"The great problem for anybody who's been in and got out is to show continuity, consistency—a sort of logic, even pushed to extremes, even doggedness, a resolve not to 'give way.' They want to seem in control of the situation."

"Sure. That's one of his pet phrases. 'I'm in control of the situation.' "

"So he minimizes the risks. He overcompensates. He has the thing out of balance."

"He certainly damn well has."

"He equates his demonstration of control over the rig, over

169

the drilling, with showing he is in control of himself. He's on top of both. He has tied his recovery to this job. If he fails, I mean if he is manifestly inadequate, falls down badly, it's going to destroy his self-assurance, show he is mistaken and not cured. And of course if the Company thinks he has failed, if he can't prove to the Company that he is all they think he is and more, it'll amount to the same thing. That's why he's been so touchy about reports to the Company, about making do without the gear you needed and so on."

"Quidd come into this somewhere?"

"Quidd is some sort of adjunct, helps his control in some way. He must have picked Quidd up somewhere along the road."

"In the nuthouse probably," Gainer said.

"There's an odd sort of symbolism in that game, have you noticed?"

"What, Fox and Geese?"

"Yes. Isn't that the game where one player has to try to trap the other?"

Gainer nodded. "One's alone, his opponent has a line of men. The one alone has to try to break through the advancing enemy line which is out to corner him, trap him. Doc, it's childish."

"Not to Nolan it isn't. He's got to get out. He's got to escape the trap. Has he ever lost, what happens?"

Gainer shook his head. "Hell, I don't know how to play that kid's game. Anyway, he's a demon player. And he is all right after he's won, sort of relaxed."

"Yes."

"You know that cabin of his wasn't on the rig originally. He had it specially built for himself, I suppose because he wanted to be able to hole up."

The doctor nodded. "He's got to be alone. Must be at times when he can't face the situation, when he has *lost* control of his nerve, his ability to face the struggle and he thinks he's going to give himself away and break down—show he is unbalanced."

Gainer said, "You know something else? I believe he knew the extent of the damage to the gearing all along. He knew that there was a fifty-fifty chance of our not being able to lower on Spud three once we were up in position, but he decided to go ahead anyway."

"Yes. I think there's some tremendous challenge for him in this whole thing."

"But what in hell do we *do*, doc?"

The doctor obviously did not have a ready-made answer. "He'd dead scared now that there's going to be a crisis with the rig and it's going to push him over the edge—make him lose control for good."

"But it's damn well here, doc! We've got to get clear of that gas. Whatever we try is going to be the most almighty risk with a sea like this. But we have to do something. We have to get a radio out for urgent assistance from two tugs."

"I thought Quidd operated the radio?"

"He does." Gainer was looking at him evenly.

"What are you getting at, Larry?"

"You know damn well what I'm getting at."

"Suppose you clear up any doubts."

"We lock them up—Quidd and Nolan. Take charge."

Guggendorf said, "Then who's going to send the radio signal?"

Gainer hesitated. It was an obstacle he had thought of. He said, "Cummings." He knew it didn't sound convincing, even to the doctor. Cummings, the electrician, was about the one man on the rig who had anything to do with Quidd. He kow-towed to Quidd, and he was under Quidd's thumb.

"Wouldn't work," the doctor said. "Anyway, I couldn't do it."

"You mean this is mutiny on the oil rig? Don't make me laugh."

"I didn't mean that."

"You don't take that stuff about Nolan's being the law here seriously, do you? This isn't a ship, for God's sake."

"No, but it may be analogous to one."

"What? But, doc, I don't understand you. You can't mean you——"

"I mean I'm not going to do anything like locking Nolan up. I'm not going to help push him over the edge, Larry. That's what you're asking me to do indirectly. You can't drive a man insane when he's struggling to keep sane. You can't push him over the cliff and if you try it, Larry, I'm going to do everything I can to stop you!"

"You'd sacrifice forty-two men to save one nut?"

"I won't drive one man mad to save forty-two. It's different. That's the difference. You told me this morning I couldn't boil water for the man in the sick bay. It's bad enough withholding something like that. But destroying a man in cold blood—it's murder and I'm not doing it."

"It seems to me you're taking a damned high-falutin attitude about your moral responsibilities, Dr. Guggendorf. Probably your Swiss professionalism."

The doctor looked at him mildly. "Cut it out, Larry."

Gainer turned round, "Oh hell, doc, I'm sorry. It was a lousy thing to say. I apologize. Take it back."

171

They were briefly silent. Gainer said, "None of this gets us any nearer deciding what to do."

"But, Larry, the only thing *to* do is to try to keep Nolan on an even keel, to help him keep balanced. Then we stand a chance of making him see reason. It gives us a bare chance."

There was a dull explosion outside, like the firing of a single artillery round.

"What in hell?" They looked at each other.

"The gas?" the doctor said.

As Gainer pulled the door, water and small fragments showered on the deck. Gainer ducked. Chalky White and Pete, who had come out of the mess, did the same, then bobbed up again. "What was that?"

"Something went up."

Beyond the platform, the gas was still erupting, the two areas of boiling sea now nearly meeting. Then Gainer saw the helicopter platform lurching over the side, the supporting struts buckled and hanging loose.

They raced across. Joe Havenga and Sowerby and three others were already at the rail. Nobody knew what had happened. Joe and another man had seen a spout of water thrown up by the explosion. It had seemed to be underwater. They sent three men hurrying below but there was no damage there. The explosion had torn away the struts of the helicopter platform which had collapsed, half crushing the mud lab and the small deckhouse adjoining. Nobody was hurt.

Gainer hung over the side with the others.

"That ain't no gas, sir," Joe said.

There was no boiling of the water as in the other areas. Nolan pushed his way through the men now crowding around. The loose struts, the uprights of the safety net and small parts of the damaged structure were banging against the side in the wind. The lopsided platform, caught by the wind, was creaking loudly. Nolan looked normal.

"Explosion," Gainer shouted. "Seems to have been underwater." A shower of spray came over, dousing them all.

Nolan was gripping the rail, his eyes screwed up, peering looked down at the sea. A mighty wave reared and they stepped back, receiving the top as it broke green against the rail. Nolan leant over again, then turned round.

"Where was it from?"

Gainer shrugged. "Can't have been gas. Miracle it didn't set the gas off."

Men were pressing into the mud lab and the adjoining radio hut. Willis came out. "It's a mess in there all right."

"Mist' Nolan, that BOP okay? I wonder if it ain't mebbe good to take a look."

172

Abruptly Nolan was stock still. He was looking at Joe. There was a tense pause. They had not thought of the blow-out preventer on the sea bed. Gainer looked from Nolan to the doctor and back again. If the blow-out preventer was damaged and didn't hold, they were going to have a wild gas well blowing directly underneath them. They could never live with it.

Gainer and Joe Havenga pushed through the men. They ran for the BOP control panel, checked there, then for the control room. Gainer pulled open the door, bent at the TV set and switched on. The screen flickered, became grey. He manipulated the controls. But they could make nothing out except the dimmest outline of the blow-out preventer stack.

"I can't see a thing, boss, kin you?"

"Not a damn thing, Joe."

Gainer switched off and they went out. Gainer went down the steps to the main deck. He walked towards the men round the lopsided helicopter platform. He saw Nolan talking to a girl.

Gainer stopped in amazement. For a few seconds it was like an illusion. Then he saw it was the Kellman girl. She and Nolan were standing apart from the rest. The girl was talking earnestly to Nolan and gesturing with one hand.

Gainer slowed up. He was looking at the girl. She was unrecognizable as the girl he had seen come aboard from the disabled boat. She was wearing a man's shirt and a pair of jeans that the doctor had evidently borrowed for her. The jeans were tight. She was barefoot. Her blonde hair was blowing across her face. She was called Karen. The doctor had told him. Even in those clothes she looked rich. She had full lips and darkish eyebrows. Boy, Gainer thought. Boy, is that a looker. He was watching her. Is that just one looker.

She was evidently pleading. He heard her say, "Will you please—please?" Men kept turning and looking her up and down. Gainer went closer.

Then Nolan said, "Miss Kellerman, you'd oblige me by getting back to the sick bay."

She suddenly flared, "But that's all you can say! The sick bay! The sick bay! I can't stand it any more. That man is dying. He's just on the other side of the curtain. He keeps turning and turning in his bed and bumping me. He doesn't stop moaning. Your doctor is doing nothing for him. I can't lie there and listen to it day and night, day and night. He weeps. He says ugly dirty things—I can't stand it. I can't! I can't!"

Nolan was obviously losing patience. His brow furrowed. "We haven't any stateroom accommodation on board this rig,

173

Miss—uh. And I have no time to devote to your personal fantasies. You've been assigned to the sick bay. Now get back there or I'll be obliged to have you put back."

"Why haven't you sent me to my father? I'm grateful that you saved me. I'll tell him what you've done. But I want to get away from here. This frightens me. I want to go."

"Miss, right now I don't give one goddamn what you or your father want. Now if you'll—"

She lifted her hand swiftly and struck him hard across the face. Nolan didn't even blink. She gave a small gasp of frustration and rage and flung away. Nolan watched her go. He turned back to Gainer, "Well?"

"You can barely see the stack. Impossible to tell if it's weakened. From the panel it seems all right."

"Yeah, well we'll know soon." Nolan's voice had the usual sarcastic drawl.

Gainer looked at the sea. The two areas of bubbling gas had joined.

As Nolan was about to move across the cabin, the girl said, "No, you said you'd stay over there."

"Sure." Nolan got up and sat on the bunk beside her. "That was about an hour ago. Clear this off." He leaned forward and took the dish with the remnants of food which Quidd had left behind off the wall flap and put it on the floor. "Quidd ain't exactly the head waiter at the Ritz."

Quidd had brought them dinner in Nolan's cabin and forgotten the dish when he had cleared away the rest of the things.

"Please can't I smoke?" she said.

Nolan laughed. "Miss Kellerman, you certainly are a persistent trier."

"Kellman. My father's—"

"Yeah. Sure. You told me. The guys must get sick of it if you're always throwing up about your old man, baby."

He was looking at her. She sat on the end of the bunk against the bulkhead. She was wearing the same man's grey shirt and jeans. He looked her slowly up and down. "Come to that, I haven't heard you say this is any better than the sick bay yet."

"It is. I am grateful."

"Yeah? You're not exactly expressive, baby, are you? Seems to me I've done the talking tonight. How about entertaining me some? A gal who's grateful ought to entertain a guy."

"I—I would give anything to smoke. Please?"

174

"Baby, you couldn't get a smoke for anything. Not here. Not for any damn thing."

She avoided his eyes. She made to get up. He touched her arm. "Take it easy."

Silence.

"How old're you, baby?"

"I've told you."

"Tell me again."

"Twenty-four."

"Yeah." Nolan looked at her.

"I'll bet you're a good hotassed lay."

She didn't say anything.

"I could give it to you good, baby."

She didn't look at him.

"I guess you laid some pretty rich guys, uh? Don't always get it so good, though. Ain't it so, baby?"

She was looking down at her hands.

"How about them rich guys? You light 'em up, all right, uh?"

Silence. His hand was on her thigh, smoothing her thigh under the thin, taut, washed-out material of the jeans. She didn't move.

"You know something? I never had a gal who had any dough. I never knocked up any gal who had dough. They were all hard up mostly. I have to have the dough to make 'em. Sure, sure. They like me to throw it around. Okay. Those babies are on the receiving end. They're a lot of tramps. A baby like you—a gal with the real dough's, you know—kind of inaccessible. Yeah. Like a woman who's wearing one of them long evening dresses, when they look at you like some goddamn duchess or something and they want to seem, what's it—in-vio-late. Yeah. In-vio-late. That's why I think you're interesting, see? You violate or in-vio-late, baby?"

He reached out. He caught two fingers in the front of her shirt, paused, looking at her—sprang the button off. She got to her feet, pushing him away. He caught her and she hit him hard in the face.

"Baby, you're getting it."

He caught her and pushed her back on the bunk. She was struggling wordlessly with small cries and exclamations. He pressed her down, held her with her shoulders flat on the bunk. He sat on her knees.

"You're gonna treat me good, ain't you, baby? You can calm me down, uh? I start something with a woman I can't finish. Ever had it with a guy who can't finish? Won't with you, though." He lay over her. She lifted herself, wriggled, threw him aside momentarily. She bit hard into his forearm.

"You hotassed little bitch," Nolan said.

He lay looking at her. Her face was turned away.

"You can't talk, can you?" he said with scorn. "You're goddamn dumb, uh? You're thinking in Swede, maybe? Yeah. Sure."

He ran his eyes over her. "You bet. I don't give a goddamn what you're thinking in, see. You're the kind, sure. Like Jesus you're the kind. You're rich, baby. Sure you're rich. Don't let any of these guys tell you you're good, though. You're no goddamn good to me. I got a tramp who's better, see? Yeah. I knocked up any number of cheapskate flopped-out whores better'n you, baby. Yeah!"

12

MARGIE FIELD was arranging her hair in the glass. The office door to the corridor was open. It was half-past twelve and she had a shopping date. She hoped this last-minute thing wasn't going to be long. She didn't want to be late. Mike wanted to see her afterwards. Perhaps; she didn't know. He was being persistent lately. She didn't see where it was leading, but it was agreeable. No news from Larry. She sighed. She wondered where *they* were leading. If there had been a date with him, she'd have been in no doubt about going.

Behind her she saw Anderson, the chief driller, in the doorway. He had rung up ten minutes before asking to see the Chairman or Mr. Stoneman urgently. Anderson raised his chin in interrogation. He was a tall, craggy man who made a predominant effect of eyebrows; they stuck out big and bushy from the flat white cliff of his face.

Margie turned around. "Yes, five minutes. He's got a lunch outside, so you'll have to be smart." She led the way into Meldreth's room. Stoneman was standing in conversation with Meldreth beside the desk. They did not look round until Anderson was half way to the desk.

"Yes?"

Anderson said, "I have a man below, it's Parrish, the pilot from Mister Mack, who says he has some information about Mister Mack but won't give it to anybody except a member of the Board. He says it's important. I've tried to get it out of him but he won't say. He confirms that the weather's very bad out there and that they're carrying on, but he insists that what he's got to say is highly important and relevant to the operations and something you must be told personally—or somebody else high up."

Stoneman, who had begun to move away from the desk towards his own room as Anderson had begun, had stopped and was looking at Anderson. "What's his name, do you say?"

"Parrish. He's the helicopter pilot."

"He has come in with the reports then. Where are they?" He stepped back towards the desk, hand extended.

"No, sir, he hasn't anything. Naturally, I asked him. He says he wants to give his explanation to an executive director. I thought——"

"If he hasn't brought the reports, what's he doing here? Have you been in touch with North Scully?"

"Yes sir. They say they haven't seen him. The helicopter's there all right but Parrish didn't report there. They were ringing me yesterday about it. Nobody saw Parrish. I told them I didn't know where he was. I expected he would turn up there. Now he has turned up here."

"Bring him up," Stoneman said.

"I'll tell Miss Field." Anderson went out.

They waited. In a few minutes Anderson came back with Parrish. Parrish was in a dark blue suit with white breast pocket handkerchief, grey tie, shiny black shoes. He looked very self-assured. The bald scalp on either side of the crest of black hair was shiny. His stance with his backside thrown out added to his cocky air. Anderson made the introductions.

"You have something you wish to say to us, Mr. Parrish?" Meldreth said when they were seated.

"What are you here for?" Stoneman corrected sharply. Stoneman had remained standing.

Parrish said, "I brought in the helicopter from Mister Mack yesterday to North Scully. I did so on my own authority. Mr. Nolan did not know I was coming off. In fact, I've every reason to suppose that if he had he'd have tried to stop me. That wouldn't have made any difference, wouldn't have made me change my mind. There's a howling gale out there as you know. I'd already told Mr. Nolan that conditions were getting too bad and that if they kept up I'd have to take the helicopter off as a matter of security. I'm responsible for the helicopter. If I hadn't taken it off yesterday, I probably shouldn't have been able to get off at all. I also took off because I was fed up with the conditions aboard and sick and tired of making complaints that never got dealt with."

Stoneman's look was flinty. He plainly had no sympathy for these arguments. His eyes narrowed and his face was set in grim lines. Meldreth was looking severe and Anderson embarrassed.

Stoneman said between his teeth, "Is this what you insist on saying to an executive director?"

"It is."

"Then let me tell you, Mr. Parrish——"

"And something else." Parrish said firmly and loudly.

Stoneman pulled up, obviously staggered at being interrupted. He was fixing Parrish. Quietly he said, "Go on."

"I brought the mud engineer off with me, a man named Bradford."

"Bradford came off——?" Anderson began in a surprised tone. Nobody took any notice.

"I was coming away with the aircraft. He guessed it and came with me—to get away. I didn't ask him why. He had kept on telling me how fed up he was with the platform, the conditions on board and so on and so forth—a long rigmarole. He kept on about it. I could see enough myself to understand it. Make no bones about that. Finally when he knew I was taking the helicopter, he wanted to leave with me and I said it didn't worry me, he could come or he could stay behind, it was all the same to me. *I* was going." Parrish's glance did a quick tour of the faces, sizing up the reactions. They were all frozen. But Parrish had not lost any of his rather testy cockiness.

"The point is that when we had taken off and were on our way inshore, Bradford began to talk as if he had left for some other reason. The way he spoke was suspicious. There seemed to be something behind it. He wanted me to land at the Atlas base, said there were good things in it for us. Said we both ought to go to Atlas. When I wouldn't play and asked why Atlas, he closed up. At least, he said one more thing, something about Mister Mack being "fixed." But he seemed to see he had gone too far with me and shut up, wouldn't say any more.

"He did a crude cover-up about not meaning Atlas especially, and then he said he was taking a holiday. The point is— and this is what I'm insisting on—if anything goes wrong, I am keeping myself in the clear. I'm not being associated with Bradford, I am not going to be accused of being an accomplice of Bradford's simply because I took him off in the helicopter. It was a mistake. I admit it. If I'd known, if he'd handed me this line of talk beforehand, I'd have steered clear of him. But we were away and it was too late. And since I did bring him ashore, I've been thinking about it. I decided it was best to come and say so frankly. I've no reason to get myself in a sticky position because of Bradford. That is what I wanted to tell you."

Stoneman was rigid. "He said specifically Atlas?"

"Yes."

"Anybody by name?"

Parrish shook his head.

"When he spoke of Mister Mack being "fixed," did he say or did he give you the impression that he'd *done* something?"

Parrish shrugged. "He didn't say. I don't know what he meant."

"Sabotage?"

There was a crackling silence. Parrish looked from Stoneman's face to Meldreth's and back. Stoneman continued to stare at Parrish. Anderson coughed.

"Where is Bradford now?"

"I don't know. I left him in North Scully. He wouldn't give an address."

Stoneman said, "You said you wanted to talk frankly, Mr. Parrish. So will I. I believe you have come here with this story to cover yourself. You've got cold feet. You want to opt out now. You want to buy yourself out, isn't that it? And you reckon that the little matter of your leaving the rig without authority and deserting your job is going to be overlooked by your grateful employers. Isn't that it?"

"No."

"We aren't likely to believe you were not his accomplice just because you *say* so. Where is the evidence that you weren't in with him?"

"You think I'd have mentioned Atlas if I had been?" Parrish said. But he had lost some of his assurance.

"Mr. Parrish," Stoneman said. "I have a recommendation to make to you. Don't underestimate the consequences of what will happen to you if you open your trap outside this room. You are to report your movements daily to Anderson. The Company reserves its entire right to treat your conduct as a breach of contract and hold you responsible for trouble your absence may cause on the rig. If I hear you have breathed a whisper of this you'll be for the high jump. And it'll be bloody high, Mr. Parrish, make no mistake. Now get out."

Parrish turned. Anderson was on his feet. The two of them marched out in silence. Stoneman waited until the door shut, then erupted. "Get me Julius. Quick! Tell Anderson to leave that man below with somebody and come up here." He rang for Margie, "Miss Field, call me Voyss at North Scully. In my office. Urgent."

"Same again," Bradford said to the woman behind the bar.

"Double brandy, dear. More ginger?" Bradford shook his head. She was tall and gaunt, about sixty. She had a pink rinse with a velvet bow on top and a long row of beads round her neck. The private bar was empty except for Bradford. It was still early and quiet. He could see round the partition into the public; only three customers there, drinking steadily, rustling a paper, picking the winners. Would have been a nice half-hour if he hadn't got all this on his mind.

"There we are, dear." She took his money. "Ta."

Bradford looked out over the top of the frosted glass door panel into the wet street. Not far beyond, round the corner, stretched the desolation of the Euston Road. He hated the district—the Room to Let signs, the tea shops and slop pails, the arctic bay windows, the greyish light, torn newspapers blowing about and the general genito-urinary look. It was getting him down. The thought of Mexico only made it grimmer.

A man with a grog-blossom nose came in. Bradford sipped the brandy. Raymond was late. Bradford had suggested they meet in the Hansom. But no, Raymond had said, definitely no. That was Out. Definitely Out. Bradford had had endless difficulty getting hold of Raymond in the first place. Never in. And when he was in—who was it wanting him?—he was always in a meeting. Tied up. He was in meetings all bloody day.

At last Bradford had got him. Raymond had said they could meet in the pub here.

A couple more customers came in, two beefy types with thick hands and pill heads talking earnestly together. Bradford had commandeered the end place and stool so that he and Raymond could talk in peace. The two new customers were blocking the way. He cursed under his breath; no use Raymond missing him. The bar was going to be crowded shortly. Why couldn't Raymond turn up on time?

He took a step back so as to remain in sight of the door. Another customer came in and dived for the vacant end space and Bradford had to step smartly up to the bar again to keep it.

"Eow. So'y," the newcomer said. He was wearing a camel hair coat and Brute aftershave.

Bradford stabbed out his cigarette end and lit another. He wanted to tell Raymond all about the operation. Atlas were entitled to know. They were paying. He wished he had had more time to deal with the mud balance. In the end, it had been a rush job. The talk with Parrish, bringing him around to the idea of taking off, had all taken too long, left him no time to falsify the balance as skilfully as he had intended. He wasn't going to say as much to Raymond, of course. He'd tell Raymond he'd done a precision job.

Otherwise, the operation had worked perfectly. The timing had come out beautifully. They were bound to have trouble with the high-pressure gas they were holding down.

Another customer came in. Hitler moustache, bowler hat. Bradford cursed, finished his brandy and ginger ale. What were they playing at? He had never been so miserable in his life. No Judy. Couldn't relax. Couldn't sleep. Last night he had almost gone to the Hansom, picked up one of the girls; would have been company. Then he'd thought maybe of running into Ambrose there, or Raymond; no sense in playing it wrong now.

He saw Raymond shouldering through the customers towards him. Everything immediately became brighter. "Raymond, old boy. Thought you weren't going to turn up. How's life? How's the old chum, eh?"

Raymond was nodding, bending forward, his frog-mouth pursed. "Ssh! Go easy on the names. No names, no pack drill, eh?" More gravel-voiced than ever. He was gripping Bradford's biceps, wheezing, smelling of liquor, pepper and tobacco. He had certainly had a couple already. His nose looked fatter. He leant closer in a cloud of the combined smell and croaked in Bradford's ear, "How's the old hunkey-dorey?" recoiled, looking at Bradford, leaned in again and recroaked, "Get it? Get it?"

"Oh. Yes. Fine. Fine!" Bradford laughed. They laughed together. Bradford didn't know what they were supposed to be laughing about. But he played up. "What's yours Ray—er, what's yours, old man?"

"Usual. Double *soixante-neuf.*"

The woman behind the bar looked down her cigarette holder. "It's yours, love." Raymond wheezed and went into a wet fruity cough. He sounded as if he were going to cough one lung up.

"And a double brandy-ginger."

Bradford grabbed Raymond's coat lapel and put his lips to Raymond's ear and whispered that everything had been done, carried out to plan, that trouble was certainly on the way for You Know Who, that he had—but Raymond, nodding his head, gripped his wrist, pushed him away, waved him quiet with open palm, saying, "Ssh" and "Yesh-yesh-yesh-yesh. No need. Everything understood. Okay-okay. Fine. Fine. Okeydoke. Tickety-boo, Bob's your uncle, son of a gun."

Bradford dried up, surprised. He hadn't got across a fraction of what he wanted to say. He didn't know what to think. He shrugged. The drinks came. Raymond sank most of his in one swallow. He had an unobtrusively practiced manner with a glass; he hardly seemed to drink, just tipped it smoothly down. Bradford lit their cigarettes. He stood looking at Raymond who was standing with one hand on the edge of the bar, finger and thumb round whisky glass, little finger (signet ring) separated. Raymond was not his old genial self. Bradford made to lean in and whisper again but Raymond had his palm on his chest pushing him off, nodding, nodding, pursing.

They finished the drinks. Bradford ordered another round.

Raymond looked at his gold wristwatch. "Mush be going." The camel hair Brute went, leaving them a few inches more space. Then, as Bradford paid, Raymond put his mouth to Bradford's ear.

"Can't make contact again yet. Too obvious. Mustn't associate. Can't do anything yet. Too risky. Have to keep Quiet. Eh? What money? Don't know anything about that. Not my pigeon, old man. Never touch the stuff, (wheeze). Keep your head down for the time being. Eh? Understand? When? Can't say. Depends. Keep it quiet, eh?" He retreated and in a natural voice said, "Is that the time. I got to be going. Well—keep smiling, old man. All the best. Regards to the missus." With a final nod he was shouldering through the customers for the door.

Bradford watched him go in dismay. He reached for his drink. Raymond's glass was on the bar. He had even left some of his whisky.

The world, the pub, everything darkened. Bradford felt abysmally miserable. What was he supposed to do now? How long was he supposed to wait until Atlas decided it was safe enough to get in touch with him? He had carried out his side of the contract. Ambrose had said . . . He realized how hopeless it would be to try to find Ambrose or Harry. Worst of all was not being able to see Judy. He dared not. He was supposed to be on the platform. How was he going to explain having left? It suddenly occurred to him that he hadn't worked out a water-tight story with Parrish. Somehow, in the rush to get away, then later ashore, they hadn't gone over it. He had been too pleased to be off. But if the platform had a blow-out? Of course, he could say ten different things; they could never check. But he needed a story that would chime with Parrish's.

He began to feel prickling on the top of his head. He ought to have settled all this with Parrish before they had parted. Ought to have got it all sewn up. Oh God. It was a very bad mistake. Where had he put that note of Parrish's address? Had to find it. Had to get in touch with Parrish straight away. See Parrish and settle their story. Maybe once he'd seen Parrish, he could ring Judy. Yes. See Parrish urgently.

"Same again d'you say, love?"

"No thanks." Bradford hurried out.

The wind was screaming through the derrick. Gainer was on the rig floor waiting for dawn. The arcs were on. He had rigged up a searchlight in the direction of the gas to keep a check on its progress in the night. It shone out on the water, on the tremendous seas rising and breaking, the boiling gas area and the jets pulsing as if some marine creature of great size were approaching. Heavy intermittent hammering came from the other end where the men were trying to disengage the damaged helicopter platform.

Two hours earlier Gainer had seen the Kellman girl come out of Nolan's cabin. She was in oilskins. Nolan had taken her to the sick bay and then returned. Gainer had been puzzled, then shrugged it off.

The platform itself was being regularly doused with sea water. Far away to the north there were the lights of a ship. The rest of the sea was empty.

Nolan came up the steps. He hunched in the shelter of the doghouse, looking out at the gas. He held the collar of his short coat tight up round his neck. Gainer saw he had a twitch at the corner of his mouth. Nolan shouted, "We'll have to kill it."

"Kill it?" Gainer looked at him.

"Skid the derrick back, drill a slanting hole into that upper porous horizon we struck earlier and pump the gel* through till it kills the gas hole."

It was a classic method for normal circumstances. But Gainer shook his head. "Never do it—anyway, we haven't got anything like the gel we'd need. (He was sure Nolan realized this.) We haven't got above one hundred and twenty tons. Gene, for Christ's sake listen to me. We can't possibly drill in this anyway. We're going to need assistance any hour now. Call up the base and get two tugs out fast, will you? If we can't get the rig away from this hole, we've got to get the men off." He was going to add, "This is an emergency," but pulled himself up. Better not.

Nolan clutched the neck of his coat to his throat. He was hunching almost to stooping. Gainer noticed the subtle change of manner which announced another mysterious swing of mood, a coming crisis. Nolan said something Gainer couldn't hear.

"What?" Gainer shouted.

"Our radio is out."

"Out?" Gainer stared at him. The radio hut was next to the mud lab and the damaged helicopter platform had collapsed on both. That he knew. "But we——"

"Quidd says he can't operate."

The searchlight showed up a double jet of water rising and dispersing in spray. Nolan wet his lips. He let go his collar,

* Gel. The rig name for bentonite, a grey powdered material used to make mud, in this case heavy mud.

fished inside his coat and brought out the dark glasses. He flipped them on. "We skid back, drill at an angle, kill it."

Gainer shouted, "How in hell do you expect to drill in this weather? We had the travelling block hitting the derrick already. You stand back pipe in the derrick in this gale and you'll have the derrick down. You can't even *pull* pipe, Gene. For Christ's sake, we've got to batten down, stand by and get Quidd working on that radio——"

"We're going to kill it as I said, and like it."

Nolan stepped into the doghouse and the door slammed. The next moment his voice came over the loudspeaker, "Get me Willis up here on the floor. Willis on the rig floor. Willis."

Gainer took two steps towards the doghouse. He reached for the handle, checked himself. He turned and went quickly down to the main deck. There were pools of sea water. He went towards the rail but the heavy spray drove him back. He was baffled and restless with anger and anxiety. He told himself that he had to take over. The doc was wrong. Yet what would they gain if the radio was genuinely out of commission? If it were not damaged, Quidd would quite probably have removed some part by now and made sure it couldn't send.

The sky was paling. A green wave came over the rail and showered the deck. Gainer dodged. He went along towards the men working on the broken struts. They had been trying all night to free the circular helicopter platform which was now hanging over the side, giving hold to the waves and wind and increasing the pressure on the rig structure.

Joe Havenga and Frank were in charge. They could have cut away the mass of steel in a couple of hours with acetyline cutters but couldn't use them because of the gas. The men were on improvised scaffolding slamming away with sledgehammers. They had wrapped the heads of the hammers in rags and sacking to avoid sparks. They were soaked and chilled by the spray and wind.

Gainer pitched in and helped them get a steel line from a winch round part of the damaged structure. They stood back, threw in the winch and managed to pull the toppled platform lower. By the time they had finished, Gainer was wet through.

Gainer headed across the deck. He could see Willis and Sutherland on the rig floor. He went down the hatch and turned along to the engine room. Ransome was drinking a thermos of tea. He looked frightened.

"How much longer we sticking this?" Ransome said.

"Sid, I'm going up to the control room. When I give you the signal, I want you to jack up ten feet on all."

Ransome looked at him in surprise. "What? This Mr. Nolan's order?"

"Hell, no. It's mine. What's the matter?"

"But Larry, we can't climb up Spud three hardly at all. We're nearly out of leg."

"But they're taking 'em green on the helicopter platform."

"Can't get up more than three feet. Hardly make a difference."

"What? You mean we can't jack the platform up more than three feet above this?"

"Not on Spud three we can't because she's sunk. Got no more leg."

"Christ!"

"If we try jacking up on the other two, we're going to give ourselves a list." He paused. "Larry, when are we getting shut down? I been up all night. Some of the lads been sitting up in the mess. Don't want to turn in."

Gainer had seen the group when he had come on deck himself at half-past four. There would have been trouble if Joe Havenga, Frank and the other drillers hadn't been there too during a break from the work outside. The drilling teams and roustabouts were controlling the rest. It couldn't last.

"Larry, are we——?"

"I'll be back." Gainer turned, lifting a hand in salute. He did not want a discussion. On deck he climbed to the gearing. About three feet of the massive toothed rack on Spud three extended above the gearing. The tops of the other legs were higher. If Spud three sank again, they could no longer jack up more than three feet to keep the platform level. They would go over.

He looked down. The platform seemed barely above the water—as if the sea had risen under it. They were not sinking. But it looked as if they were. It *felt* like it. He saw Willis, Sowerby and some of the others on the rig floor. Below him, the port crane swung out. A group of men was waiting to move pipe.

Gainer jumped down to the deck. It was lunatic to think of drilling! He *had* to force the issue. There was no sign of Nolan on the rotary floor. He looked up at the control room. Not there either. He crossed rapidly to Nolan's office, opened the door. It was empty. Alongside, the cabin door was shut. He rapped on it. No answer. He tried it. Locked.

"Nolan! Open up. Gene." No answer. The cabin was in darkness and the jalousie up inside the window. He believed Nolan was inside and he wished he didn't.

He bent down trying to see through the slats. He couldn't see anything. Then, shifting, he made out a white patch in the gloom—Nolan's face in the shaving mirror, staring fixedly at some point. Gainer straightened up. He knocked at the door again but Nolan didn't answer.

He stood there not knowing what to do. The impulse for a decision had been blocked. He saw Jackson on the rig floor with the others now. They were obviously discussing the drilling. He crossed the radio hut under the collapsed helicopter platform. The door was locked. The hut was a light prefab. The roof had been crushed and one of the supporting struts had gone through. The damage could well have knocked out the set.

There was a shout from above. Gainer backed out and looked up. It was Joe Havenga, on the scaffolding, soaked to the skin. He raised an arm pointing out to sea. A geyser of water was shooting high into the air from the gas, much nearer the rig. The top of it was blowing off in the gale.

The men under the derrick had stopped to watch. There was another group including the cooks at the door of the mess. Gainer went up the steps to the derrick floor. Jackson came over.

"It's moving closer in." He wasn't smiling for once. "Seen that one out there?" He pointed at an angle. Another small area of sea was boiling.

Gainer said, "Listen, Jacko. I'm telling you not to move the derrick and not to shift any pipe. We're not drilling."

Jackson squinted at him. "We've got Nolan's orders."

"I know it. I'm giving you different orders. You can forget what Nolan told you. We're not going to drill."

"You mean that?"

"I do."

Jackson grinned. "Boy, what are you going to do about Captain Bligh?" A tremendous gust of wind had them grabbing for support. Moisture—rain? sea?—whipped at them out of the wind, stinging like hail.

Jackson shouted, "He's going to see you hanging from the highest yardarm in the British navy."

"Tell the others. Tell Willis he's not to shift any collar or pipe. Everything lashed down. Get some extra lashing round the travelling block—and those tongs."

Another fierce prolonged gust. Jackson put both hands to his mouth and yelled, "Getting bloody worse."

Gainer nodded grimly. Spray showered high above the forward end of the platform. He ran to the doghouse, grabbed the mike. "Joe, Frank. Get some rope around you. Double up the scaffolding lines. Every man has to be roped up. You hear this?" He pushed open the door, stood looking out. Joe waved.

"Jacko, get these slips stowed."

Gainer moved about the deck supervising. Willis was inclined to argue, saying that Nolan was boss. But Gainer saw that he had not been looking forward to the attempt to drill and kept watching the gas.

At noon they saw a freighter passing about five miles off, the nearest a ship had been for days. Gainer ran back to the doghouse and signalled madly with the rig lights. The ship was taking a pounding from the seas with the bridge disappearing at times. He switched over to the loud-hailer, shouting, "Am in need of assistance—in need of assistance." But the wind snatched the sound away. She passed without a sign. He hung up the mike, let the door slam behind him.

There was a metallic jangle and he saw the helicopter platform, broken away by Joe and the others, pitch over the side. But instead of falling free, it hung there, like a great target, still attached by something. He crossed to the steps down and as he reached them Quidd's head appeared. Quidd came up. "Mr. Nolan wants you."

"The hell with him."

Quidd's face stiffened. Gainer brushed past and went down. Then on impulse, he headed for Nolan's cabin. Get it over. He'd tell Nolan himself.

The door was shut. He was about to knock when it was opened by Nolan inside. "Oh, come in, Larry." Nolan stood with his hand in his trousers pocket.

This is it, Gainer thought, and stepped in. Now he's going to get it. He said tautly, "I've just given orders to Jackson and Willis to stop——"

"Yeah, sure. Wait a minute, Larry. Come on in. Siddown, will you? Shut the door. Yeah, thanks. Siddown."

"I'd rather stand."

"Nah, siddown, siddown."

Gainer took the chair. Nolan smiled. In a casual voice he said, "Look, Larry, we haven't played a game for a while, uh? How about it? Uh?"

Gainer felt the shock like a punch. "What now, for Christ's sake?" He couldn't help himself. *"Now?"*

Slowly Nolan's smile faded. He looked at Gainer. There was a slow change of expression. His chest rose slowly, as if he were filling his lungs with air. Gainer caught himself.

"Okay. Sure. Why not?"

Nolan's look lingered on his face for a moment more. He broke his stance. "Great." He gave Gainer a sidelong glance, bent down and pulled open the drawer, brought out the board and draughtsmen. He sat down on the bunk opposite Gainer.

There was a lash of spray against the window.

Nolan was pinching his lips up as if he had eaten something sharp and sour. He was sitting tense over the board.

The sick bay was dimly lit through the jalousie.

The doctor came out from behind the white curtain dividing the small space and twitched it to behind him. The girl who had been sitting on the bed got up. She looked mute inquiry at him. Guggendorf said, "He's sleeping."

"Can't you keep him under?"

Guggendorf nodded.

"Is there any news of them coming for us?" she said nervously.

"I haven't heard yet. You should try to lie down, not worry."

"No. No. Are we going to get away soon?"

"Oh yes," he said with spurious confidence. But he did not think he was really deceiving her. She had tried to cover up when he had noticed the bruises on her arm. He knew she had been to Nolan's cabin. He had given her an opportunity to explain but she had shied off. She had a strange reticence about herself.

"You should rest," he said. "You're much too strung up. Would you like me to give you something?"

"No. Please. I want to be able to help myself."

There was a knock on the door and Gainer's voice, "Doc. You there?" Gainer's head came round the door. "Sorry, doc. Can I see you right away?" Gainer glanced at the girl. No mistake, she was beautiful.

The space was so small that she had to retreat between the bed and the bulkhead to allow the doctor to get out. He stepped outside, pulled the door shut behind him. Gainer took his arm, led him two paces away. The wind surged over them from the sea.

Gainer said, "I've just left Nolan. Been playing that damned game again. Doc, it's no time for ideal solutions—we *have* to do something about him fast. He's mad crazy—he's already over the edge. He's started on one of those mad upswings again when he gets wild excited. You have to move in, doc, and no delay now. Or I damn well will, I swear it."

The loudspeaker along the deck blared muzzily. The sound carried away in the wind and the noise of the sea. Gainer paused, trying to catch it. It sounded like somebody calling for Nolan. The voice seemed urgent.

He shouted, "Hold on, doc," and went to move closer to hear. The deck under his feet became unstable.

The whole platform listed sickeningly to one side.

There was the multiple smash of things falling. Gainer and the doctor were struck motionless.

"Christ—we're going!"

The door of the sick bay flew open, the girl ran out. Then Gainer raced along the deck and sprang up to the control room just as Nolan came up the hatch. A moment later, they were at the control panel together. Gainer slammed on the general alarm bell. Ransome was white-faced, staring at the dials.

"Spud three. Started going very slowly, I called you. Then she went all of a sudden—too fast to jack up. We're practically out of leg there. If she goes again, we're over."

They stood barely moving, their eyes fixed on the dials and the inclinometer. Nothing moved again yet. Gainer looked out of the window. Men were at stations on the upper deck in answer to the general alarm. The doctor and the girl were together. The list was not great but it made everything look extremely precarious.

"Could be the gas," Gainer said. He looked sideways at Nolan. Nolan was tightlipped. Gainer knew that his mood was rising from the trough to the peak of inner excitement.

"We could get trim again if we lowered on Spuds one and two," Ransome said.

"In this sea?" Gainer said. "Look at it now."

The sea was breaking over the lower side. Nolan said "Mr. Ransome, go down below and check with the damage control party." Ransome went out.

"Mr. Gainer, I want to know the men who are not at emergency stations."

"The hell you do!" Gainer said angrily. "The only emergency station I'm interested in is the radio—getting the transmitter going. I'm going to take every man who can handle a radio repair and put them to work on it right now—and if you don't like it, you can stick it."

"Yeah?" Nolan looked at him. He had a key in his hand and tossed it in the air and caught it. Then, to Gainer's surprise, he said, "Okay okay. I have no objection. If you feel that way about it. Maybe we do have to do that anyway. I'll have Quidd go to work on it right away. This is certainly where we have to keep right on top of the situation—reduce this downtime to the minimum. You got something there. Yeah. Damn right."

"What?" Gainer couldn't believe it. "Do you mean to say that you're *still* reckoning to keep this rig in position?"

"Uh? Oh—now wait a minute. Wait a minute now. You're getting me all balled up. Did you think I was going to get the transmitter fixed so as to put out that we were folding? Uh?

Call up the Company, say we have a gas strike here, maybe the biggest gas strike in the whole entire North Sea but we want to be pulled out? So as Atlas can come up and horn in? Yeah! You bet your sweet life. Sure, sure. I mean that. Yeah!" He laughed.

Under his breath Gainer said, "Christ."

"Nobody in his right mind, Mr. Gainer, would think of leaving a hole like this except under absolute imperative necessity and we certainly haven't reached that yet. No sir. Maybe you haven't had very extensive experience in trying to find a hole again offshore. Well, I tell you, it's pretty often as much as any goddamn driller's time is worth to try to do that, even when you're sitting damn nearby direct over it. Yes sir. Damn right."

He was gabbling excitedly, his mood on the upswing. "What would anybody think we had all that G and A structure down there for if it was so easy to find a hole? If we were to pull and go by some unfortunate accident, we certainly could not leave all that equipment on the sea bed—and that would make it certain, if we pulled it, that we shouldn't be able to find the hole again. See?

"You know how much you can miss oil by. You can hear how the French made that strike at Hassi Messaoud, in the Sahara? That big strike there? Ever hear that? Well, yeah, these operators, see, were bound by contract to drill so many holes in every block. They'd drilled a hell of a lot of dry holes in this area and they were pulling out, see. Then somebody says, 'Hey, you guys, wait, this deal says we gotta drill 8 holes each block and we only drilled 7 in this one.'

"So, okay, they leave behind a drilling crew just for the sake of the deal—and whoosh! they strike the biggest goddamn oilfield in the whole entire Sahara. Yeah. The whole Sahara. You miss it like that on land and boy, you can miss it a whole lot easier offshore. Yes sir. That gas hole is just going to cave, the weather'll blow itself out and we'll be sitting okay—okay."

Gainer turned away, too sickened and furious to listen to more. Then he flung back, "You think with that gas out there, the rig going over, you're going to—You're crazy, Nolan. I'm taking control of this rig. You're clean off your nut!" Unable to contain himself, he stalked past Nolan to the door. He was through with Nolan. He was going to take over and the hell with the doc. He reached for the handle.

"Not yet I ain't. I'm still on this side." Nolan spoke from down the room behind him. The voice was quieter, shaking with the effort at self-control. Gainer turned around. Nolan was facing him, solitary and scared.

"But I'm going to beat that too, see? You think this is maybe just a drilling for me, uh? Turning to the right. Making hole?" His words gradually gathered pace again; he spoke in a low voice, intensely, slightly raving.

"I been on my way to hell, Gainer. But I'm pulling out, I'm pulling out. You know I was eighteen months away. In a beautiful nut-house? You know that? Yeah. I was a volun-tary patient, what they called a volun–tary inmate. You ever been inside one of those places, Gainer? They got beautiful grounds. Yeah. They got bare rooms with bare walls and the walls and the floor all polished by these nuts rubbing their hands over 'em, their bodies over 'em and lickin' 'em, no glass windows, no hooks where you can hang yourself. They don't want you to hang yourself, see. They want you to live. Yeah. I was inside for a year. The head doc, a guy name of Kuhe, he says if I try to discharge myself—since I was a volun–tary inmate, see?—he's going to have to put me into a public institution and they'd keep me.

"He was a big old guy with a bald head. So I'm keeping myself screwed right down and it's not so good. It feels like I'm going way out over the top, never coming back and I can't take it.

"I'm paying my way, see, too. So they have my dough tied up and it's running out and I can feel they're going to send me down to the State nuthouse. So I have to try to keep screwed down and sweet Jesus I can't do it . . .

"Then one of the guys—he was the doctor's assistant—he starts coming to me and talking to me and helping me. I guess he doesn't tell Kuhe. Sometimes I'm sort of okay at these examinations and the other doc talks Kuhe round. Then this Kuhe gets himself killed on the street by an automobile. It's Easter Sunday. After two weeks I get a discharge for my-self. Only provisional, see. They have the drop on me. But this doc, he says I'm better and it's okay to go outside.

"Then, so help me, I see what the deal is. They've had all my dough, see? They've collected. And now they're going to tip off one of the State guys to pull me in. Just like that. Yeah. So I start hiding. I gotta lock up. Jesus! Then I've got to get back in oil, see. Got to get back fast; fast as hell. Only thing I can do. Yeah. But I'm going to show 'em I'm still the best goddamn pusher ever was and no nut, see. I'm the best goddamn shooter and crooked hole specialist and I'm gonna get oil and they can't beat me any more than any goddamn oilfield ever did, see. I have six majors coming for me in a month. Yeah. For a nut! So there's this offshore job, okay okay. It's tough. So I go right out for the tough job, see. Now do you see?"

He paused fractionally. "I'm in control of the situation. I'm not being tied by any goddamn gas well, Mr. Gainer. I'm Pusher on this rig and if you think you're going to take over, sa–a–ay, you're goddamn wrong, wrong as all hell."

He grabbed the mike, "Will you for Christ's sake, come in, Ransome? Where's the damage control report?"

Distorted and unreal, Ransome's voice came over, "Cement mixer's overturned. Harrison's underneath. Looks as if he's dead. Doctor's here. AC switchboard damaged . . ."

The door suddenly burst open in a gale of wind and the papers of the control room blew about in chaos.

At the moment Mister Mack took the list, Jackson was in the magazine. He had locked the door and was sitting on the edge of one of the sawdust-filled bins of explosive. He was only three parts drunk. He looked with great affection on the bottle of whisky, still half full, on the deck at his feet. Shutting one eye, concentrating on his watch, he made out the time, two-thirty.

The sudden list pitched the bottle over. Jackson sprang forward, reaching for it as it rolled. Boy! Lucky it was stoppered. Good old Buchanan. He retrieved it, only then realising that the whole platform was tilting to one side.

The glass he had poised beside him on the edge of the bin had fallen inside. He stood looking around the compartment. Some of the gear had shifted in the racks. Well damn me, Jacko, he said to himself; what d'you know? We're lopsided.

He took the glass out of the bin, wiped it, blew the last sawdust off. He looked around again. What the hell had happened? It came back to him, like a mental double take, that there had been a pretty loud crash not far off outside, something broken loose. He could hear voices out there.

At that moment the general alarm rang. Jackson stood there with the empty glass in his hand. Men began running past outside. He could hear others clattering up or down the steel ladder. Well, well. No time to fold the old tent and steal quietly away.

He took out a packet of cigarettes and lit one. He was always tickled by the rush to panic stations but today it seemed funnier than usual. The real cream, though, was the parting shot he was leaving behind for old push-face Nolan. He poured himself another whisky, recapped the bottle, put it on the deck.

Joyfully he imagined the scene when Nolan discovered the other bottle he had prepared and planted. He looked down at it—a bottle of Black and White lying ready for discovery, in the lower rack. It was three parts full of petrol and he had also managed to squeeze in a little of the gelatine dynamite from a cartridge in the bin. The dark-tinted glass was perfect. One petrol bomb. One of Mr. Molotov Jackson's cocktails. Maybe he should tie a fancy presentation ribbon round it. Silently Jackson was laughing. Oh boy oh boy, just to see him smash it to the deck. "No goddamn drunks on my rig." Wham! Oh boy! But by that time, Jacko would be fa—ar away.

He sang, "If I had the wings of an a—a—a—an—gel, Over these prison w—alls I would fer—ly, Oh I would fly."

He sat down on the edge of the bin. He drew on his cigarette. It stuck to his lip when he made to take it out and burnt his finger. He flipped his hand painfully, sending half the lighted tip into the bin.

Jackson looked muzzily round, half overbalanced backwards, caught himself. He snickered. Peering down, he trod out the fragment of cigarette tip on the deck. He puffed the cigarette slowly into life again and took a drink. He looked round uncertainly, vaguely remembering something and saw a light among the wood shavings in the bin. The edges of several shavings were glowing.

They looked a bit like litmus paper. Fireworks as a boy. "Apply match to touch paper and stand back." He laughed. A breath of air and they would be in flame.

Jackson watched them. Smoke began to rise. The cartridges of gelatine dynamite were a few inches away. There was a tiny pop and one of the shavings became flame. He spat, missed it. Others burst into flame. His chin dribbled spittle.

"Hey now, boy. Hey—" Lurching over the bin, the cigarette in his mouth, Jackson reached out a hand to blot out the suddenly growing nest of burning shavings. He lost balance, tipped over. His right forearm, carrying his weight, plunged into the bin. At the last second he managed to check himself with his other hand by gripping the edge of the bin. His drink pitched into the shavings. His forearm landed alongside the nearest cartridge, slightly dislodging it.

He said a delayed-action "Whoops" and chuckled. He concentrated hard, looking down at the cartridge, carefully withdrew his arm. The cartridge resettled itself. Lil bit tight, Jacko boy, he told himself. Hail Buchanan. He heaved himself upright. His upset drink had put out the shavings. Boy oh boy, Jackson thought.

There was a creak.

"Jesus," Nolan's voice said from the door.

Jackson slurred round. Quidd was in front of Nolan. There was nobody else. Quidd's face glowed with triumph. Nolan pushed past him into the compartment.

Jackson tipped himself off the edge of the bin, just caught his balance and stood facing them, swaying. Nolan's hands were shaking as if he were making an immense inner effort.

"Smoking——" His voice was a croak.

"Ah—this non-shmoking carriage, inspector?"

Nolan's eyes shifted. He saw the bottle of whisky on the deck, lunged forward and let fly a kick at it. The bottle cracked against the bulkhead, didn't break. Nolan bent down for it, threw it again and smashed it this time. A bottle of beer stood farther along. Wildly, Nolan swung to it. His foot grazed the bottle. It spun into a corner.

He saw the bottle of Black and White in the rack. Nolan stepped forward. Jackson extended an arm. "Now wait a minute. Now that's a Buchanan special. You want to keep that f' special occasion."

Nolan turned and in seconds was out of the compartment. His steps went fast up the ladder to the top deck. Jackson dropped the cigarette to the deck, trod it out. He leaned back against the bin, facing Quidd. "Piss-faced little skunk, you." Quidd backed to the door.

Something obscure worked in Jackson's mind. He chuckled, forgetting Quidd, swung round, picked up the bottle of petrol and gelatine explosive. Quidd recoiled as Jackson advanced and pitched out of the door.

Holding the bottle, Jackson went up the ladder. As he reached the top deck, Nolan charged out of his cabin. He had a pistol. He didn't see Jackson for a moment. Jackson spotted him first and ran past him aft. A shower of spray came over the deck. Jackson skidded but kept up. Men were gathered in groups.

Then Nolan saw him; but Jackson had a good start. He raced towards the derrick, jumped up the steps, stumbled but was on the rotary floor before Nolan had covered the main deck. Nolan scrabbled up the steps with the gun in his hand. The men were gaping. As Nolan reached the top, Jackson shouted something and brandished the bottle. If Nolan had been intending to use the gun, he hesitated now—perhaps he had caught Jackson's words? Then he charged forward.

Jackson ran crabwise across the floor and started up the derrick ladder. He was laughing. Nolan shouted at him from below, then went up after him. Gainer coming up the hatch from below saw them climbing in the wind. The derrick was slightly inclined by the list.

"What the hell's going on?" Then he guessed. Jackson was clowning on the ladder, waving the bottle and baiting Nolan. Two shots smacked flat and small in the wind, too close together, as if the second were unintentional. Jackson hooted, waved the bottle wildly. Gainer saw Joe Havenga move across the derrick floor below and start up. Jackson was climbing again.

The wind was tearing at the three figures. Jackson reached the fourble board and went on up. Nolan reached it in turn, paused, saw Joe coming up and shouted at him. Joe stopped on the ladder, looking up. Then Nolan continued up after Jackson.

Spray swept over the men on deck watching. Gainer looked quickly around; he couldn't see the doctor or the girl. Quidd was standing alone by the hatch, looking up.

Jackson reached the top platform—the crow's nest. He moved to the rail and stood looking over. He waved, did a zig-zag lurch, grasped the rail steadying himself. He turned, looking down the central opening in the platform at Nolan coming up. Nolan was a few feet below. Joe Havenga was climbing again after him, not far behind.

Gainer had to shift to keep Jackson in sight. Jackson had moved to the far side, away from Nolan ascending, ducked under the rail and was lowering his legs. He no longer seemed to have the bottle. He lowered himself, chest on the platform floor, his feet searching for support on the braces below. The crow's nest platform, shaped in a square, extended out beyond each side of the main derrick structure. Jackson's feet therefore hung in the void.

Nolan's head reached the top. Jackson slipped and fell— Gainer flinched, half turned away, then looked back and saw that Jackson had not slipped but had swung himself inward to reach the main structure. He had a foothold on a brace and was hauling himself inward with his fingers through the open steelwork of the crow's nest flooring. He reached the main framework of the derrick and clung to the outer side of it.

Nolan was looking over the rail. Jackson, out of reach beneath him, was clowning again. Nolan swung one leg over the rail, then the other; he bent down, kneeling on the outer edge of the crow's nest platform, heels in the air, preparatory to trying to swing himself to the lower braces like Jackson.

Joe Havenga appeared at the rail. He seemed to be pleading with Nolan. Nolan took no notice. Abruptly, Joe reached over and made a grab for Nolan but Nolan swung away. Joe hitched a leg over, then the next. Nolan was nerving himself before dropping his legs into space and swinging himself in towards the braces under the crow's nest.

Joe edged towards him, lowered himself—and lunged. His outstretched arm caught Nolan round the middle. Simultaneously, Nolan wrenched himself away or dropped. Joe's one-handed grip came away and the two slipped. They seemed to hang there for a fraction of a second. Then they were falling, blown clear of the rig.

Gainer did not see them hit the water. He was racing toward the steps to the derrick floor. Chalky White and Pete were ahead. In a moment there were twenty men on the derrick floor and others underneath at the edges of the slot. The waves were heaving up green into the slot. They were wet through in a few minutes. They could see nothing in the high seas. They tore the lifebelts out of the fittings and threw them into the water. Frank and Pete were tipping planks overboard, throwing in anything that would float. One of the men up the derrick ladder shouted that he had seen a head—but nobody else got a glimpse. It was obviously hopeless. Nobody could survive in such a sea for more than minutes.

Chalky White stood apart, scanning the sea for Joe. "A guy like that has to go. A guy like that." He was weeping. Somebody touched Gainer's arm. It was Willis. He jerked his head. "Jackson's down."

Gainer came to himself. "Sutherland went up for him." Gainer turned. Jackson and Sutherland were crossing the main deck between the groups of men.

"Jacko! Jacko!" Gainer called out; but Jackson didn't hear. Gainer couldn't think. He was momentarily overcome by what had happened. He went into the doghouse. He stood with the door shut. Then he picked up the mike. "This is Gainer speaking. I want anybody who can do a radio repair up here at once. We've lost the Pusher. I'm taking over. Somebody look at the pipe lashing. Ransome—Sid—put a full-time watch on Spud three in the control room."

The doghouse door opened. The doctor and Sutherland were outside. "Larry, Jacko says he's left a sort of petrol bomb up there."

"What?"

"He left a petrol bomb—it's a bottle of petrol and gelatine up on the crown block platform."

"What?" He couldn't take it in. "What the hell are you saying? Jacko's drunk."

"It was some joke he was going to play on Nolan. He's still tight all right but he swears he's not fooling on this."

Sutherland nodded earnestly. In seconds, Gainer was outside. They ran down to the deck and looked up. They couldn't see anything. The doctor came back with binoculars. "There it is. I can see it." He passed the glasses to Gainer. Gainer focused. "Christ Almighty."

The bottle was rolling in the wind. As Gainer watched, it

197

rolled towards the central opening in the platform, rolled back.

Willis shouted, "Wind's veering. We're getting the gas over here."

"If that thing falls, we've had it," Sutherland said.

Gainer was still looking up through the binoculars.

"Get those men off the rig for Christ's sake!"

The light was failing. The men were standing back in groups on the main deck. The wind blew their clothing. They were watching Gainer climb the derrick. He has passed the fourble board. It was starting to rain.

Gainer's cap blew off and soared away. He hunched against the rain and went on up. They saw him climb out on the crow's nest platform, stoop and pick up the bottle. The next minute he was emptying the petrol out on the wind. He slid the bottle into his shirt and turned to come down. Then they saw him pause. He stood looking out across the sea to the west for several minutes, then came down.

The rain swept across the inclined deck. The doctor, Willis and a dozen others had come up to the derrick floor. They gathered round Gainer. Gainer's face and hair were running.

"Switch on your rig lights, all of them," Gainer said. "Signal on and off. Keep it up."

"What's the idea?"

"Aircraft out there. On the horizon. Ship in trouble or something. He's circling over it. Chance he'll see us." He was numb with the wind. He handed the bottle to Willis. "Fill it with sand. Sink it over the side. Take it easy. Who's got the key to the magazine?"

"Quidd. Nobody's seen him."

"Find him and get it."

Gainer went to the doghouse. He waited a minute, recovering from the climb and the numbness.

He picked up the mike. "This is Gainer speaking. This is a general call, Gainer speaking. We're in an emergency and our safety depends on everybody doing what he's told and acting quickly. We're doing our best to get help out here. Those of you who have emergency working posts below decks are supposed to be down there now. Get down there right away. The rest of you stand by in your quarters or in the mess. Every man get his lifebelt and keep it by him. That clear? All keep your lifebelts with you. The gas is now blowing this way and an accidental spark or flame means extreme danger for all of us.

"We're hoping to get a radio signal away. In the meantime, you'll all help, fellows, if you take it easy and stand ready.

Okay? Now I want Chief Ransome, Sowerby, Sutherland and Frank Curtis up here right away."

Outside the doctor came up from the main deck. "Cummings says it'll take him three or four hours. He reckons he can make a job of it. Can't tell for sure. The other man's not much help."

"Where's Quidd?"

Guggendorf shook his head. "Haven't seen him."

"Doc, do something. Go and tell Chalky White—you know, the little floorman?—tell him to stand by in the radio hut. If Quidd tries to interfere with Cummings, tell him to fix him."

"He doesn't need telling. Quidd won't appear. They're all out for him. He's on his own now."

"Do it just the same. Then come back here, will you?"

The men had dispersed when Ransome and the others grouped on the rig floor. It was nearly dark. The lights going on and off above flickered on their faces. The wind blew the rain over them. Sutherland, Frank and Sowerby had their lifebelts slung over their shoulders.

Gainer had to shout. "We have to get some life rafts made and rope lines out. Take up this rig floor here, use all the planks we can. There's the roof over the draw works. Get the tables out of the mess on to the deck."

The loudspeaker from the control room blared, "Aircraft coming over." They broke off and looked up.

"There he is." They could only see the lights. The aircraft came over. Gainer yelled to the man on the doghouse switchboard. "Make SOS. SOS."

The man turned helplessly.

"Three shorts, three longs, three shorts!"

The man signalled. The aircraft circled, coming in.

"For Christ's sake I hope he doesn't come any lower."

"Don't start firing flares, mate," Frank said.

"Stop flashing! Stop flashing!" Gainer yelled, seeing his mistake too late. They stood tense and silent while the aircraft completed another circle. Then it made off westward. They watched it vanish.

"Oh God." The sudden destruction of their hopes had affected them all. It was crazy but they had to pray he did not come back.

They stood discussing what they could do. At last Gainer said, "We're going to need everything we can take ahold of if we get into the water. Let's make the rafts, get the tables out. All the furniture that'll float. Any doors not essential, take 'em off the hinges, lay 'em on deck. Get it all out ready to float off. If we have to——"

"Chief—Mr. Gainer—Spud three——" The loudspeaker from the control room was rasping again. "Spud three alert——"

Slowly and horrifyingly, the platform began to slide over.

Above them, the derrick creaked and shuddered with the strain. They stood unable to move, electrified. Loud cracks came from the draw works behind, as if it were going to break loose. They could hear the clang of pipe shifting on the deck and faint crashes of other things falling.

The platform seemed to be going right over.

A surge of water smashed over the lower side. The group was suddenly released from its rigidity. Men came running out on deck. The list had stopped. The deck now sloped steeply. Waves were coming over the rail solid.

Gainer was at the doghouse mike. "Everybody on top deck. Up on deck. Cummings keep at the radio. Everybody else out."

The searchlight shone desolately on the gas beyond.

13

BRADFORD stepped toward the window and looked out once more. The hotel bedroom was on the first floor. The bay window was draughty. There was a loose floorboard and every time he stepped on it, the glass-fronted wardrobe alongside gave a groan, the board creaked and the stuffed chaffinch under the glass bowl opposite vibrated madly on its perch. The bowl stood on a twisted wood column in the bay window. Bradford had tried moving it because the bird's joggling got on his nerves; but the chambermaid always put it back. Bradford believed they put it in the room so that somebody would smash it and have to pay for it as an 'antique.' It was a fifth-rate, slop-pail-smelling hotel, a glorified boarding house. But he was sticking it out since it was the address Atlas had. He had tried to comfort himself with its cheapness and anonymity. Now he had sent the address to Parrish and Parrish would be replying any day—any hour, he hoped.

Outside, the weather was still bad, the rain and storms continuing. Bradford stubbed out his cigarette into the already overflowing ashtray. He had asked Parrish for an urgent reply. The room had no phone. He hoped Parrish would come here.

He lit another cigarette. If nothing happened soon, he was going to The Hansom. He was going to start having meals there every day, maybe getting Judy along, then telling Angelo to 'charge it to Raymond'. He could live there. He could run up an account as long as your arm. What could they do? Nothing. He'd been square. What did they think they were playing at?

He moved back to the window. There was a bedroom window opposite which was occasionally profitable. A brunette who undressed. Not bad. Didn't pull the curtains. It was about her hour now. He looked out. She didn't seem to be there, though he could see movement through an open door beyond. Perhaps she was coming in?

A knock at the door behind him startled him. The moustached chambermaid was holding the door. "Two gentlemen to see you. They said you was expecting them."

"Yes?" Bradford said eagerly. Then he saw them behind her and had a stab of mistrust. Two? They were already inside. Neither was Parrish. They were big men. They had gabardine raincoats. One looked faintly familiar.

"Afternoon Mr. Bradford. Hope we're not disturbing your afternoon nap. This is Jim Case. Mr. Case is from our personnel department. My name's Douglas Duggan."

They shook hands. "How d'you do?" Bradford said. Duggan turned heavily and made sure that the maid had shut the door. Bradford retreated into the room.

"What personnel department did you say?" Bradford said.

Duggan grinned. He had his trilby hat in his hand. He put it on the wobbly Victorian table with the red plush runner which encumbered the middle of the room. He had thick black hair. "You should know that, Mr. Bradford."

"Well I don't. Suppose you tell me."

Another grin. "You're quite right. Quite right. That's the proper attitude. We hope Jim here will be taking care of your own personal matters before long. Eh, Jim?"

"That's right." Jim was standing at the farther end of the room, nearer the bed. He was looking round, sizing the place up.

"I don't get it," Bradford said. "You from Parrish or aren't you?"

Duggan checked his movements. He looked at Bradford. "Parrish? Who's Parrish?" He turned massively, looking with mistrust at Case, turned back. "I'm sorry. We don't know Parrish."

Bradford felt suddenly weak. He wanted them out of the room. "What do you want? Who are you from? Will you kindly state your business, Mr. Duggan, and then if there's anything to transact we can do it downstairs. This is my bedroom and I don't like people saying they're expected and coming in here like this. It's an abuse. This is a private room. Now what is it you're after?"

Duggan was smiling benevolently again. He nodded. "As I say, you're quite right, Mr. Bradford. We're glad to see it, aren't we, Jim?"

"Right."

Duggan leaned forward, threw out his neck and said in a whisper "From Atlas." The word stretched his mouth. "Atlas. That make you feel any better?"

Bradford's mouth opened silently. He took a long breath, leaning over backwards, tipping chin towards ceiling. "Mister Duggan. From Atlas. Of course. I'm sorry. Well, well. Of course. Got you mixed up with somebody else. Why now, sit down, sit down. Take your coat off. Mr. Case, make yourself

202

at home. I mean, hope you don't mind if I call you Jim. This is a dump but—you know I had to watch it. Rayond agreed it was best to be careful, you know. How is old Raymond? Things must have got moving pretty fast since I saw him. I didn't expect to see you so soon."

"Oh Ray's all right. Boozy old sod."

"Double soixante-neuf."

Laughter.

"We got the office to put a move on."

"Can't help feeling I've seen Jim somewhere before," Bradford said. He felt enormously relaxed.

Case, who was still idly examining the back of the room, said, "You know the oil business."

Duggan sat down. The chair wasn't really big enough for a man of his size but he settled himself cosily. "So it all worked out with Mister Mack?"

"Worked like a charm. That's fixed all right. Timing perfect."

"I heard something but no details," Duggan said, grinning. "What exactly did you do to that rig of theirs?"

Straddling a chair, Bradford grinned. He cocked his cigarette up at a jaunty angle in his lips. "What we agreed—Ambrose, Harry and me. Precision job on the mud balance. Knocked the calibration very carefully to buggery. They've been drilling through high pressure gas, holding it with the mud. A blow-out's a near certainty, I mean it really is a certainty. I was thinking of a time bomb at one time but there were snags. You know. Wasn't easy."

"I bet it wasn't."

"I can tell you it wasn't. Have you heard anything? I mean, if they've had a blow-out?"

Duggan shook his head. "Nope."

"I've been expecting to hear it on the wireless or something. Terrible weather. They've had soft-bottom trouble there too. I tell you, they're going for the lot. Believe me."

Duggan laughed. "Sounds just the job."

"It was."

"So that when they think they've got eight thousand psi mud, they've got, say six thousand—five thousand?"

"That's it. And whoof, she goes."

"And they're in gas?" Duggan said.

"Hand me my asbestos pajamas," Jim said from behind. They laughed heartily.

A small question which had been nagging at the back of Bradford's mind formulated itself. "But, Doug, listen. How come you never heard of Parrish? I mean, this was the arrangement with Ambrose and Harry. Part of the job. This was how we worked it out. I came off in the helicopter Parrish was piloting. I mean, Ambrose and Harry and Raymond knew all along——"

"Well, I don't know what it's like with you, but in Atlas everything's so bloody compartmented and departmentalized and security-minded—Christ they're mad on security!—you can't get any information out of anybody. You wouldn't credit it. Wouldn't credit it. There's that bloody great warren of a building to start with. I never heard of Parrish and I don't think Jim did (Jim was shaking his head). This is what we're up against all the time. It's chronic. I dare say Ambrose has made arrangements with you that nobody'd think of telling us unless we asked—and I mean, kept on chasing. I mean, you have to chase the buggers hard. It's like that in Atlas. Drives you balmy sometimes. Honest to God."

Bradford said, "Well, that's just it. We agreed, you know —terms for the job. It's done. Tell you the truth, Doug, I'm not too flush. I mean, you know, I've had expenses. Not all profit, this sort of thing. Raymond said it wasn't his pigeon. But I need the rest of the money and I want the job in Mexico quick."

"Job in Mexico?"

Jim interjected from the back, "Didn't we hear something about that, Doug?"

"Come to think of it," Duggan said.

"Ambrose agreed within two months," Bradford said. "I was thinking of taking a bit of leave out there and going straight on the job, so I'll have to have the cash right away."

"What was that?" Duggan said.

"What?"

"The cash. How much?"

Bradford hesitated. "Ambrose knows all this. I mean——"

"Course he does. It's none of my business. Doesn't concern me. But if you want me to do something about it . . ."

"Well." Bradford hesitated further, then said "Seven."

"Thousand?"

Bradford nodded. "And there'll be a bonus. On top. So you can see I need it."

Silence.

"You're going to get it, too," Jim called over.

Duggan grinned broadly. Bradford noticed his big feet. Duggan was looking at him and grinning. A change had come on him. The grin didn't mean what it seemed. Duggan got to his feet. He seemed about seven feet tall. "Well Mr. B. Bradford, we've got you good and cooked now, haven't we?"

"Eh?" Bradford saw Jim pull his suitcase from under the bed and flip it on top of the bed to open it.

"Hey, what are you doing?" He made to move across and was gripped by Duggan's hand on his collar and almost lifted from the floor. He struggled but Duggan's grip was choking him.

"Let—what the——?"

Case was rummaging in the suitcase, taking out items. He struggled harder. Duggan shook him. Bradford fell out of his grasp backwards over a chair, hit his head excruciatingly but before he could scrabble up, Duggan's great hands were grasping him again. Duggan hauled him upright and, holding him, gave him the heel of his hand hard under the nose. Bradford nearly passed out. He gasped with pain and fear. Case was turning out drawers.

Duggan hit Bradford twice more. After the second, he left him on the floor. Bradford lay feeling warm blood running down his face. He did not move. His eyes were shut. He seemed to be one mashed and throbbing nose and lip. Muzzily, he could hear the two searching the room, speaking together.

One of them kicked him painfully in the back.

"Get up, squirt."

He had to open his eyes. They had opened a second suitcase and thrown its contents abouts. The room became dark, he felt a mass rising from his stomach, a cold chill on his forehead.

"Get up, do you hear?"

Bradford stirred and vomited. They stood looking down at him until he had finished, then kicked him again. He fell forward into the vomit. He got to his feet shaking, with running eyes, trying to wipe the blood, mucus and vomit from his face and clothes.

"Get your hat and coat, Mr. B. Bradford. We're making calls."

"Please—can't——"

Case weighed a packet of letters in his hand. "Do we give your adorin' Judy the treatment, slob? Or shall we just leave her to the court?"

"No—no. Nothing to do with it. She wasn't——"

"Save it, popeye. You have a lot of talking to do tonight yet before you're finished. A lot of very serious talking. Get moving."

Walter Meldreth opened the door of Stoneman's office and stood holding the knob. Stoneman was on the phone but promptly rang off. "Come in, Walter. I have John Julius coming through."

Meldreth shut the door behind him. He had been observing

205

the briskness of Stoneman's movements, the other small signs of a dangerous mood. Stoneman motioned him to a chair. Then to his surprise, Stoneman produced a box of Henry Clays, flipped open the lid and paper cover, and held them out. Meldreth took one. He looked up over the box at Stoneman's level stare. There was a glint of amusement in the eyes. It was like hard electric illumination on ice.

"Any answer from the platform yet?"

Meldreth said "No. North Scully keeps on trying but can't raise them. The radio may have broken down."

"Then we must——"

One of the phones on the desk buzzed. "Yes?" Stoneman said. "Put him on. Hello, John? Well, how is it? You've got the affidavits? Good. Good. In detail? Excellent. We want it as circumstantial as possible. Yes, yes. That's all right, my men know what to do. They are looking after him. They'll see that he comes to no harm . . ." He listened, interjecting a word from time to time.

Meldreth watched his face. Then he reached for a pad and wrote in block capitals THE WOMAN? He held it out to Stoneman. Stoneman went on listening, then interrupted. "What about the woman? A statement from her? Good. Full? Yes. Well *keep* her scared—keep her bloody scared. She knows about the letters? What? Fur coat . . . I see. No cheque, I suppose? No, the bastards, too much to hope for. Still, it's excellent, excellent. Of course we shall want everything prepared for court, but I don't think an action will be necessary . . ."

Meldreth saw Stoneman's look go past him to the door. Then Stoneman turned his back in irritation. Meldreth looked round. Margie Field was just inside the room. It was Stoneman's strict rule that he was never interrupted. Meldreth waved her away. Margie fluttered a small sheet of blue paper at him. Meldreth got up and went to her.

"Walter——" Impatiently Stoneman held the phone away from him, then said into it, "John, I am being interrupted. It seems I can't—One moment."

Meldreth was reading from the paper in his hand. He stepped hurriedly to Stoneman's side, held it out. "Radio message from Mister Mack—badly garbled. North Scully have added a service message."

Stoneman took it.

Gau blowinqt wrgene need asshs assistanye nolan fost caswapeies send tgu ts tugs all posblee a sjeet oainer. Attached was a service note. This seems garbled version—badly sent— for following: *Gas blowing or blow-out. Urgent need of as-*

sistance. Nolan lost. Casualties. Send tugs all possible speed. Gainer.

Stoneman laid the phone on the desk. The ridged lines of his face set. He turned, looking across the room. Margie and Meldreth waited in silence while he stood there. Julius's voice on the phone said, "Hello-hello?"

Then Stoneman snapped round. He picked up the phone. "Call you back," and hung up. "Walter, get North Scully. See that the tugs have gone. They've had this radio. If they've not gone already I want to know why. Get the helicopter out. Tell Voyss to raise another helicopter, two, if need be."

Meldreth hastened out. "Miss Field, get me Anderson up here at once. Tell North Scully I want constant contact by radio maintained with the platform. Ask Gainer for a further report. Who received this message? If any syllable gets out to the papers, I'll have somebody's guts."

As she was on her way out, he called after her, "And get me Warren Neal. On the private line. Do it first. Utmost urgency. I don't care if he's in bed with his wife. Get him!"

He snatched up the message, reading it again, then moved out restlessly across the room. At the window he twitched the curtain back and looked down at the street and out over the deserted and rainsoaked park. A few minutes passed.

Meldreth came in, a little breathless. "They've gone—tugs have gone. Fierce weather. Gale, very high seas."

"Any other message?"

"Not yet. I've told them to let us know the moment there's word."

"I am calling Neal. This'll settle it. It's straight sabotage. Criminal indictment. Our Mr. Bradford is truly in for it now."

Meldreth said, "That may not be the cause of the blow-out. We don't know. We're only——" He stopped. Stoneman was looking at him intently. Quietly Stoneman said, "Walter, I would not repeat that, if I were you. I wouldn't even think it." He paused. "Do you understand?"

The phone rang.

"Do you, Walter?"

"Yes. Of course."

"Keep it in mind—whatever happens hereafter. Bradford caused the blow-out and nothing else. Is that clear?"

Meldreth nodded.

Stoneman reached the desk and took the green private line phone. "Stay here, Walter. Hello? Jack? Well, it's as we feared, alas. We've just had a radio message. They've had a blow-out. Brought on by Bradford's sabotage, of course. They've asked for urgent assistance and we've got two tugs

207

on the way. They've had casualties. They're in gas. It's probably very serious. We're waiting to hear more. But I think this evidence is more than enough, don't you? We have affidavits from the man, all the details. It's Atlas all the way through. He was paid £3,000, was to get £7,000 more. I told you that last night? Yes, yes. Good. I thought you'd agree. It is certainly the clincher. Good. I knew you'd feel that. Will you come round here at once then? Bring your document and the tape. Excellent. I'll have Julius here. I think we have to move smartly. As soon as you and Julius are here and we've been over it, I'm going to call Moreno. I want a forcing confrontation, a showdown tonight, in the next few hours. I shouldn't think we'll have to threaten, though we'll threaten everything under the sun if necessary. But Moreno knows when he's beaten. And of course, if anything worse happens to Mister Mack, he'll be in deep. Right then. Be expecting you."

He put the phone down. He half-swivelled the chair, tipped it back. He looked grimly satisfied. He sat contemplating Meldreth on the other side of the desk. He smiled thinly.

"Walter." Meldreth tautened. "I want you to call up Moreno. I want you to say you have a personal communication to make to him. *Personal.* Make it sound a *li–ttle* . . . equivocal . . . you can do it so well, Walter—as though you could be induced to leak something . . . as though you're losing your nerve. H'm, Walter? Make sure he keeps an hour free to see you tonight."

Meldreth swallowed. "Is it necessary tonight?"

Stoneman gave him a crocodile grin. "Doesn't it occur to you that you've supplied the reason yourself? I am settling this thing once and for all before those men are brought ashore."

The wind got up further still after dark. They moved about the sloping triangle, soaked to the skin, shifting planks and furniture to the deck, improvising rafts.

An hour before dawn, an aircraft flew overhead. They switched off all lights and waited horrified in the wild darkness of the wind and the sea, watching the tiny blinking navigation lights above. The aircraft circled, using its searchlight. Its assurance seemed to mock them. At last it flew off.

At daylight, Gainer stood over Cummings in the small deckhouse. They had got the signal away.

"Any reply?" Gainer asked.

"I'm no good at receiving Morse. Nor sending. Honest, Mr. Gainer, I can't even tell you whether they're calling us."

"Where's Quidd?"

"I don't know," Cummings said. "I've been on this."

"Mr. Gainer—Larry, oh Christ, it's a tug—two—two tugs coming up!" It was Ransome's excited voice over the intercom from the control room. "It's the tugs—tugs!"

Gainer ran slipping across the deck to the derrick steps. Some of the men had gathered on the rig floor, as if the extra height gave them more security. The tugs were smashing their way through the sea about four miles away. Men were running out of the mess and the dormitory deckhouse. They made for the rig floor.

The tugs had seen the gas and were steering for the clear side. Their approach was interminable. The men were hunching and moving about to keep warm and get out of the fierce wind. The tugs seemed to be making no progress. Then they sheered off again. The men shouted and waved. The tugs manoeuvred. One was signalling with a lamp. They couldn't read it.

"Where in God is that bastard Quidd?" Gainer said.

But both tugs were turning away, keeping clear, obviously afraid of exploding the gas.

The doctor was beside Gainer. "Are they coming in for us?"

"Whether they do or not, we can't live much longer."

Jackson went through the deserted mud compartment on the deck below, climbed over the washing machine which had pitched in from next door and negotiated the sacks of cement and chemicals piled up by the list. Mud spilled from the tank lay in a pool. Jackson waded through and made for the magazine compartment. He slid on the sloping deck, scrabbled up. There was nobody about. The whole deck was deserted. Gear was piled up everywhere in confusion. Most of the lights were still on.

He reached the door of the magazine, took his key out and opened the door. The compartment was in darkness. He reached in, switched on the light. He grinned faintly, shut the door behind him. He hesitated, then locked it.

On the far side of the compartment, he knelt and reached behind the bottom rack and pulled out a thermos flask. He stood up. His jaw and lips were working in anticipation of the drink. He took the cork out, poured the cup-top full of whisky and drank. He shuddered, screwing his mouth up, feeling the shot go home. Slowly, his stance relaxed. He poured another, tipped it down. The flask had been full and there was still plenty.

He put the cork back, propped the flask carefully upright against the rack, then stood still. A soap box was standing upended on the deck. He knew it had not been there before.

Then just beyond, in the darker corner of the compartment, he saw a boot. A tarpaulin was hanging from the top of the rack. The boot was under it.

Jackson stepped over, pulled a fold of the tarpaulin aside. Quidd's hot frightened eyes stared at him from behind it. He was standing stiffly to attention, arms rammed to his sides, squeezed into the corner. He still wore his hard hat and he was obviously very scared.

Jackson grinned. "Well! Lord Quidd. Lord Justice Quidd. Hi!" Quidd stood there rigid, motionless, his eyes fixed on Jackson.

Jackson lifted the tarpaulin aside. "So this is where you've been. They were looking for you all over."

Quidd stepped out. Something metallic fell to the deck. Quidd looked jerkily down but the next instant sprang back as if Jackson was going to hit him. Jackson bent and picked up a key, tagged *Pusher. Magazine.* He grinned. "Hi, Quidd, L.J."

He put the key in his pocket, pulled over the soap box, sat down. "They're still looking for you, Quiddie boy. Why'nt you go up and join your old pals?"

Quidd was staring, wordless.

Jackson picked up the thermos, poured himself a drink. He drank some, recorked the flask and stood it down again.

"This is nice and cosy, eh? Quite a snuggery. You don't happen to have any extra hooch stashed away, boy, do you now? Oh yes, wait a minute. Where's that bottle of beer Nolan was kicking around the last time? How about finding it for me, Quiddie, eh? Must be around somewhere. Unless you've sunk it. You sunk it, you little rat?"

Quidd edged away.

Jackson took another drink. He put the cup down, dipped in his pocket and brought out a packet of cigarettes. He took one. He was facing Quidd. He produced a box of matches, struck one, lit the cigarette. He inhaled deeply, blew the smoke out. He waved the match feebly. He was grinning at Quidd. "Hiya, Quiddie."

The match was still burning. Quidd was staring at it. He seemed to shrink physically. He said, "No—no—don't!" He reached a red, bony hand towards the match, now curling but still alight.

"Oh this?" Jackson seemed to notice it for the first time. The flame was touching his fingers. He waved it gently. The match went out. "What's the matter, Quidd? You scared?"

Quidd suddenly sprang past him across the compartment, slipped on the lopsided deck but was up at once wrenching at the door. He twisted the ring handle frantically for a moment, realized it was locked, twisted himself round defensively, back to the bulkhead.

Jackson grinned at him. "Hiya, Quiddie. Have a drink?"

Pleadingly Quidd said, "Let me out."

"Out? What's the matter with the snuggery, boy? You wanna smoke?" He held out the cigarettes.

Quidd pressed himself back, not taking his eyes off Jackson.

"Honest to God, Quidd, you're not your old sparkling self. Querulous Quidd, me old tried, true and trusty. Cheer up, Querulous. What's getting you?"

He poured himself another whisky and sipped. "How about finding that bottle of beer, me old? Come on now, get down to it, find that bottle, Querulous. Go on." His gesturing hand brushed the rack, knocked the cigarette end off.

Quidd started forward, recoiled.

"What?" Jackson said. He put the cigarette back in his mouth, puffed vainly. He took it out and looked at it. He looked down at the floor. The cigarette end faintly glowed. "Oh. Yup." He trod massively on it, grinding it out in a prolonged way under his foot, looked up again at Quidd. "Yup. Have to be careful. One little spark in that bin there—set those shavings alight—and whoof! Eh, Quidd?"

Quidd moistened his lips.

Jackson took out the matches again, struck one and lit the stub of cigarette. He exhaled the smoke, holding the lighted match. "What's the matter? Oh this? Okay, blow it out for me."

Quidd advanced a step, bent down blowing frantically and grotesquely at the match. Jackson was chuckling. He moved the match slightly. Quidd was sweating. He blew again twice. Jackson dropped the match on the deck. It went out.

"You didn't get it. Okay okay. We'll give you another chance in a minute."

Quidd dropped to his knees. He twisted his hands together, pleading. "No, no. Let me go."

"Get up, you little bastard." Jackson's voice was a lash. Then he was grinning again. "What's the hurry, Querulous? The tugs are out there. You know that? They're all off by now. We're alone. Just you and me, boy. And we're going to keep turning to the right, ain't we, Quidd?"

The men were crowding the rail.

"She's coming in now." They had been waiting with rope lines all morning for the leading tug to approach. The other tug was standing farther off, apparently on orders from the first.

The secondary gas crater had subsided abruptly at eleven

211

o'clock and they thought this had improved their chances. On the other hand, the list of the platform had worsened. The derrick could not stay up much longer.

As they waited, first Willis then others came to report oil on the sea. They could see oil spreading among the gas areas. Oil was blowing wild under pressure. They looked at each other.

"What a way to bring a well in," Willis said. "There it is though, if we ever get out of this."

The leading tug moved slowly closer. The voice of the loud-hailer came over the water. "I cannot come in for you lads. Gas zone is too close. Assistance is on the way. We are expecting a helicopter. Hold on."

Gainer jumped over to the doghouse loud-hailer. "We can't wait. Can't hold on. Must have assistance now. We're going over." The sound blasted out across the sea. "Come in now. We can't hold on any longer."

The tug was turning away.

"You damned fancy fair-weather sailor!" Gainer shouted. "This platform is going to turn over any minute. This is our last chance!"

The tug sank in the trough, smashed into a high wave. It was heading away. Slowly it came round. The men at the rail gave a ragged shout. The tug came round further. The loud-hailer voice said, "If I set that gas off we're all going to be blown to kingdom come."

"Are you going to stand by and see us go?"

"I advise you to hang on till the last minute. This is a damn bad sea. Can't you manage it?"

"It's now or never. Come on in for Christ's sake."

There was an interval of several minutes. Then the tug said, "All right. Am approaching on starboard side. Scrambling nets down my starboard side. Get your men down as fast as you can. Throw your lines inboard. I can't tie up and I don't want that bloody derrick falling on me."

Another cheer from the men. The second tug kept its distance.

On deck, the doctor was bending over the sick bay patient. He had roped two lifebuoys round him. Frank Curtis was going over with him. The Kellman girl was alongside with another lifebuoy. Gainer gave her a pair of driller's gloves. Yet he found he had to grit himself to tell her to go. "Use them for getting down the rope. If you wait you'll get scared. Get down and strike out for the net."

The tug nosed in. Men climbed over the rail and stood crouching and tense by their rope lines, ducking away from the spray. One or two jumped too soon. "Hold it! Hold it!"

Their heads were below, bobbing in the sea, riding the side of the great waves. The tug came close to, swung, presenting its starboard side, and then in one mass movement, the rest of the men were swarming down the lines, some falling prematurely, some disappearing in the water, others thrown to the tug.

But none of them had measured the true fierceness of the sea, the risks of the escape. The tug rose and fell sickeningly alongside the platform and swirled and smashed dangerously in. The sea spouted against its side. Seamen on deck had men torn away as they tried to drag them on board.

Gainer turned and saw the girl clinging to the platform rail. He shouted "Get down the rope!" Below there was a confusion of struggling men, breaking waves and shouts and the lash of foam. He saw a man like Frank reach desperately for the net then disappear. The sick man had gone.

The girl was still holding back. Gainer did not know what to do. Could she live in it? Yet to hesitate was probably fatal. He grabbed her, lifted her over the rail. "Get down the bloody rope!" About a dozen men were left to go.

The tug's telegraph was ringing as it manoeuvred to stay within reach. Then there was an extra swirl and it began to move away. Gainer gripped the girl, held her on the edge. They all shouted and waved madly.

The loud-hailer blared. "Can't stay. Look at the gas aft of you." Gainer swung round. There was a pulsing spout where the second crater had subsided earlier. The area of oil had spread. He turned back.

The tug was already well off.

Jackson crossed his legs and poured himself another drink. "What you feeling so hot about?"

Quidd had discarded his overall coat. He was wearing a singlet. He was sweating. All at once he threw himself on the door beating and kicking it.

"Mr. Gainer! Come and get me. Mr. Gainer! Mr. Ransome! Cummings . . . Cummie . . . Cummie . . ." A spray of sweat flew off his head as he hammered.

"You mean Mummie." Jackson was chuckling.

He took out his matches, struck one. He watched Quidd over the flame. He put the flame to his cigarette and inhaled. He held the match upright.

"Blow, Quiddie?"

Quidd hunched forward. The compartment tipped violently to one side. There was a great crash outside against the bulkhead. Things showered from the racks. Jackson lurched sideways on the box, dropped the match, then was on his feet.

Crashes echoed from the spaces beyond the door. A carboy of acid broke free with a creak and rolled across the compartment. Quidd was hanging rigidly to the racks.

All the lights went out. In the silence there was the sound of their breathing.

Jackson chuckled. "They can't fool us. We got a light, eh, Quidd?"

The match flared in the dark. It showed Quidd's face.

"Blow, Quidd?"

Quidd screamed.

The great platform was dying. It was slowly pitching over, like a dying sea monster sinking to the depths.

Gainer, the girl, Pete and eight other survivors, stood in the spray on the jointed ladder below the decks. It was mobile equipment in the first place and the sea had twisted and broken it. Gainer had brought them down. After the fresh list, the derrick was going to collapse at any moment.

The tug was moving in again. "I'm giving you two minutes. Sling your line for'ard. Pay out the slack. Watch it—watch it."

Gainer threw the line—wide. The tug lifted on a mighty crest and the next moment the men in the bow had the line.

Pete went first. Halfway down, the tug rose, the line went slack. Pete let go and dropped. His head hit the side; they saw him briefly, then he disappeared.

They looked at the girl. She shook her head.

"Next!" Gainer shouted. Cummings went. He landed safely. The girl went third. Gainer got a spare line round her and they lowered her, guiding her with the other line. She got down. The rest went one by one. Gainer was last. Just as he went down, the tug dropped and sheered away. He fell short, grabbed for the scrambling net. He felt the mighty arms of the sea dragging him back. He hung on but he was smothered. He felt himself going—then other arms were pulling him aboard.

The loud-hailer was calling for any more. "I am leaving. Any more of you up there? Last call. Last call."

Gainer shook his head. He was staring at the deck. He didn't want to hear. It was hideous.

"You all right, Larry?" It was Chalky White.

"Sure. Thanks, Chalky."

They felt the surge of the engines as the tug headed away. They were all crowded together on the deck, in the shelter of the deckhouse, in the engine room, searching for who was there and who wasn't.

"Seen Chalky?"

"Over there."

"Where's Lofty?"

"You seen Sutherland?"

Gainer saw the doctor.

"Anybody seen Willis?"

Gainer could not get Pete out of his mind. "Frank! Thought you hadn't made it."

The sea came over them from the bow.

"We didn't lose, though, Larry, did we?" Chalky said.

"Lose?"

"There's the gas and the oil there. We hit the pay sand."

"Sure," Gainer said.

"Could be the big time for Contram."

"You'll be back for the completion, kid."

"Reckon somebody will. Not me, though. I'll be some-where else. Turning to the right."

The distance increased. The lurching platform stood out against the sky. The derrick was still standing but as they watched, it heeled over majestically and fell, showering braces and steel components.

Suddenly there was a great igniting flash. They caught the thud of the explosion. It lit up the sky and the sea seemed to heave up in it. Mister Mack was enveloped in a billow of flame.

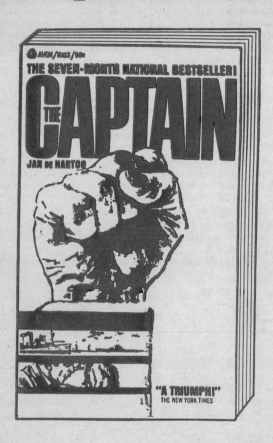